MW01247178

The Art of Love

D.J. AUBUCHON

FIRST EDITION

Published by D.J. AuBuchon, Springfield, Missouri, USA, in 2024.

Library of Congress Cataloging-in-Publication Data has been applied for.

ISBN 979-8-9914965-1-3
ISBN 979-8-9914965-2-0

Cover and Interior Design by Estevan Torres
Cover Art by Bob AuBuchon
Edited by Amanda Filippeli

Manufactured in the United States of America.

www.djaubuchonauthor.com

Acknowledgments

Darryl, I couldn't have written this book without your encouragement and support.

To my amazing kids, Josh, Brittney & Emily for your support and feedback.

To my best friends, Lisa & Dawn, who read the first draft, giving me the courage to turn the story in my head into a real book. Lisa, you've been my biggest cheerleader for over 38 years, and I couldn't have done this without you asking me for more chapters.

To my friends, who are fellow authors:
Mickey Miller, your encouragement and help through some difficult scenes really pushed me to be a better writer. Your friendship means a lot and thank you for all of your help. Heidi Spark, your guidance and feedback have provided the inspiration I needed to get through the business side of being an author. Thank you. Eva Holt, for always cheering me on and for being my first Beta Reader.

To my editors, Amanda & Christa. Thank you for believing in my book, for walking me through the process, and –pushing me to become a better writer. This book would not have happened if it weren't for the two of you.

To my brother, Bob AuBuchon, for the amazing cover art. It means so much that you captured exactly what I wanted and I can share a piece of your art with the world.

To my friends, who put up listening to me talk non-stop about this book and the writing process. Your excitement and encouragement mean so much to me.

To Estevan Torres, you took my idea for the cover and brought it to life. Your help with formatting and adding your special touch to the pages of this book, made it all the more special and made it a work of art. Thank you doesn't seem enough.

I could not have written this book, without my muse; the music. The songs at the beginning of each chapter either inspired that chapter or fit perfectly.

A very special Thank You goes out to Justin and Slavo of Fly by Midnight for writing songs that not only spoke to my heart but gave me the idea for this book. Your encouragement and friendship have meant the world to me.

Dedication

To the women of GenerationX, who sacrificed their wants and needs for their family.
This is our time to make our dreams come true and thrive.

"Art, like love, moves the heart in unexpected directions."
Marty Rubin

Chapter 1

"This Song Should Not Exist" by Ruxley

The bedroom was shrouded in darkness with the heavy curtains drawn shut, blocking out even the faintest hint of light. The bright blue pillows laid in the corner of the room, where they had been thrown long ago. Dust collected on every surface, only showing the occasional handprint. The room used to be filled with life and sunshine. That ended when the doctor said the words that no one is ever prepared to hear.

Julie cocooned herself in the covers as her body laid motionless except for the shallow rise and fall of her chest. The air was heavy with the scent of stale sadness, a palpable reminder of the three months that had passed since Jim's death. The room felt frozen in time, a silent witness to Julie's grief as she remained trapped in a world of memories and pain.

Julie stared at the ceiling as her hand reached out to Jim's side of the bed, and the tears streamed down the sides of her face into her graying brown hair. She heard a knock on the bedroom door and glanced over, wiped the tears away with the sleeve of her sweatshirt, and looked up at her daughter.

"Mom, I have to go. I want to make sure that you're up and alright before I leave," said Ashley with a tenderness in her voice. She had been the sole caretaker of her mother for the past few months.

"I know, honey," Julie responded quietly, without moving.

"You'll feel better if you take a shower," Ashley suggested. "I can start it for you."

Julie reluctantly got out of bed, following her to the bathroom. Ashley reached for a towel and hung it on the hook next to the shower door before turning the water on. Julie waited until Ashley left the room to undress. She didn't have to look in the mirror to know that she had lost too much weight and didn't want to alarm Ashley. Julie startled when she climbed into the shower and the water hit her bare skin. Julie took a deep breath and let out a heavy sigh as she let the warm water run over the back of her head. Something caught her eye on the counter… it was Jim's electric razor. A wave of grief hit her and she began to cry uncontrollably.

Ashley knocked without opening the door, "Mom, how are you doing?"

Julie wiped her eyes, as if it made a difference. "Be right out."

"I'll lay some clothes out for you. Let me know if you need any help," suggested Ashley.

Julie peeked her head out of the bathroom door to see if Ashley was still in her bedroom. She emerged once the coast was clear and walked over to the bed. Julie rubbed her hand across her stomach as she slipped on her jeans and sweater, knowing that the jeans would be too large for her now tiny frame. She tried to avoid looking at Jim's side of the closet as she reached for the closest belt. But it was inevitable. Tears welled up in her eyes as she reached out to touch his dress shirts. Holding one of the sleeves up to her nose, she breathed in the remaining scent of Jim. She was pulled out of her trance when she heard Ashley opening the front door of the house. She moved back to the bed, putting on the belt and the sweater.

"Mom," Ashley picked up a blanket, folding it. "Ben and I are worried about you. You can't stop living just because dad is gone."

"I just need time," replied Julie without looking over at Ashley.

"It's been three months, Mom. We don't know how to help you and I feel incredibly guilty leaving you home alone."

Julie glanced over at Ashley and sighed, "You shouldn't feel guilty. I'll be fine. No need for you and your brother to worry. I'm 58 years old. I know how to take care of myself."

Ashley sighed with frustration, "Carla said that she would come over tonight to bring you dinner. She mentioned something about going on a trip and wants you to go with her."

Julie didn't have the energy to deal with Ashley's pushback of how she should be grieving, so she stayed quiet.

"Okay… well, I need to get going. I have an appointment with my advisor," said Ashley.

Julie took Ashley in her arms to hug her goodbye. "I love you, Ash."

Ashley patted her mom's back in the embrace and said, "Please eat something. You've lost too much weight. Ben and I can't lose you too." She stood back and looked Julie up and down. "I love you mom."

"I love you too sweetheart," said Julie as she walked toward the front door with Ashley.

"I'll call you later, okay?" Ashley kissed her mother on the cheek.

Julie turned the radio on when she walked into the kitchen. "Every Breath You Take," by The Police, filled the room with music as she picked up a glass and walked to the fridge.

She and her best friend, Carla, were in a bar that they were too young to be in, but Carla was dating one of the bouncers. Julie swayed to the music, sipping on a wine cooler, when she noticed the tall, dark-haired man walking toward her. He had lazy, hazel-colored eyes, a big smile, a dimpled chin, and was holding a bottle of Bud Light. When he moved in front of her, he dropped to one knee and started to sing the chorus. It was like something out of a John Hughes movie. She immediately became embarrassed and reached out to get him to stand up, but he persistently sang to her as a crowd started to gather around them, making Julie blush even more. She never felt comfortable being the center of attention, but this handsome boy made her feel like she was special in that moment. When the song was over, he stood up introducing himself as Jim Anderson, her future husband.

Julie smiled at the memory. It was the first time she had smiled in some time. Walking through the house toward her bedroom, she grabbed Jim's favorite bright blue checked cardigan. She stripped her clothes off and wrapped her small frame in the sweater. Holding it closed with one hand, she steadied herself as she pulled out a pair of sweatpants before moving to the bed. The darkness was her solitude, where she could grieve him without judgement. Easing herself back onto the bed, she pulled the covers over her head. She sniffed as she drew the sweater up to her nose. This one didn't smell like Jim, but it didn't matter. Julie remembered the last time Jim wore it, which was the last time the two of them walked around the neighborhood before he was too weak. She closed her eyes and willed herself not to cry. Rolling over, she put her back towards Jim's side of the bed and drifted off to sleep.

When Julie woke up, she reached for her phone and noticed a text from Carla.

Carla: What sounds good to you for dinner?
Julie: I'm not hungry, so get whatever you want.
Carla: Liver and onions ok with you? LOL
Julie: Gross.

Carla: See you at six.

Carla let herself in and was surprised to see Julie sitting on the sofa staring into the fireplace. Julie didn't notice Carla until she set the bag of Thai food down on the coffee table. Bending down to join Julie at the fireplace she said, "If you're waiting for Santa, you've got a few months."

Julie looked at Carla and smiled. "Food smells good."

"Are you actually going to eat?" Carla asked.

"Depends on what you brought and where it's from?" Julie replied as she watched Carla start taking containers out of the bag.

"Uh, Chiang Mai. Only the best for you, my friend. Drunken Noodle for you and Spicy Basil Chicken for me," Carla handed Julie the container.

"No steamed dumplings?" asked Julie.

"Bitch, would I let you down? I got two orders of dumplings. I figured whatever we don't eat tonight, you can heat up tomorrow," Carla plopped down next to Julie on the sofa. "Is Ash still staying with you?"

Julie smiled. "No, I insisted that she get back to her life," Julie said before putting a bite of noodles in her mouth.

Carla watched her eat and said, "It's about time you eat something. I can see your bones."

Julie rolled her eyes as she picked up a dumpling. She moaned at the explosion of flavors in her mouth. "Jim doesn't…" Julie caught herself before continuing, "Didn't like Asian food."

Carla put her plate down and reached over to put her hand on Julie's knee. "Remember the time in college when we talked him into going to that sushi restaurant?" she said with a slight laugh.

Julie looked at Carla and smiled, "He was mortified

at the thought of eating raw fish. Never could understand the appeal."

"He was so grossed out and I couldn't stop laughing," Carla chuckled.

Julie became quiet as she leaned onto Carla's shoulder, "Things were so different then."

"Yeah, but you've got two great kids, a beautiful home, and a lifetime of memories. You'll eventually recover from this, Jules."

"You think?" Julie asked, her voice softened to a whisper.

"I have no doubts. You are one of the strongest people I know," Carla said as she moved to hug Julie.

"I don't feel very strong. I feel like I break a little more with each breath," whispered Julie.

Carla pulled back and wiped the tears from Julie's face. "We need to get you out of this house. How about a trip to the beach?"

"I can't go on a trip like that. You know how Jim is about stuff like that," said Julie as she put her head down.

Carla frowned, searching her mind for the right words. "Jules, he's not here to tell you no," she paused before continuing, "I've talked to the kids, and we all agree that getting away would be good for your mental health."

Julie didn't respond for a moment but finally said, "I don't know if I'm up for a trip, Car." She looked up with look of desperation across her face. "Where would we even go? What would we do?"

Carla smiled sweetly at her dear friend. "We can go and do whatever you want. This is your trip."

"Jim and I used to take the kids to Destin Beach in Florida," said Julie.

"Do you want to go there or someplace new? We could go to Venice Beach in California. I went there a few years ago for a conference."

"Hmm, somewhere with no memories?" contemplated Julie.

"Yes, a place to refresh your mind and spirit. You need this, Jules. You can't keep shutting yourself in that room. It's not healthy."

"My head knows that, but my heart hasn't caught up yet," said Julie as she put her right hand over her heart. "I just don't know how to do anything without him. He and the kids were my entire world and now he's just gone. And… and I'm left sad and angry. His sister, Charlotte, said that he's in a better place now with God." Julie shook her head side to side, "If God is real, then I'm so fucking angry that he or she took him away from us. I don't know how I can ever move on."

Carla hugged Julie. She pulled back and looked her in the eyes, "That's what I'm here for. We've been through everything together. I'm not going anywhere. We will get through this."

Julie grinned a crooked smile and mouthed, "Thank you."

Carla reached into her purse and pulled out a piece of folded paper. "The last time I came to see Jim, he handed me this note."

Julie looked up with a puzzled look on her face. "What does it say?"

Carla handed the note to Julie, who opened it carefully and stared at the words. It didn't even look like Jim's handwriting. The cancer had ravaged his body and caused his hands to shake, making it difficult to read.

Dear Carla,

My time is coming to an end and I need your help to make sure that Julie doesn't die with me. I know that sounds a bit dramatic, but I want her to continue living, and love her life. We've had 37 years together and 35 years of marriage. I know that I haven't always been the easiest to live with and I've made my share of mistakes, but it's her turn to pursue her dreams. I'm so proud of the life we built together but I need Julie to know that it's ok to move on and continue living her life. Don't let her pull the covers over her head and grieve too long. You are the one person that I know I can count on to make this happen. She is stubborn and won't listen to the kids when they tell her these same things, but you are the one that can force her to go on even when all she wants is to fade away. Teach her how to live without me. I'm counting on you Carla. She needs you now more than ever.

Love, Jim

Julie put her hand up over her mouth and looked up at Carla while tears streamed down her face. Carla reached over and rubbed Julie's shoulder. Together they sat in silence, neither knowing what to say. Julie wiped her tears away and smiled at her friend.

Nodding her head, Julie looked Carla in the eyes and said, "Thank you for sharing this with me. He tried to tell me some of these things toward the end. I made him stop every time he brought it up because I thought it meant he was giving up the fight. I wasn't ready to hear it."

"He was finally willing to let you go, Jules. I believe that at the end, he truly wanted nothing more than your happiness," said Carla quietly. "I don't know all the ins and outs of your complicated relationship, but I think he was remorseful in the end." Carla took Julie into her arms for an embrace.

Julie took a deep breath and hung her head down. "I wasn't perfect."

"There's no such thing as a perfect marriage or relationship, Jules. You were a good wife, and you are an amazing mother. You both did the best you could."

Looking at the fireplace again, Julie quietly said, "Maybe."

The air was suddenly heavy, but not with sadness. It was filled with a lifetime of regrets surfacing for the first time in years. Julie rested her face in her hands while rocking slowly back and forth. Carla patiently sat and let Julie take the lead in what happened next. Julie thought back to the first time Jim put his foot down and told her no. Being an only child, she had grown up getting her way most of the time and that worked for at the beginning with Jim. She would bat her eyelashes and give him a big kiss. This time was different. She wanted to go with Carla on a girl's trip with some of their college friends. When Julie brought it up to Jim, he immediately said no. He continued that she was married now and those other girls were nothing but trouble. She tried everything to get him to change his mind to no avail. Maybe Carla was right. In his death, he was trying to set her free to live the life she wanted.

Finally, Carla broke Julie's thoughts, "Jules, do you want me to stay here tonight?"

Julie looked over at Carla, shaking her head no. "I'll be ok."

"Are you sure?" Carla asked with concern. "I don't mind at all."

"Let me think about the trip, ok?" Julie asked.

"Absolutely," replied Carla. "I'm at least going to clean up dinner." She stood up, starting to gather the food containers.

Julie tried to stand but flopped back onto the sofa. "I'm really tired, Car. I'm gonna go lie down. Lock up before you go?"

"Sure thing. Get some rest. I'll call you at lunch tomorrow," Carla watched as her friend stood and walked back toward the bedroom.

Chapter 2

"Healing Hurts" by Blu Eyes

Julie found herself standing in a vast field surrounded by swirling mist. Echoes of Jim's voice called out to her from the shadows. Her mind filled with memories of his constant guidance and love. The weight of his absence pulled her down like a sorrowful anchor. As she gazed into the mist, she began to see flickers of light. Glimpses of a world beyond her grief. A strange sense of liberation and a freedom she hasn't known in years. Without Jim's watchful eyes, she realized that she can make her own choices and follow her own path. The conflicted emotions swirl within her. The grief for the loss of her beloved Jim battled with a growing sense of empowerment at the prospect of forging her own destiny. As the mist began to part, she took a hesitant step forward fully unsure of what lied ahead.

Waking up, she instinctually reached over to Jim's side of the bed but remembered that he wasn't there. She looked over toward the closet and sighed. Getting out of bed, she walked over to Jim's side of the closet. She just stood there looking at his neatly stacked jeans and sweatshirts, and at the racks of pressed shirts and sweaters. He loved order and hated chaos. She moved some of the jeans so that they weren't so neatly stacked. "There," she said quietly. It was her first sign of starting to heal. As an artist, the chaos made her feel alive and creative. Jim's love of structure always overshadowed the messiness of life that she craved. A piece of her old self took root in that moment, and she smiled. She walked back over to the bedside table and picked up her phone to text Carla.

Julie: Let's plan that trip to Venice Beach.
Carla: Hell yeah! When do you want to leave?
Julie: As soon as we can.
Carla: Okay!
Julie: I'll come over tonight and we'll plan it out.

Julie felt a wave of exhilaration come over her as she set her phone down. She walked into the kitchen. As quickly as the high of the previous moment happened, the next wave of grief and guilt hit her when she looked out the window toward the swing set Jim had put together for the kids when they were little. He had wanted to tear it down, but Julie insisted on keeping it up in case they had grandkids someday. She didn't cry this time, as if her body had finally run out of tears. He was everywhere in this house, a ghost that couldn't find his way to the afterlife. Turning toward the coffee pot, she poured the water in and hit the brew button. She took a seat at the island to wait. Her mind was waging a battle by debating this trip with Carla. Should she cancel or go? It had only been three months since she buried Jim, but sometimes it seemed like a lifetime ago. Time had played tricks with her mind over the past two years of Jim's battle against cancer. She could vividly remember their wedding day but couldn't remember her last fight with Jim.

The coffee pot overflowed, which caused Julie to jump up and wipe the counter. Cleaning up the mess gave her comfort and made her feel like he was nearby watching her. She fought back tears before pouring herself a cup. Walking out to the front porch, she sat down on the bench swing and adjusted the blue pillow behind her. Blue was Jim's favorite color, so she made sure to use as much blue as she could stand to make him happy. She stretched her legs out in front of herself to push off from the brick banister that surrounded the porch. She felt like a little kid when she sat there. It always brought back memories of this same swing being on her parent's back porch. Rays of sunlight touched her bare legs each time the swing moved her forward. The warmth felt good and made her smile. Two neighbors walking their dog waved as they passed, and Julie waved back.

Suddenly, Julie was aware that the world had continued and now she was indeed all alone. Something she had secretly feared when the doctors gave them Jim's diagnoses of liver cancer. Thinking back, she wondered if she was scared of losing him or scared to be alone. She had never lived by herself. When she dreamed about being able to call the shots in her life, it was wildly different than what she was experiencing now. A tear ran down her cheek, but she brushed it away quickly.

Taking a sip of her coffee, she noticed a bright red Cardinal had landed on the ledge of the porch near the swing. Legend says that if a Cardinal visits you, it is a sign that a loved one who has passed is with you in spirit. Julie stared at the bird before asking out loud, "Is that you, Jim?" She smiled at the thought of him returning to her in this way because he had loved taking the family to St. Louis Cardinal baseball games in the summer. The bird flapped its wings to take off into the sky, and Julie watched it fly until it disappeared. Shadows danced across the long porch as her gaze fixed on the slivers of sunlight that seemed to chase them. The rhythmic creak of the swing echoed through the stillness, a lonely melody that matched the ache in her heart. She traced the grain of the wooden slats absentmindedly while lost in memories of happier times. Her fingers paused momentarily over the spot where Jim used to sit. The heaviness of the grief pressed down on her, leaving her feeling hollow and adrift in a sea of sorrow. With each sway of the swing, she found herself sinking deeper into the emptiness that now filled her days. The world around her faded into insignificance as she surrendered to the overwhelming tide of sadness.

She pulled the pillow from behind herself to prop it up on one end of the swing before lying down. She kept one foot dangling from the porch swing to push off when it started to stall.

Julie looked up when she heard a car approach. It wasn't a car she was familiar with but was relieved when she saw Ashley stand beside a young man with longer brown hair. He immediately put his arm around her as they walked toward the porch.

"Hey, Mom," called out Ashley. "Wanted to stop by to check on you." As they approached the porch Ashley added, "This is Jordan."

Julie stood up and stretched her hand out to shake Jordan's, but he didn't remove his arm from around Ashley. Julie let her hand slip back down to her side. "Nice to meet you, Jordan."

"We can't stay," Jordan said in a curt voice.

"Okay," said Julie as she leaned forward to give Ashley a hug.

"Jordan has some things to do, but I wanted you to meet him. So, I talked him into driving me over," said Ashley.

Julie asked, "Did you meet at school?" Something about Jordan didn't set right with her. Ashley's smile seemed tight, "Yeah."

Directing her question to Jordan, "You're in the same architectural program?"

"Something like that," he said, before looking at Ashley. "She's okay. We gotta bounce."

Ashley smiled, "Yeah, we only had a few minutes to spare. Love you, Mom."

Julie watched as the two walked down the steps and toward the car. Julie noticed that Jordan's arm never left Ashley's neck until he walked to his side of the car.

Her mother's intuition realized that something was off with Jordan as she watched them drive away.

Julie walked toward Carla's apartment door with Jim following behind. "We don't have to stay long," Julie reassured Jim.

"We're only staying 10 minutes," Jim replied.

"Jim, she just had a fight with Christian. She needs me," Julie looked up at Jim while pushing her bottom lip out in a pout.

"God damn it, Jules. Don't pull that shit. I said 10 minutes. Not a second more. I don't want to hear you two, blabber on about the Douchebag of the day."

"I said you didn't have to come with me," Julie said sternly.

"Oh right, and have her talk you into going to a bar to pick up men. That's not happening."

Carla's house was an older red brick home in South St. Louis with a large front porch and black shutters. She met Julie at the door and ushered her inside.

"How was your day?" Carla asked.

"It was fine," Julie replied.

Carla looked at her and rolled her eyes. "Fine? Your favorite word to describe anything and everything," she said sarcastically.

Julie gave Carla a nudge, "Oh, you hush."

They sat down at the small dining table adjacent to the living room. Carla opened her laptop to Google flights to Los Angeles. She looked over to Julie and asked, "How are you really doing?"

"I'm fine. Really," she replied. Julie reached over and placed her hand on Carla's arm. "Really."

"Are you trying to convince me or yourself?" Carla asked as she lifted her eyebrows and cocked her head to the side.

Julie took a deep breath and sighed, "I. Am. Fine," she said slowly.

Carla rolled her eyes again, but this time even more exaggerated. "Bitch, please."

"That's all I have to say right now about it," said Julie firmly while smiling at her friend. "Let's talk about our trip."

"When do you want to leave?" Carla looked back down to her computer.

"Yesterday," Julie replied before letting out a little laugh. "Whatever works best for your schedule. I don't really have anything going at the present time."

Carla switched the screen over to her calendar. "I can move a few things around so that we could fly out on Thursday."

"As in two days?" Julie asked.

"Yeah, you said yesterday."

"True, but that seems fast. How much is this going to cost?"

"I have plenty of American Airline miles," Carla opened another page on the internet browser. "I should have enough for two round trip flights. It's one of the perks of owning my own business and going to a lot of conferences." She typed in the details and said, "Wala! There's a flight at 7:10 am with a short layover in Dallas. I have enough points to cover our flight."

"I can pay for a hotel," offered Julie.

"Nonsense, I'll book a rental. Our flights are pretty much free," assured Carla.

"Carla, let me pay for something," Julie insisted.

"You can buy the booze," Carla responded with a wink.

Julie laughed, "Trying to wipe out my savings?"

Carla narrowed her eyes at Julie and smirked. "Now you're a comedian?"

Julie shrugged her shoulders.

Turning her attention back to the original topic. "How long do you want to stay?"

"Not long, because…" stammered Julie.

"Because you have so much going on here?" Carla said with a slight laugh.

"Hey, that's not fair," Julie reminded her.

"Sorry," Carla looked back at her computer screen. "Three, four, or five days?"

"Four?" suggested Julie.

Carla took in the look on Julie's face. "That gives us two days the explore. Wanna go for five days?"

"I guess five days would be ok. Two days for travel and three days to do whatever we're going to do there," Julie said with a nervous look on her face.

"Anything in particular you want to do while we're there?" asked Carla.

Julie shrugged her shoulders. "Sitting on the beach sounds good to me."

Tapping the keyboard, Carla said, "Bingo, how about a cute little house on one of the canals in Venice Beach? A short walk to the beach." She turned the laptop around to show Julie the photos of the house.

Julie's eyes grew big when she looked at the photos on the screen. The first photo looked like an art studio with paintings displayed on easels. Nodding her head yes Julie replied, "That looks perfect."

Carla saw the excitement in Julie's face. "That's just the sunroom off to the side of the house. Scroll through the rest of the photos," she encouraged.

Julie looked through the other photos and her smile grew with each one. When she came to the beach photos she said, "I just want to lay on the beach and soak up the sunshine with a Pina Colada."

"Throw in a cabana boy and you've got the perfect vacation!" Carla exclaimed with a chuckle.

Julie rolled her eyes and gave Carla her best 'mom'

look. "Cabana boy?"

"A girl can dream. A young hot stud to wait on us hand and foot," joked Carla.

"I wouldn't expect anything less from you," said Julie as she smiled. This felt good to her, like old times, but she knew that moments like this were fleeting.

"We're all set! The flights, car, and rental are all booked," Carla picked up her wine glass to cheer with Julie. "We're going to have so much fun!"

Julie didn't look so sure but forced a smile anyway.

Carla reached over and patted Julie's hand. "We are going to have fun. You need this, Jules. Don't overthink it, ok?"

Julie sighed, "Something happened earlier today."

"This doesn't sound good," remarked Carla.

"Ashley stopped by with her new boyfriend," Julie said with a concerned face.

"What's he like?" asked Carla.

Julie considered, "Something seemed off."

"Off? What do you mean by that?" Carla said with concern.

Julie thought back to her earlier memory of Jim. "He seems controlling."

Carla drew her head back, "That's a big judgement for meeting someone once."

"It's a gut feeling," said Julie.

"Young love. She'll either put him in line or it will fizzle out. I wouldn't be too worried," said Carla. "But then again, I don't have kids. So don't listen to me."

"Yeah, maybe," said Julie. She wondered if she was bias because of her experience with Jim.

Chapter 3

"Lovely" by Billie Eilish & Khalid

Julie stumbled her way to the kitchen. She flipped on the overhead light and squinted as she covered her eyes, not fully ready for the bright light. Looking up at the clock, she realized that it was four in the morning. Julie yawned and stretched her arms up over her head. She pushed the button on the coffee maker, thankful that she thought ahead when she got home from Carla's last night. Sitting at the island, she propped her head up in the palm of her hands. The aroma of coffee quickly filled the room. Breathing it in, she looked back toward the kitchen doorway and half expected Jim to come walking in ready to head out the door for work. She let out a heavy sigh and forced herself up to get a note pad and pen. If she was leaving tomorrow for her trip with Carla, she'd better get organized. It was second nature to her after years of family trips. Jim always insisted that she write things down to keep her on track. Sitting back down at the island, she sipped on her cup of coffee and wrote the word PACK in bold letters on the top of the pad. Staring at it, she took another sip before inhaling.

"I shouldn't be going on a trip. I should be making a list of all the things that need to be done around here." She pushed her mouth into a half frown as she pondered her options. "Did I send thank you notes for the flowers and plants from the funeral?" she asked aloud. "I'll go. Carla already has everything booked. Do people even expect thank you notes after a funeral? I'll go," she said as she got up, coffee cup in hand and walked toward the bedroom.

Standing in the closet, she stared at Jim's clothes and smiled at the neat stack of jeans that she had purposely messed up. Turning to her side of the closet, she started pulling out anything that she thought would fit her. She froze as a familiar scent enveloped her senses. It was Jim's cologne, unmistakable and haunting. With trembling hands, she dropped the clothes onto the bed and began to search. Her footsteps echoed throughout the silent house. She moved room by room, hoping against hope to find him even though she knew he was gone. A ghostly presence that refused to fade, the scent lingered and led her deeper into the memories of their life together.

She took in a deep breath, "It must have been a piece of clothing, that's all," she said trying to reassure herself. Closing her eyes, she scratched her forehead and concentrated on her breath. Her stomach growled and caused a distraction. She forced herself to make some breakfast.

Julie stood in front of the bed surrounded by the clothes she needed to pack for her trip. Each item seemed to mock her, a reminder of the life she had lost. Tears welled up in her eyes as she picked up a shirt that Jim had bought for her on their last vacation together. The memories flooded back and overwhelmed her with grief.

How could she go on this trip without him? How could she face the sunshine and the laughter of others when her world had been shattered? She sank to the floor and clutched the shirt to her chest as sobs wracked her body. Every item she touched brought back a wave of memories, a painful reminder of the love she had lost. The simple task of packing felt insurmountable. A mountain of heartache she couldn't bear to climb.

Julie: I know you're busy, but could you come over after work to help me figure out what to pack?

Carla: Do you know what time it is?

Julie: Sorry, I've been up since four.

Carla: It's a good thing I love you. LOL Yes, I can swing by after work for a bit.

Julie: You're the best, Car.

Julie busied herself cleaning up the mess she made with the clothes. When she went into the garage to get her suitcase, she noticed some boxes that were collapsed and leaning against the wall. She picked up a box and quickly glanced over to Jim's truck before going back inside. Taping the box together, she set it down outside the closet in the bedroom. Julie pushed the scent of Jim's cologne away as she carefully folded some of his shirts. As she reached for another sweater, a small stack of papers slipped from the pile of sweaters and fluttered to the floor. With a furrowed brow, she reached down to pick them up as her heart pounded with curiosity and dread.

Among the papers was a letter. Its edges were worn and creased from being folded and unfolded countless times. Most of the papers were in Jim's handwriting, but she picked up one with script she did not recognize. Julie's hand trembled as she read the words scrawled across the page.

My sweet Valentine,

I wish we could be together today. I love the diamond necklace you gave me. I wear it every day and think of you. I miss your touch and your kiss, my love. The time we get to spend together is beyond magical and I can't wait until our trip next month. Just to have you all to myself is a dream come true, even if it is only for a short time. I can still feel your gentle touch when I close my eyes and long for the day that we can spend the rest of our lives together.

All my love, Andrea

Julie sat there dumbfounded. She stared at the letter as it floated out of her hand and landed on the floor. She was in a state of shock. Her mind reeled as she struggled to process the betrayal. How could she have been so blind to the truth? The clothes in her hands suddenly felt heavy, weighed down by the deception and lies. She wanted to call Carla, but she couldn't move from Jim's side of the bed. Her mind yelled to get up! To move! To do something besides stare at the goddamned note! Breathless, she curled up into the fetal position. She didn't even recognize the sounds coming out of her as she sobbed and rocked back and forth.

Julie wasn't sure how long she laid there. When she felt strong enough, she sat up in bed and looked over at Jim's pillow. A surge of anger came over her. She punched his pillow before jerking herself out of bed. Walking over to the closet, she started pulling Jim's dress shirts down, not caring if the hangers broke or of the mess she was making. She searched for more love notes, trinkets, or anything he could have kept from this woman.

She abruptly stopped as it dawned on her that she knew Andrea. She was the girl from his office that couldn't quit crying at the funeral home. Her hand shot up to her mouth in shock. Andrea was just a few years older than Ashley. Her mind was racing again. What trip had he planned with her? Did they spend long lunches together at her place or a hotel? She let out a blood curdling scream as she dropped to the ground in the closet. Sobbing, she fell against the door frame.

The memories came flooding back. Jim had cheated shortly after they got married. It was another pretty, young, blonde girl from his office. He denied it when Julie confronted him. He turned the tables on her and made her think she was crazy for even suggesting that he would cheat on her. She thought about all the times when she traveled with the kids to visit her parents in Austin without Jim. His excuse was always work. Was he cheating on her then? Did he have someone else in their bed when she was gone? Her mind unraveled with all the scenarios. Each time she asked him about any little thing, he always turned it around to make her think she was just being insecure and possessive.

"How many were there, Jim?" she screamed. "How many fucking women did you screw behind my back?"

She felt nauseous and stumbled toward the bathroom. Sliding down onto the cold tile, she hugged the toilet as she cried. Wiping her mouth when she stood up, she marched in and grabbed her phone.

Julie: I need you.
Carla: What's going on?

Shivers ran down her back as she looked at the bed she had shared with Jim. A wave of nausea crested in the back of her throat, but she swallowed. She did not want to give him the satisfaction of making her ill yet again. She moved out of the bedroom and toward the sofa in the living room. Lying down, she closed her eyes and willed away the tears. She was done crying for this man. He had ruined her, their life, and their family. Closing her eyes, she thought of Ben and Ashley. They both loved and adored their father. She wanted to call them and tell them what she had found. It would break their hearts to know that their dad wasn't the perfect father they knew. Deep down, she knew that wouldn't make her feel any better and would only traumatize them. She stared back towards the fireplace.

Jim was weak and shivered in his recliner. Julie carried in the wood from the back porch and began stacking logs into the fireplace.

Jim coughed, "Make sure you check the damper and stack the wood crisscross to create an air pocket to feed the flames."

She rolled her eyes, "I've made plenty of fires with my dad when we went camping."

"I know what I'm talking about, Jules. I'm a fucking engineer. You only have a stupid art degree."

She restacked the wood to his demands, not wanting to cause more stress on his cancer riddled body. Lighting the stack, she turned around and walked out of the room.

Carla arrived and let herself into the house to immediately start looking for Julie. Her text was alarming and Carla had no idea what she was walking into. Calling out her name, Carla walked toward the bedroom.

"In here," Julie called out. Her voice raspy and soft.

Carla rushed toward the living room to find Julie on the sofa. "What happened, Jules?" she said as she sat on the floor and began pushing the hair out of Julie's face. "Jules?"

Julie looked up with tears in her eyes and said, "Andrea."

"Who is that?" Carla asked.

"Jim's mistress," said Julie softly.

"What the fuck are you talking about, Jules? A mistress?"

Julie just replied, "Letter." Pointing toward the bedroom.

Carla got up and hastily walked into the room to find the letter still on the floor. Picking it up, she read it before rushing back to Julie. "What the fuck? Where did you find this?"

Julie sat up and pulled her knees close to her body before motioning Carla to sit down. "I was…" she stammered. "I was putting some of Jim's clothes into a box when that fell out."

"Are you sure this was to Jim? Maybe he was holding onto it for someone else."

Julie cocked her head to the side looking at Carla and asked, "Why would he have kept it if it wasn't for him?"

"I'm grasping at straws here, Jules. I have no idea. I just don't want this to be true. I am so sorry, babe," she said as she rubbed Julie's leg. Trying to console her friend she said, "Maybe it was a one-time fling."

Julie turned her gaze up to Carla's face. Looking into her dark eyes, she said, "She wasn't the only one."

"What do you mean? How do you know?" Carla asked in confusion.

Julie took a deep breath. "It started a few months after we got married."

Carla had a look of shock on her face. "Jules, that can't be right. You two were head over heels in love. He worshiped you."

Julie shook her head as the memories came back to her. "He called to say he was working late on a special project and me being…, me, I made him dinner and took it to his office to surprise him. I rounded the corner off Clark Street and that's when I saw them. He had his arm around a cute blonde intern and they were walking out of the office building and headed who knows where. They were laughing and he stopped to kiss her."

"Why the hell didn't you tell me?" Carla asked.

Julie shrugged her shoulders before speaking. "If I said it out loud, it would make it real."

"Did you ask him about it?" Carla leaned in.

Julie nodded. "He told me I was mistaken and that it had been someone in his office named Brad. He was in his office working like he had told me when he called."

"You believed him?"

"What else was I supposed to do, Carla? I was married and only had a part time job. What was I going to do?"

"Talk to me. Tell your parents," Carla said. "Why did you stay, Jules?"

"I chose to believe him. I couldn't tell my parents. They loved Jim. I didn't want to hear my dad tell me that if I had only gotten a real degree then I would have had more options."

Carla sat there quietly, "I'm so sorry, Jules."

"I hoped that it was just a fling and that once we moved out of Chicago, it would stop."

"Did he stay in touch with her after you moved?" Carla asked gingerly.

"I don't know. Now that I've triggered these memories, I'm sure there were more."

"Wow. I consider myself a pretty good judge of character and wouldn't have guessed that he was like that. He missed his calling. He should have been an actor," Carla said angerly.

"We. Were good actors," Julie said in a whisper. She sat there quietly with her head in her hands.

"Fuck him," Carla said breaking the silence. Getting up from the sofa, she walked into the bedroom and grabbed the suitcase along with an arm full of clothes. "Let's get you packed. You're staying at my house tonight. No arguments, Jules," Carla demanded.

Chapter 4

"A Little Bit Yours" by JP Saxe

Sunlight dappled across the ugly carpet. Julie sat mesmerized by the way it danced over the faded colors. Turning her head, she noticed an airplane taxiing toward the runway. Her mind was still reeling from the events of yesterday. She swallowed hard as she replayed finding the letter again.

The air was thick with tension as she searched for the right words. Her heart pounded in her chest, but as she looked into his eyes, she only saw evasion and denial.

"I know what I saw, Jim. I'm not blind," she yelled as she crossed her arms.

He reached out to caress her arm, but she jerked away. "You're just being paranoid with the hours I've been working. You were probably just tired."

"Jim, it was you with your arms wrapped around the blonde girl from your office," Julie insisted.

"Don't be like this baby. Why would I cheat on you? You're carrying our first child. You're beautiful, why would I stray?"

Carla plopped down in the seat beside her. "I bought water, popcorn, trashy mags, and look, Twizzlers! Remember how we ate Twizzlers until we puked our freshman year in college?" Carla busted open the package of candy and handed one to Julie.

Julie smiled at the memory and took a bite of the licorice. "I think it was the vodka not the Twizzlers," she said with a slight laugh, happy for memory that wasn't painful.

"You know I couldn't stand the sight or smell of them for years afterwards, but I still like vodka, so I think you're wrong," Carla said before taking another big bite.

Julie rolled her eyes. "Is there any liquor that you don't like?"

"Uhm, Jager," Carla said, as she made a nauseated face.

"Don't even go there. Talk about not being able to stand the smell of something," replied Julie, with a disgusted look on her face.

"Do you remember when we got into trouble trying to sneak some into the basketball game our freshman year?" laughed Carla.

"I remember getting caught. Then my parents threatened me to go to community college and give up my art major," replied Julie.

"Your dad never understood your art. He wanted you to quit as soon as you started," Carla shook her head before taking another bite into a piece of candy.

"True, but he was so happy when I started dating Jim." Just saying his name was like a dagger to Julie's heart. She tried to stop the tears by taking a deep breath, but it didn't help.

"Don't do that," Carla said, as she put her arm around Julie, "We're gonna have a great time, I promise."

Turning to look at Carla, Julie tried to smile and said, "Thank you for always being here for me."

Carla's face dropped, "Don't go getting all sappy on me. You know I don't handle that well. Besides, we just need to concentrate on getting you laid sooner rather than later." She immediately started laughing.

Julie rolled her eyes and looked around to see if anyone else had heard Carla's crass remark. Turning back toward Carla, "I don't need another man."

"Okay, we can stop and get you a vibrator," Carla joked as she laughed out loud again.

"Stop!" Julie said, her cheeks flushed with embarrassment. "Good thing I love you."

"I love you more, bitch." Carla leaned her head next to Julie's. "Can I ask you something?"

"Anything," Julie said immediately.

"Have you thought about telling the kids what you found?" Carla tried to keep her voice low.

Julie bit the corner of her lower lip and looked over at Carla. "I don't know."

"They deserve to know the truth," Carla said with a tinge of protectiveness in her voice.

"Maybe," Julie paused. "It won't change anything other than tarnishing Jim in their eyes. Or it could make them angry at me for keeping it to myself if I don't tell them."

"Do you think Charlotte knew how he was? It makes me wonder if he did that to girlfriends before you, like in high school," said Carla.

"I doubt she knew. She and their mom, Jenny, are so religious, I don't think he would have shared that with his family. Who knows? Maybe Craig cheated on Jenny," Julie said with a shrug of her shoulders.

"You didn't deserve this. You know that, right?" asked Carla. She turned toward Julie, looking her in her eyes. "You did nothing to deserve this," Carla said sternly.

Julie nodded her head in agreement. "I tried to be a good wife. I kept everything the way he liked it, neat, tidy and organized. I even used his favorite shade of blue when decorating the house," she said with a hint of disgust in her low voice. "Anything to keep him happy."

"Well, you're going to forget all about it. We're going to lay in the sun and get our tan on!" announced Carla.

Julie just smiled before taking another piece of candy from the bag.

***

The rental house was a cute bungalow with pale green paint and dark green trim. Sitting her bag down in the hallway, Julie walked directly toward the artist sunroom area. Her hand flew to her mouth when she saw the seaside paintings sitting on easels. Each one more beautiful than the next. Julie couldn't help herself. She reached out to touch a beautiful orange and pink sunset over the water. Stroking the painting with her finger like a paint brush, she imagined seeing that sunset in person. Standing in awe, she wondered if the owner of the home was the artist. Julie leaned in closer to take in the tiny brush strokes and the intricacies of the artwork. After her close observations, she took a step back to observe all three together.

"It's the same spot," she said.

Carla yelled from the other room, "What'd you say?"

Julie didn't respond, making Carla come looking for her. "What did you say?" she asked as she entered the room.

Not taking her eyes off the paintings, Julie repeated herself, "It's the same spot."

Carla looked at the paintings, "What?" she said with a slight hint of annoyance.

Julie grabbed Carla's arm bringing her close to where they could stand side by side. "The paintings. They are all from the same spot, just different times of the day. Sunrise, mid-day, and sunset. See?"

"Oh yeah," patronized Carla.

Julie looked over at Carla and laughed, "You're an artist, Carla. Doesn't this excite you?"

Carla looked at Julie through hooded eyes, "I'm a graphic designer."

"Still an artist," assured Julie as she smiled at the paintings. "We have to find this spot and some drawing supplies. I wonder if there's an art store nearby?"

Carla smiled and said, "Food, booze, art supplies. In that order."

"At least you put food before booze. You might actually be growing up after all," teased Julie.

"Mehehehe," Carla said mockingly as she turned around. "What room do you want?"

"Doesn't matter to me, just tell me where to put my things. I want to check out the canal," Julie said pushing past Carla.

The small deck area looked out over on the canals. Looking to her left, Julie noticed a picturesque scene with a small, white rowboat tied up to a post attached to the white bridge on the other side of the canal. She smiled at the sight before turning around to see two lounge chairs and a small grill that sat ready for use. Closing her eyes, she took a deep breath of the fresh sea air. This felt like heaven to her and she wondered why she had second guessed coming on this trip at all. Carla joined her on the deck where they sat back on the lounge chairs and took in the warm sunshine on their faces.

Suddenly, the excitement of being in California wore off and Julie's mind began to think back to the letter and her memory of that day in Chicago. She tried to recall if there were other women in Jim's life besides those three. She questioned every family activity and every work interaction. Her mind flipped from one event to the next. She wondered if Andrea went on that trip to Seattle that Jim took last year. An ache slowly started taking over her head and she abruptly got up and walked inside. Picking up her bag, she walked toward one of the bedrooms. Shutting the door, she moved toward the bed to lay down. Closing her eyes, she forced her mind to concentrate on the pinkish color of the back of her eyelids. She would do anything to make the memories and questions go away. Finally, her mind quieted long enough for her to drift off to sleep.

***

Julie walked into the kitchen, "What's all this?" she asked, looking at the array of groceries, booze, and a smattering of tablets, charcoal pencils, and colored pencils.

"You said you wanted drawing supplies, so I bought you some. Are they not the right kind? I tried to think back to some of our classes to remember what you liked," said Carla.

Julie smiled sheepishly and asked, "You did that for me?"

Carla stopped putting the groceries in the fridge and turned to look at Julie, "Bitch, you know there isn't anything I wouldn't do for you. Do you feel better after your nap?"

Julie rubbed half of her face and sighed, "At least my headache is gone."

"That's good. I picked up a pizza and some beer for dinner. I didn't think you'd feel like going out."

"Thanks Car. You're right, I think a night in would be good. What can I do to help?" Julie asked.

Carla opened the fridge door and tossed a can of beer to Julie. "Just sit."

***

Julie was unusually quiet as they ate and watched a movie. Carla had tried several times to discuss the hot guy on the screen, but Julie was clearly distracted and didn't

engage. Feeling frustrated, Carla paused the movie and said, "Get it out."

"Get what out?" asked Julie.

"Whatever is in your head. Get it out!" demanded Carla.

Julie stared at the television. "Just finish the movie, Car."

"No. You're gonna talk to me. It's not healthy to keep it all bottled inside. You've buried things for thirty-five years. It's time to get it out and get a clean slate."

"I miss him," she said slowly and softly.

"That's understandable, but I will not let you go back to pulling the covers over your head and not living. He wanted you to be free to live your life. Even if he was a fucking wretch of a human being and cheated on you!" said Carla.

"I'm so angry at him, but I also miss him. I feel like I'm going insane. The fires of anger are doused by waves of grief, and I feel like I'm caught in the middle drowning," Julie cried.

Carla let out a sigh, "Oh Jules. That's why you have to talk about it. You can't keep all of that inside of you."

"I feel so guilty," said Julie.

"Guilty? What do you have to feel guilty about?" asked Carla.

"I knew he was cheating and I stayed! I had three children with him!"

"Wait…three? What are you talking about, Jules?"

Julie realized what she had said. She brought her hands up and rubbed her forehead, knowing that she had said too much. "When Ash was two, I found out I was pregnant, like super early pregnant. I found out that Jim was…,"

"Fucking someone else?" Carla interjected, seething with anger.

Julie closed her eyes as the tears ran down her cheeks, "Yeah. I knew he always ate lunch at a restaurant around the corner from his office and I wanted to surprise him with the news. He wanted a big family, so I was excited to share the news. I saw him sitting with a red headed woman. He reached across the table to hold her hand. I was heartbroken and didn't know what to do, so I got in my car and drove to Planned Parenthood to get information about an abortion. They helped me set it up for the next week."

Carla scooted over to hug her friend. "I'm so sorry, Jules. Why didn't you tell me? You didn't have to go through this by yourself."

"It was something I had to do alone," whispered Julie.

"Did you ever tell him?" asked Carla.

"No. You're the first person I've told. I wanted to tell him. To hurt him as much as he had hurt me. God, how can I hate him so much and yet miss him?" Julie asked with exasperation.

"Why did you stay with him, Jules?" Carla asked.

Julie looked down at her hands. They were shaking. "I loved him," she said quietly.

Carla sat stunned and not knowing what to say, so she leaned over and took Julie in her arms. Julie hugged her back so tightly. Her life depended on that hug.

Chapter 5

"Six Feet Under" by Billie Eilish

Julie wrapped herself in a pink, fuzzy blanket as she sat on the deck to watch the brilliant sunrise. She reached her arm out from under the warmth to pick up her mug of coffee. She was awake most of thc night with dreams about that summer day in 2000 when she walked into the abortion clinic all alone and scared. She was exhausted but thankful that she was here with Carla and not at home, alone. Lifting the mug to her lips, she sipped as she stared across the canal at the houses, all dark with only the occasional porch light on.

"I'm just as lonely now as I've been for the past thirty-five years," she admitted in a whisper. Her eyes darted around to make sure no one else could have heard her admission. Birds started to chirp in nearby trees and she smiled at the sound.

Movement caught her eye from the huge windows in the house directly across from her. It was a young mom carrying her toddler into the kitchen as she flipped on the light and sat the child on the counter. An older child soon joined them. Julie watched the mom scurry around the kitchen making breakfast. It brought a smile to Julie's face reminiscing of her kitchen at home, making breakfast for Ben and Ashley, and planning their day together. Ben would ask for bacon and Ashley only ate pancakes. Closing her eyes, she pictured Ashley's blonde hair always a mess in the mornings, but Ben was always so put together as a child with combed hair. Jim was busy working while Julie raised the kids. Glancing back at the house, she noticed the husband had walked into the kitchen across the way, sending a cold shiver down Julie's back. She frowned as she took another sip of her coffee before leaning her head back.

Carla appeared in her robe, with her cat-eye glasses on and her black hair a mess. "It's cold out here."

Julie looked over and laughed, "Grab a blanket from the living room and join me." She waited as Carla turned around, shuffled back inside before returning with a mug of coffee and a big blanket.

"How long have you been out here?" Carla asked as she wrapped the blanket around her and sat down on the other lounge chair.

"Before the sun came up. I had trouble sleeping," explained Julie.

"Last night was rough," Carla reached her hand out from under the blanket and placed it on Julie's covered arm. "I'm glad you trusted me. It had to be so hard keeping that to yourself for the past twenty-four years. Now that you've remembered it, what are you going to do?"

Julie shook her head slowly, "There's really nothing to do."

"Have you thought about talking to a someone, like a therapist?"

Julie smiled and looked over at Carla, "Isn't that what best friends are for? Free therapy?" she joked.

Carla had a serious look on her face. "I know our generation scoffs at therapy and talking about our feelings, but you might need help processing this, Jules. It's a lot."

"I'll think about it," Julie said with a slight grin. She and Carla knew that 'thinking about it' was basically a no.

Changing the subject, Carla asked, "Beach Day?"

"Sounds good," replied Julie with a slight smile.

***

Packing a cooler with sandwiches, waters, and a few hidden adult beverages, they headed for the beach. Carla picked out a spot that was away from the crowds trickling onto the beach. Julie carefully laid down a big beach blanket they found at the house along with an umbrella. Dropping down onto the blanket, they put their feet toward the Pacific Ocean.

"How are you doing?" asked Carla.

Julie rolled her eyes under her dark sunglasses. "How often are you going to ask me that?" annoyance in her voice.

Carla edged her sunglasses down her nose to peer above the lenses at Julie. "As often as I need to."

"I'm fine. I'm really fine," Julie stated, moving her gaze out toward the ocean. Taking a deep inhale of the sea air, she let it out slowly and repeated, "Fine."

"Have you thought about what you're going to do when we get back?" asked Carla.

"I'm considering an art class through one of the community colleges," Julie said in a somber voice. "Not really sure, yet."

"Hmmm, that would be a good place to start," Carla agreed.

"Ben suggested that I move to Atlanta, but I'm not ready for big changes like that, plus Ash still needs me close."

"What about when Ash is done with her Masters? Is she considering staying in St. Louis?" asked Carla.

"I doubt that she will. She wants to move to Chicago," replied Julie. "But then again, so much has changed recently. I have no idea what's going to happen with her career or if Ben will stay in Atlanta," said Julie.

"Thought any more about telling the kids?" asked Carla as she stared over at Julie.

Julie looked straight ahead toward the ocean and

took her time to respond. "Not really. I might tell them someday. Honestly, I don't want to talk about it anymore. Let's just have fun."

"Ok, I'll drop it. Promise me one thing. That you will move on with YOUR life and do the things that YOU want to do, okay?" asked Carla.

"I will give it my best shot, that's all I can promise," she said trying to smile as she looked over at Carla.

"Okay, then," said Carla. "Want a trashy mag or a book to read?" Holding out a worn book and one of the magazines she picked up at the airport.

"Book," said Julie as she took it from Carla's hand.

Julie had a hard time concentrating on reading. Putting it down beside her, she propped herself up on her elbows. Carla had laid back with a magazine covering her face. Julie looked back out across the beach to her left and noticed a young couple. The young man couldn't keep his hands off his girlfriend as she just giggled. Turning her gaze back to the waves crashing into the shoreline, she slowly closed her eyes and breathed in the salt air.

Carla noticed the change on Julie's face. "Thinking about him?"

"Yeah," Julie said with a sigh. "I feel like if I move on, I'm somehow betraying him."

"After what he put you through, nothing you do is betraying him," Carla consoled Julie.

"It's all so foreign to me. I didn't date much in high school and the only guy I had been with before Jim was Darren. You know how badly that ended." Julie chuckled, "Besides, I'm too old now to have a man interested in me."

"That's preposterous," said Carla, raising her voice. "You have so much to give to a partner and you're young, bitch. I know because I'm the same age as you and I'm not too old for anything."

Julie couldn't help but to laugh. "What would I do without you?"

"Not sure, but your life would be a hell of a lot less interesting," Carla said with a wink.

***

Carla stood in the kitchen making dinner with a glass of wine in one hand as she poured the box of pasta into the boiling water. "Dinner will be ready in ten minutes," she yelled.

Julie had just gotten out of the shower. Slipping on a gauzy dress, she walked toward the kitchen, put her hair up into a messy bun, and strolled through the door. "What can I do to help?"

"Not a damn thing. Pour yourself a glass of wine and take a load off," Carla commanded.

Picking up an empty wine glass, Julie gave herself a heavy pour before sitting down at the little table. She opened one of the charcoal pencil packages and flipped open a page in her sketch book to start doodling. Julie examined the kitchen some inspiration, fixing her sight on the bottle of wine, fresh tomatoes, a bulb of garlic, and an open jar of half gone tomato sauce. She started sketching the still art.

Carla walked over to the table. "Damn, you've still got it," she stated as she glanced over Julie's shoulder.

"I don't know," Julie said with a hint of disappointment in her tone.

"Stop. You always were your worst critic. Well, other than your dad and Jim," Carla said with a raised brow. "Sorry," she said through gritted teeth.

"You're right, and my perfectionism has only gotten worse over the years," she dropped her attention back to the drawing. "This is crap."

"No, it's not, Jules," said Carla as she walked back over to the stove. "Spaghetti is done. I'm just waiting on the bread sticks. Come make a plate," invited Carla.

Julie cleared the table of her drawing mess before getting a plate of food. She was quiet during dinner, tired of spewing her feelings over the past few days. She was tired of hearing herself speak.

"Cat got your tongue?" Carla asked, tilting her head and furrowing her brow.

"Just lost in my thoughts," said Julie.

"Moving on doesn't mean you're turning your back on the good times in your past, right?" asked Carla.

Looking down at her vibrating phone, Julie answered and pushed the speaker option, "Hey Ash. You're on speaker."

"Mom," Ashley's voice trembled.

"What's going on Ash? Why are you crying?" asked Julie.

"Jordan and I had a huge fight. We were at Imo's Pizza and this girl walks in alone. He starts staring at her and totally ignoring me. I snapped my fingers in his face to get his attention. He fucking grabbed my arm and twisted it until I was in pain." She stopped momentarily before continuing, "He said, I could fucking get over myself before getting up and walking over to talk to that other girl."

Carla chimed in, "What the fuck, Ash? You're better off without a jerk like that!"

Julie calmly asked, "What did you do, Ash?"

Ashley stopped crying just enough to answer, "I just sat there, frozen, not being able to believe what happened. He slid into the booth with the girl, putting his arm around her. I didn't know what else to do, so I left."

Julie took a deep breath, "I'm so sorry, Ashley. You'll find someone better."

"I love him, Mom! I don't want anyone better." Ashley sobbed.

"Ash, you deserve someone who wants to be with you more than anyone else," said Carla, as she looked over at Julie.

With a raised eyebrow she mouthed, 'Your kids need to know about their dad.'

Julie shook her head no, before saying, "Ash, what can I do to help?"

"Can I stay at the house? I really don't want to talk to him tonight and if I go to my apartment, he'll just come over later."

"Of course you can, honey. It's your home, you can always come back. Are you okay to drive?" Julie asked.

"I'll just Uber. Thanks, Mom. Love you!" said Ashley before hanging up.

Carla shook her head, "You have to at least tell Ashley so she has a fighting chance to get away from this douchebag."

Julie looked down at her hands, "I can't ruin the way they remember their dad. I just can't do it, Car."

"Jules, they need to know so they don't end up in a bad relationship. You have to stop the cycle," Carla urged.

"I'll think about it, but hopefully this Jordan boy has just fizzled out of her life," even as Julie says it, she knows from her own experience that the words are not true.

After cleaning up dinner, Julie excused herself to the sunroom. She stood in silence with the paintings. She wanted to find the spot on the beach that was represented in the paintings. Julie looked around the room and started digging through books and drawers to find any photos that would give her a clue as to where to find the answers to her questions. She felt that if she could find the spot, it might be a sign to help her move past the weight of grief, anger, and turmoil that plagued her mind. She sighed in disappointment when she couldn't find anything.

Walking back toward the kitchen, she heard music coming from the back deck. She smiled as she walked out to find Carla with a glass of wine and a joint. It reminded her of their college days lounging on Oak Street beach in Chicago. Julie began to sway back and forth to the music, causing Carla to get up to join in. Together they twirled, sang, and laughed just like they did back before life got too complicated. Julie's heart and mind still felt heavy thinking about what Ashley was going through. She wondered if knowing the truth about Jim would help or hurt the situation.

Chapter 6

"4:35" by Gemma Hayes

A slight fog hung over the canal, giving the porch lights across the way an eerie vibe. Julie found herself in another sleepless night sitting on the deck and wrapped up in that same fuzzy blanket. The dreams forced her to relive times when she found evidence of Jim's infidelity. Pulling the blanket up closer to her neck, she took a deep breath and held it before releasing with a big sigh. Her thoughts shifted to Ashley and the situation with Jordan. She struggled on whether she should tell Ashley and Ben the truth about their dad and her relationship with him. She bit her lip, thinking about how she could even broach the subject of aborting their sibling. Her heart and mind felt so heavy. Julie struggled to catch her breath as tears began to fall and she felt unable to move. Closing her eyes, she focused on breathing, counting between each breath, until she relaxed.

Carla peeked her head out of the door. "Will you make some coffee?" she called out.

"Be right there." Thankful for the distraction, she picked the blanket up and made her way into the kitchen.

"Not sleeping again?" Carla asked.

"I never sleep good in strange beds," Julie covered her truth.

"Hmmm, okay," Carla responded sarcastically knowing that Julie was lying. "It's our last full day. What do you want to do?"

Julie thought for a moment before answering. "Let's ride bikes."

"The fuck? You really want to go bike riding?" Carla asked, clearly annoyed.

"Yeah… but if you don't want to, we don't have to," Julie said as she pouted, sticking out her bottom lip.

Rolling her eyes, Carla said, "Fine, but we have to go out tonight. I saw a flier about Archie's Bar having an 80's music night."

"Deal," said Julie as she poured Carla a mug of coffee. "I'm going to go lay down for a bit, if you don't mind."

Carla reached up taking Julie's hand, "You, okay?"

"Yeah," Julie said as she nodded her head before turning around.

Carla crept into Julie's room, laid down on the bed, and snuggled up to her friend. Julie woke up but didn't move. She closed her eyes again and concentrated on having a warm body near her. A wave of loneliness crashed over her, causing tears to fill her eyes and fall onto the pillowcase. She sniffed, alerting Carla that she was awake.

"I'm here, Jules. You can always count on me," assured Carla.

"I know, Car. I'm glad you're in my life," replied Julie through the tears.

"You are not alone. I know you feel lonely, but I'm here. Life will get better, I promise."

"It doesn't feel like it. It feels like my worst fear is coming true. I'm really alone."

Carla sat up in the bed, sitting cross legged. "You didn't let me feel alone when I divorced Christian. You invited me into your home. I know Jim wasn't crazy about the idea, but you stood your ground for me. I've loved being your friend from the moment we met. I wouldn't be where I am now if it hadn't been for our friendship. It's my turn to show you that I'm here for you, through the good and bad. Let me be the one you turn to, Jules."

Julie sat up, wiping her tears away with her hand. She leaned over and put her head against Carla's. "I would be rotting in my bed right now if it weren't for you. I love you, bitch," she said with slight grin.

"I love you more, bitch," replied Carla. It was quiet for a moment before Carla asked, "Do we really have to ride bikes?"

"Yep," answered Julie with a laugh.

***

The fog faded before they made their way to the bike rental near the beach. Julie picked out a light pink cruiser bike, while Carla opted for a bright blue one.

They both got the giggles when first hopping on the bikes. "Stop making me laugh!" screamed Carla as she shakily tried to get her bike under control.

Julie laughed harder until she started to fall over. Catching herself with her foot, she eased off the bike and placed it on its side. Bent over in laughter, she squeaked out, "Oh my god! Don't make me pee my pants!"

Carla pulled up beside where Julie was clutching her chest, laughing. "I don't remember riding a bike being so hard! Why the hell do people say, 'It's like riding a bike?' Fucking A, this is awful," she said with a hardy laugh.

Once they got going again, Julie felt brave and let go of the handlebars. She stuck her hands out to her sides and mimicked an airplane. "Look ma, no hands," Julie yelled out to Carla.

"If you fall, I'm not taking you to the ER!" Carla threatened. "Now, I remember hating bike rides as a kid. How did you talk me into this?"

"You're doing great!" hollered Julie as she sped around Carla.

"I hate you for making me do this!" yelled Carla as she started to lose control of the handlebars. "Help Jules!"

Julie stopped her bike and watched Carla struggle to catch up. She couldn't contain her laughter. It was one of those deep belly-laughs that felt so good and so natural. Carla stopped beside Julie, hoped off the bike, and turned it around. She started walking back toward the rental office.

Julie turned her bike around to catch up to Carla. "Oh, come on, it's not that bad."

"I'm done. We tried it and I'm hungry," she said angrily.

Julie hopped off her bike to walk next to Carla. "At least you tried something new and I had a good laugh," she said as she winked at her friend. "You wanted me to laugh and have a good time," she reminded Carla.

Carla looked over at her with squinted eyes. "Not at my expense."

"Oh, honey, I wasn't laughing at you, just the situation. Please don't be mad at me," Julie begged.

Carla rolled her eyes and sighed. "I'm not mad at you. I'm just over this forced form of exercise."

***

Julie took a seat at a small outdoor table, while Carla ordered coffee and their breakfasts at the beachfront café. Carla returned, setting the drinks down on the table. Julie smiled as she sipped the fresh hot coffee.

"So, you're good with going to the 80's night at that bar tonight?" asked Carla as the server placed their plates of eggs and bacon down in front of them.

"Yeah, it could be fun," Julie said before taking another sip of coffee.

"You are a menace, choosing hot coffee while

sitting near the beach in the heat. You should try cold brew. It makes more sense," teased Carla.

"I've relied on hot, black coffee for over forty years. Why stop now?" retorted Julie. "I should call Ashley and check on her."

"Does that asshole know where you live?" asked Carla.

Julie sighed, "Yeah, she stopped by with him the other day."

"What was your take on him?" Carla asked looking up at Julie.

"Hmmm, I had the feeling that he likes to push boundaries and was borderline rude. He's not what he says he is."

"So, you don't like him. Ash said that she loved him, which happened quickly if they just started dating, don't you think?"

"I think she's still grieving and searching for something or someone that is hers," added Julie.

"Hopefully it's over, before it really begins. I want to break the little fucker's arm for trying to hurt her!" said Carla with an edge to her voice.

"Yeah, me too," said Julie.

***

"Let's Dance" by David Bowie
"Everybody Wants to Rule the World" by Tears for Fears

They could hear the music outside of the bar, making the girls feel giddy with excitement. Carla turned and said, "First round is on me!" as they walked inside.

"What are you going to have?" Julie yelled over the loud music.

"Sex on the beach!" yelled Carla. "You want one too?"

"Sure. I'll find a table," offered Julie.

Walking away from Carla, Julie spotted a small table with two chairs in the middle of the room. She hurriedly sat down and scoped the place out. There was a parquet dance floor near the front with tables and chairs filling out the rest of the place. She smiled with excitement as the song, *"Footloose" by Kenny Loggins* played over the speakers. She shuffled her feet back and forth to mimic one of the scenes from the movie of the same title.

Carla carefully walked toward Julie with two very full drinks. Sitting down, she handed Julie a drink while lifting hers up to her lips.

"Cheers!" yelled Julie, trying to stop Carla from taking a drink.

"Oh, right," said Carla as she clinked her glass into Julies. "What are we drinking to?"

"Friendship," said Julie with a smile.

"Friendship!" cheered Carla loudly.

Midway through their drinks, the song, *"Let's Dance" by David Bowe* started. Both girls jumped up and moved to the small crowd on the dance floor. Neither of them had been out dancing in years. Laughing at each other's dance moves, they moved around the dance floor as the next song, *"Shake it Up," by The Cars* started to play. Julie and Carla swayed their hips, spinning their bodies, and flailed their hands to the music.

They were having the time of their lives, before making their way back to the table. This time Julie insisted on getting the next round of drinks. When she got back to the table, she looked past Carla and noticed a man with dark wavy hair, black rimmed glasses, mustache and scruff along his chin, sitting with a red headed woman. He looked vaguely familiar, but she brushed it off.

A man approached the table and asked Carla to

dance. She looked over at Julie, who shrugged her shoulder and mouthed, "Go on, have fun," before starting to giggle. Julie sipped her drink while watching Carla dance.

Carla ran over to grab Julie, "Come on, threes company!" dragging her onto the dance floor. The pulsating rhythm of the classic 80's song, *"Everybody Wants to Rule the World," by Tears for Fears*, filled the air and enveloped Julie and Carla in its infectious beat as they danced. Julie's reserved demeanor melted away and was replaced by a vibrant energy as she twirled and swayed to the nostalgic tune. With each movement, she let go of her worries and immersed herself in the moment alongside Carla, who matched her enthusiasm step for step. Their laughter mingled with the music, creating a symphony of joy that seemed to echo throughout the crowded room. For Julie, it was a moment of liberation and a chance to forget the pressures of her life, and simply enjoy the euphoria of dancing with her best friend.

Returning to the table, Julie glanced over at the man she saw earlier and noticed him looking directly at her. She felt her face flush and her heart rate quickened. She looked back at her drink, then quickly glanced up again and shifted her eyes toward the man. He was still staring at her. She felt instantly flustered and an uncomfortable feeling grew inside of her. She could tell that he was on a date with this woman, which made it worse in Julie's eyes. Her mind flickered back to seeing Jim taking the hand of the red headed woman and she panicked.

Carla sat down just as Julie said, "We need to go."

"We just got here. What's the rush?" Carla asked.

Julie scooted her seat closer to Carla's and said, "See the guy in the blue shirt with the red head, over in the corner?"

Carla didn't waste any time. She jerked her head around to see what Julie was talking about. "What a hunk!" exclaimed Carla.

"He keeps staring at me and he's obviously on a date. I'm getting creeped out and I want to leave," explained Julie.

"We are having fun. Can't we just stay a little longer? We never get to go dancing," Carla protested.

Julie looked back over towards the man in blue. The red head was no longer sitting there and he was staring directly at Julie. She wanted to look away, but couldn't. He just nodded his head at her and smiled. She turned her attention back to Carla. "I really feel uncomfortable. Can we please leave?" begged Julie.

Carla rolled her eyes at Julie and said, "Fine, we can leave."

Walking back to the house, Carla reached out and took Julie's hand in hers. "I'm sorry I was being a dick back there."

"I'm sorry for ruining our fun," Julie apologized.

"I don't want to sound insensitive, but what exactly weirded you out about the guy?" asked Carla. "I thought he was pretty hot, to be honest."

Julie thought for a moment before responding. "He was on a date with that woman, but he was staring at me. It triggered my memory of seeing Jim with that red head in Chicago. I wondered how many times Jim and I were on a date and I didn't notice him staring at other women. He wasn't nearly as blatant as Jordan was with Ashley."

Carla hung her head down, "I get it and if you didn't feel comfortable, we did the right thing by leaving. I didn't think of it from that perspective. I'm sorry," Carla said as she wrapped her arm around Julie.

The cool night air brushed against Julie and Carla's cheeks as they strolled along the quiet street, their footsteps echoing in the silence. After a moment of hesitation, Julie cleared her throat and her voice slightly trembled as she broached the delicate topic.

"Carla, there's something I need to tell you,"

Julie's words hesitant yet resolute. Carla turned to her friend, sensing the weight behind her tone.

"What is it, Jules?" Carla asked, her concern evident in her eyes.

"Jim isn't the only one that strayed. I…I had an emotional affair," Julie confessed, her voice barely above a whisper. She paused, searching for the right words to explain the tangled emotions that consumed her.

Carla's brow furrowed in surprise, but she remained silent and allowed Julie to continue.

"It was with a single dad in Ashley's first grade class," Julie continued, her voice tinged with regret.

Carla listened attentively. Her expression was a mix of empathy and understanding. She reached out and gently squeezed Julie's hand to offer silent support.

As they continued to walk, Julie recounted the complexities of her feelings, unraveling the layers of guilt and longing that had led her down this path. She felt a weight lift off her shoulders, relieved to finally share this secret with her trusted friend. Carla remained by her side, offering a comforting presence as they navigated the tumultuous terrain of Julie's emotions.

Julie looked forward to the days that she volunteered at the kid's school. When she arrived, she was surprised to see a man in the classroom. It wasn't often that dad's volunteered, but she walked toward him, wanting to make him feel welcome.

"Hello," Julie reached her hand out to him. "I'm Julie, Ashley's mom, and you are?"

"I'm Brian," he stated as he shook Julie's hand. "I'm Olivia's dad, we just moved here. It's nice to meet you, Julia, oops...Julie."

Julie smiled, "My name is actually Julia, but everyone calls me Julie. What brings your family to St. Louis?"

"My job. I'm an Art Professor at SLU," Brian waved at Oliva, who ran over to give him a hug around the legs. "Go back to your seat, baby."

Julie's heart fluttered to see him be so sweet and attentive to his daughter. "Does your wife work?" Immediately realizing that she was being nosey, she added, "Sorry, that's none of my business."

Brian looked over at Julie and grinned, "It's okay. Olivia's mother passed away a few years ago." He looked back to Olivia, "Car accident."

Julie's hand shot up to cover her gapping mouth, "I'm so sorry."

"Don't be," he said as he looked into Julie's eyes.

Feeling a flutter in her chest, she looked away and turned her attention to Ashley. "We should plan a playdate for the girls sometime. Go to the park after school."

"We would love that. Olivia is pretty shy, so it would be good for her to have some time with friends outside of class."

Julie explained that it was a knee jerk reaction to trying to deal with Jim's infidelities. Hand in hand they continued to walk back to the rental house and forget about the man at the bar.

Chapter 7

"Clear" by Fly by Midnight

Julie lazily sauntered toward the beach. The gentle breeze caressing her face mixed with the warmth of the sun made her smile. Her mood had been lifted by the sand and surf, compared to what she felt back home. It was a reprieve she welcomed from the darkness of grief that enveloped her before. Taking a seat in the sand, she watched the waves hit the shore. Pulling her knees up to her chest, she slowly rocked side to side and got lost in the sights and sounds surrounding her. "God, I'm going to miss this," she said quietly. "Maybe I need to move to the beach someday." Removing her sunglasses, she squinted as she looked back toward her path to the house. Turning her attention back to the shoreline, she noticed a sailboat in the distance. It looked so tiny as it bounced around the ocean. She felt small in this moment, and she was ok with that. Back home, she was the widow and the epitome of grief. She never enjoyed being the center of attention, and Jim's death thrust her into the core of it all. Wiping a tear from running down her cheek, she clicked her tongue as she stood up and made her way toward the beachside café.

When Julie turned around from placing her order, she realized that the creeper guy from last night was standing off to the side, waiting for his order. A sense of panic rushed through her veins, causing her heart to beat faster. She drew in a deep breath and hoped he wouldn't recognize her. Thankfully, he was busy looking at his phone. Julie put her head down and stepped to the side. She hoped that her sunglasses were enough of a disguise to keep him from noticing her. Peeking up at him she realized that Carla was right, he was very handsome and not very creepy at all. His chestnut curls hung down in front of his face as he looked down and he was taller than she expected. Even though he wore sunglasses, she could see the smile lines around his eyes. He reached up to push his hair back, and she felt a wave of excitement rush through her and replace any panic she had felt.

Looking away, she took a deep breath to steady her nerves before glancing his way again. He was tall and had a mustache and patchy scruff the same chestnut color as his hair, but with flecks of grey that might not be as noticeable if he weren't standing in the sun. He was dressed in a white dress shirt that was open and showed the top of his tan chest. He also wore dark denim jeans, brown loafers, and black aviator sunglasses. He was actually quite beautiful. Julie was lost in the moment staring at him. She hadn't felt this type of attraction to someone in so many years, she couldn't help but smile and laugh quietly to herself. "What is happening?" she said under her breath as she looked away from him. Her mouth partially open, she bit her lower lip as she casually looked back toward him. She was jolted back into reality when she realized that he was looking directly at her and smiling. Suddenly she felt flustered and nervously looked away from him. His smile was warm and friendly, and she could feel her defenses lowering just looking at him. "Crap," she said under her breath.

"Didn't I see you at Archie's last night?" he asked walking towards her.

"Maybe. I'm not sure what the name of the bar was," she lied.

"My name is Marc and yours is?" he asked holding out his hand.

"Julia, um Julie," she stammered.

"I thought that was you," he replied with a slight

laugh of excitement. "You probably don't remember me, do you?"

"I'm not from here. You must have me confused with someone else."

He smiled and said, "You remember your best friend in high school, Lizzy? I'm her little brother that used to follow you two around."

Julie's eyes grew big with disbelief and her mouth dropped open. She quickly composed herself and replied, "Oh my gosh, Marc! The last time we saw each other, you were, like… maybe ten years old. How is Liz doing?" she asked as she touched his arm and a tingle rushed through her. "I haven't talked to her in years." Julie tilted her head, returning his warm smile.

"She and her family, moved to Spain a couple of years ago. They're doing great."

"Family?" Julie asked. "I'm so happy to hear that. How many kids does she have?"

"Two boys. They are amazing kids." gushed Marc. The barista called Marc's name and he walked over to grab his coffee. "How long are you in town?" he asked when he approached her again.

"We're heading back this evening. You live out here?" Julie said while touching his arm again.

"Yes. I have a house here, but I also spend a lot of time in New York for work. Where are you now?"

"St. Louis. That's where my husband, Jim landed a job thirty years ago, and we just stuck around."

"So, you're married. Kids?" he asked as he removed his sunglasses.

"Uh," she stammered as she looked into his dark eyes. "Two," she stated proudly, her eyes lighting up as she spoke. "Ben is an engineer in Atlanta and Ashley is finishing up her Masters in Architecture in St. Louis. I'm actually a widow," the sound of her own voice startled her. It was the first time she had said the words out loud. She looked down at her hands to try and figure out why she had blurted that out and make the situation awkward. She could feel the pink flush sweeping over her face.

The barista called her name, but she didn't seem to hear it so Marc walked over to pick up the drink and came back to her. Holding it out, he said quietly, "I'm so sorry, Jules."

She looked back up at him as she took the coffee from him, her hand touching his. "It's all still pretty new. He passed away a few months ago. That's why I'm here."

Marc looked at her with a confused look on his face, "He was from California?"

"No," she replied. "He told me to travel and see the world, and my best friend, Carla, is making sure I do just that." Julie looked away as she rolled her eyes. That sentence sounded so stupid to her as she said it.

Marc pinched his lips together and shook his head in agreement. Julie finally looked back at him, and he was looking at her in the most endearing way. He reached out and touched her arm, making her swoon. Putting her hand up to her mouth, she quickly looked away as Carla approached the two of them.

"Hey, didn't we see you at Archie's last night?" Carla asked as she lowered her sunglasses to get a good look at Marc.

Julie interrupted, "Yes, uh, this is Marc Diaz. His sister Lizzy was my best friend in high school."

Carla stuck her hand out to Marc and said, "It's a pleasure to meet you, Marc, is it?"

Marc shook Carla's hand. "The pleasure is all mine," Marc quickly glanced at Carla and then returned to Julie, "Well, I need to get to the office, so I will let you ladies enjoy your breakfast before your flight home. It was nice to meet you, Carla." He paused and glanced back to Julie, "It was great to reconnect with you, Jules," he said leaning forward and giving Julie a quick peck on the cheek.

Julie immediately reached up to touch the spot that he had kissed.

As Marc walked away, Carla whispered to Julie, "I told you he wasn't a creeper!" She watched him walk away, "What a great ass!"

"Carla! He's a kid," Julie exclaimed, even though it was evident that he was no longer a child. She couldn't help but look at his butt as she watched him disappeared.

"That is not a kid, Jules. That is one fine adult man, 100% beefcake."

Picking up their sandwiches, they returned to the house. Julie was quiet the whole way back, thinking about one time she and Lizzy took nine-year old Marc to the movies. Lizzy was meeting her secret boyfriend at the time, so while the two of them made-out in the back row, Julie sat and shared popcorn with Marc. He always wanted to tag along, but Lizzy usually threw a fit about him bugging them. Julie thought it was cute how much Marc wanted to be with his big sister, especially since she was an only child.

"What are you thinking about?" asked Carla.

"Oh, just thinking back about Marc's sister, Lizzy. I haven't thought of her in years. We used to be inseparable, but college changed all of that," she said wistfully.

"I remember you talking about her when we first met, but you never mentioned Marc," said Carla.

Julie shot Carla a surprised look. "He was maybe ten years old the last time I saw him. I wouldn't have even thought about discussing him. He was a little kid," Julie reasoned.

"Marc is definitely not ten anymore," Carla chided, giving Julie a nudge. "I mean, he's a solid 10, but…you know. You did notice how hot he is, didn't you?"

"Keep it in your pants, Carla. He's just a kid," scolded Julie.

"Forty-eight is not a kid, Jules. I wonder if the

woman he was with at Archie's is his girlfriend?" asked Carla.

"Probably. Boy, did I read that situation wrong," she grimaced. "I guess he was staring at me to try and figure out where he knew me from," assured Julie, talking more to herself than Carla.

"Whatever you say," teased Carla. "I'm sure he knew who you were as soon as he saw you. You haven't changed that much over the years. Besides, he would have to be blind to not notice you last night. You looked hot!" Her comment made Julie blush.

"Carla, I have changed so much," Julie held a lock of hair to show Carla. "See? Grey hair, and crow's feet around my eyes," she said pointing to her eyes.

"You don't get it. You might look a little older, but you still look like the girl I met at the dorm mixer our freshman year of college. I, on the other hand, look like a troll doll in the mornings," Carla said in a self-deprecating tone, followed by a big laugh.

They sat on the deck for a bit, enjoying the last look at the canal. Julie watched the house across the way, looking for any signs of the young mom and her kids. She felt some kind of connection to them in a strange way. Carla was too busy on her phone to notice Julie staring toward that house. Julie took a deep breath as she stood up. She placed her hand on Carla's shoulder and said, "I'm headed inside."

Julie entered the sunroom for the last time. It was her favorite room in the house. Holding her phone up, she snapped photos of the paintings. She let out a heavy sigh as she remembered she never did figure out the spot portrayed in the paintings.

Carla walked in and stood next to Julie. "You're obsessed with these," she motioned toward the paintings.

"I am. I admit it. I need to start painting again," Julie said.

"Good. You sacrificed it for too many years," Carla turned to Julie. "You can do whatever the hell you want now. Freedom, baby."

Julie smiled before putting her arm around Carla's shoulder and turning to walk out of the room together.

"Ready to catch our flight?" asked Carla.

Julie nodded before turning around to get one more glance of this special house. She would be returning home, a little better than when she left. She still had a lot to work though, but she had some hope now.

Chapter 8

"Old Flame" by Mat Kearney

The piles of laundry were slowly getting smaller as Julie carefully folded the clothes from her trip. When she had returned home, she reveled in the fact that she didn't have to rush in and start unpacking right away. She walked into the bedroom and carefully laid the clean clothes onto the bed. Turning around, she looked over at the closet before walking past the stacks of empty boxes she had taped together earlier in preparation of donating Jim's clothing. All week, she tried repeatedly to make herself enter the closet, but couldn't bring herself to do it. Exhaling as she turned the light out, she realized that every time she entered that room, she had held her breath. She was so filled with hope when she returned from California, but she was still struggling and today was no exception. Sauntering into the kitchen, she poured herself another cup of coffee and took a seat at the island. There was a ringing in her ears on these 'bad days.' The grief mixed with the regret she felt was overwhelming. Closing her eyes, she thought back to her conversation with Marc, desperate to find that glimmer of hope again, but it seemed like a distant dream. Looking around a kitchen full of memories in a house that was now hauntingly sad.

"He's everywhere I turn now," her voice was low. She was self-aware enough to realize that this was a slippery slope and if she gave in one more time, it might mean that she would be buried under the covers for days. Moving her hands up to cover her face, she gave herself a pep-talk, "He hurt you. He hurt your heart, over and over and over," she cried out loud. "You deserve better. You've always deserved better. You can't let him win again," she sniffed through the tears streaming down her face. Mustering up enough energy to stand up, she grabbed her phone and car keys.

The sun was shining on the dashboard as Julie drove toward Forest Park. She pulled over near the Boat House and watched the geese float by, unfazed by the people in the peddle boats. The beams of sunlight glistened and made the water look like it was dancing. Julie smiled as she walked, thinking back to a particular memory of when she and Jim brought the kids here to this same area for a picnic.

The kids were begging to rent a peddle boat and Jim finally gave in. Julie stayed nearby with their picnic to watch. It started off good, with the kids peddling and Jim sitting in the back, but Ashley started to whine and plead with him to change places. She moved with grace to the back of the small watercraft, but when Jim stepped down, he lost his balance and almost fell into the lake. Ben caught his hand and helped him stabilize.

Julie turned and looked back at how far she had walked. She held her hand to cover her eyes from the bright sunlight and pictured the kids running around her as Jim chased them while pretending to be some kind of monster. She cherished those memories of the good times. She thought about the conversation with Carla on whether she should tell the kids the truth about what kind of husband their father was, and made the decision to not tell them. The good memories in her mind had a cast of tarnish on them because of the bad times, but that didn't mean that she should crush the good memories of him for her children.

***

Carla whipped open the door when she heard Julie knock. "Welcome!" she said with exaggeration, motioning Julie inside.

"I brought wine!" Julie exclaimed holding up two bottles of Pino Noir.

"Ooooh, I love Decoy. Good choice," Carla said, grabbing one of the bottles. "I'll open it now, if you're ready to get your drink on." Heading toward the kitchen, she motioned for Julie to follow her.

"How was work this week?' Julie asked as walked behind Carla.

"Ugh, I'd much rather be back in Venice Beach. It's so hard to get back in the swing of things after being away. Have you been doing any more sketching?" Carla asked while turning back toward Julie.

"I picked up some supplies but haven't really started anything yet other than my typical doodles," Julie said with a sigh.

"You'll get back into the swing of it. Creating is in your blood." Carla continued cautiously, "How are you feeling since you've been back?"

"It's still day to day," Julie said shrugging her shoulders. "Some days I want to crawl back into bed and cover my head to cry, while other days I'm able to feel a little normal. Today started out rough, but it turned around."

Carla reached across the island and put her hand on top of Julie's hand. "It will get better, once you have some distance."

"I hate feeling torn. I miss him, but I don't miss his ways of making me feel small. Does that make any sense?" Julie asked.

"Yeah, of course it makes sense. You had some major memories come to the surface over the past couple of weeks. I'm sure everything you're feeling is overwhelming"

"Thank you for taking me to Venice Beach. I don't know if I've said that or not, but I do appreciate all that you've done for me lately and for the past forty years. You've been the one constant that I can count on, and that means the world to me."

Carla smiled as she wiped a tear from her cheek. "I love you. I would do anything for you, because I know you'd do the same. Hell, you did the same for me when I went through my divorce from Christian."

Julie smiled while taking a sip of wine. Biting her lip, her mind wandered back to their last morning in California. Her facial expression giving her thoughts away.

"I feel like there is something you're not saying," Carla said with a sly grin as she squinted her eyes at Julie.

Julie rolled her eyes as she held her breath. Exhaling, she looked at Carla. "I'm embarrassed to admit that on my good days, I can't stop thinking about Marc." Her cheeks were on fire at the mention of his name.

"Called it!" Carla exclaimed with a laugh. "The man is so fucking hot."

"Did it seem like he was flirting with me, or am I just delusional?" Julie closed her eyes, but a slight smile appeared on her face just thinking about him.

"I don't know if I would say flirting, but he wouldn't take his eyes off you, even when he was speaking to me! If you're interested in him, reach out to him. What have you got to lose?"

"I don't have a way to reach out to him," Julie hung her head down.

"Does he have any social media pages?" Carla asked, picking up her phone and swiping it open.

"I didn't ask. All I know is that he has a house in Venice Beach, and he spends time in New York for business," Julie said with a disappointed edge to her voice.

"What else did you two talk about?" Carla asked.

Julie scrunched up her nose before answering. "Me. Shit, we just talked about me, well, and Lizzy. He mentioned that she and her family moved to Spain. Other than that, I blurted out that I was a widow and had two children." Julie palmed her face in embarrassment.

"You've got no game," joked Carla. "Okay, if there's a will there's a way, right?" Carla began typing into her phone.

"What are you doing?" Julie looked over to see what Carla was typing.

"Marc Diaz. Lives in Venice California, born in Austin, TX, prefers dogs over cats, an avid movie buff, loves live music and the Big Apple. He's also currently single," announced Carla with a big cheesy grin.

"What? How did you find that out?" Julie's mouth agape.

"Instagram, darling. The wonders of social media," she laughed throwing her head back at her own amusement.

"Are there photos?" Julie asked with a sly grin on her face.

"Oh yes and some are h.o.t. HOT!" replied Carla as she held out her phone.

"Lemme see," snapped Julie as she took the phone in her hand. "Oh, dear god. He's on a paddle board half naked." Julie instantly put her hand up over her mouth in shock, but did not look away from the screen.

Carla lifted one eyebrow and responded sarcastically with, "It's called swim trunks, Jules. Although, it's good to see you get excited at the sight of a half-naked man."

Julie smiled, "Carla Louise Angelo," she mock scolded her friend.

"You're finally realizing that you're still alive, and that makes me happy," said Carla warmly, coming around the island to give Julie a big hug.

Julie smiled as she embraced her friend. "Love you, bitch."

"Love you more, bitch," Carla said as she stepped back.

Julie stammered, "Uhhh…"

"Yes?" Carla asked taking a step back, waiting for Julie's response.

Julie pursed her lips before saying, "I don't know if this is possible because I'm not on social media, but is there a way for you to send him a message?" She bit the corner of her bottom lip.

"You mean, send him a DM?" asked Carla.

"Yeah, I guess. Would you be able to give him my number?"

Excitement was all over Carla's reaction. "I knew you were attracted to him!"

Taking a sip of wine, Julie looked up and tried to think of a way to defend herself. "I mean, he is attractive, right?"

"Good god, Jules, you'd have to be dead not to notice how hot this man is!" Carla said with a laugh. "What do you want me to say in the message?"

"I don't know. Maybe it's not a good idea," Julie back peddled.

"Oh no! You're not backtracking now. Grab your glass, we're moving this party to the living room so we can craft the perfect message."

After following Marc on Instagram and admiring all his photos, Carla and Julie sent the message to him.

Carla: Hey, Marc. We met at the beach café last week with our mutual friend, Julie Koffman-Anderson. She isn't on IG, and asked me to reach out to see if you would like to stay in touch with her. Her cell is 573-123-9876.

"What now?" asked Julie, as she chewed on her bottom lip.

"We wait and see if he responds," replied Carla.

"How long will that take?" Julie asked impatiently.

Carla rolled her eyes. "It all depends on if he checks IG and his messages."

"Doesn't it notify him of a message?" Julie inquired.

"Sometimes, but it just depends on his settings," Carla explained.

"Do you have that set up so we can know when he responds?" asked Julie.

"Yeah, but cool your jets. It might take a while," Carla said before taking another sip of wine. "This is really good wine, by the way."

"Thanks."

"So, what changed your mind about reaching out to Marc?" Carla said as she poured another glass of wine.

Wistfully she explained, "It wasn't a specific thing that happened, but I keep thinking about him standing there so patiently waiting on me to respond to his question about Jim. It was an awkward moment, for sure, be he had this look of kindness and empathy on his face. When he touched my arm, I felt a tingle ripple through my body. That hasn't happened in…," she paused, her face taking on a hint of sadness at the memory.

"Since you met Jim?" Carla asked.

"No, not even then. This was different." Julie said, with a questioning look on her face as she continued. "It was pure excitement. I don't know how to explain it. Am I stupid to think that a man in his late forties would even be interested in me, or am I too old?" Julie genuinely asked.

Carla's expression softened, "No, babe. You are not too old. He would be the stupid one, if he didn't want you in his life. Just don't rush into another relationship.

You need time to figure out what you want," Carla warned.

Julie just nodded in agreement as she sipped on her wine. Carla had no problem talking Julie into staying over for the night.

***

Julie woke to hearing her phone go off. She sleepily reached for it, opening only one eye. As soon as she saw the text message, her heart began to race. Sitting up in bed, she wiped her eyes to make sure that she was seeing it correctly.

Marc: Hey Jules, it's Marc. Your friend, Carla sent me a message on IG and gave me your number. I assume you gave her the ok to do that.

Julie jumped out of bed in a panic, not knowing what to say back to him, so she ran into Carla's room waking her up. "Wake up! He texted me! What should I do?" she begged.

"What is happening?" asked Carla, pushing up her eye mask.

"Marc texted me. What should I say back to him?" Julie asked, her heart racing.

Carla yawned, "This could have waited until I was awake, you know."

"I'm sorry, I just don't want to make him wait too long for an answer."

"Answer to what?" Carla replied, very confused. "Did he ask you a question?"

"No, but I should respond, right?" said Julie excitedly.

"Lemme see your phone," said Carla as she sat up in bed.

Julie handed her the phone. "What should I send back?"

Carla read the text and typed out a response.

Julie: Hey Marc, so good to hear from you. Yeah, I figured it would be fun to stay in touch.

Carla handed the phone back to Julie and asked, "How does that sound?"

"You make me sound so cool," she beamed.

"Then click send," Carla said with a yawn.

"Done, what next?" Julie couldn't wipe the smile from her face.

"All you can do is wait for his response."

Chapter 9

"Lights On" by Maggie Rogers

The sky was a beautiful shade of azure, with big fluffy clouds slowly floating by. Julie sat on the porch swing with a sketchpad on her lap. Flipping to a fresh page, she moved the charcoal pencil around, making circles that would eventually become a person. A young boy and his dad caught her attention as they rode their bikes down the street. Julie waved, exchanging pleasantries with the neighbor. Looking back to her drawing, she used her finger to smear the charcoal and create shade to an area of the face that was starting to take shape. Avoiding the eyes, she continued to work on the rest of the face.

"Why do I always struggle with the eyes?" she asked as she concentrated on the drawing. She paused and realized that she was drawing Marc. She smiled and looked back up to the sky again before continuing. She heard her phone buzz.

Marc: Good morning, Jules. I hope your day is off to a good start.

Julie couldn't help but plaster a big smile across her face and feel a flush of excitement.

Julie: Good morning. It is, thank you.

Marc: Would it be ok to call and catch up with you tonight? I told Liz that I ran into you and she's dying for an update. lol

Julie: I would love that. I don't have any plans, so I should be available anytime this evening.

Marc: I should be out of the office by six tonight, so that would be eight your time. Does that work for you?

Julie: I'll make sure I have my phone with me. Talk to you tonight.

Marc: Great. Have a good day, Jules.

Julie held her phone to her heart. It was beating rapidly, like she was some giddy teenager hearing from her crush. Closing her eyes, she shook her head no, trying to get a grip on the thoughts running rampant in her mind. Biting her upper lip, she opened her eyes and looked up to the sky again. She reached her hand up to her cheek where Marc had given her a quick kiss. She was startled by her phone ringing.

"Hello?" Julie answered.

"Hey Mom. Just checking in. How are you doing?" asked Ashley.

"I'm fine, sweetheart," Julie cooed.

"Mom, you always say your fine," replied Ashley.

"I'm really okay," assured Julie.

"I'm missing Dad," Ashley said with a sniffle, giving it away that she had been crying.

"I know you do," Julie said softly. "What's one of your favorite memories of him?"

Ashley's voice cracked, "When he almost fell in the lake at the park," she said.

"I drove by there, yesterday and thought about that. He loved you and Ben so much, don't doubt that, okay?"

Ashley sniffed but was quiet.

"You, alright?" asked Julie.

"Yeah, I just want to pick up the phone and call him."

Julie was silent as she let Ashley guide the conversation. Her heart broke while listening to the soft cries coming across the phone speaker. Closing her eyes, she couldn't fight the tears back as they ran down her cheeks.

"I just needed to hear your voice," Ashley finally said.

Julie looked down at the sketchpad. The tears had distorted the drawing of Marc's face. Sniffing before she replied, "I know, honey. You can call me anytime."

"I don't want to ruin your day by talking about Dad," Ashley whispered.

"You could never ruin my day. I'm sorry that I wasn't present much the first few months. Don't ever hold back talking to me about your dad or about anything. I love you, Ash."

"Thanks Mom. I love you too. I'll let you get back to whatever you're doing. What are you doing today?" Ashley asked.

"I'm just sitting on the porch swing and doodling. Nothing important," Julie said shifting her eyes back to the drawing. She reached down to smear the tear drop into the drawing. "How are things with Jordan?"

"Um...," Ashley paused. "It's going okay, why?"

Julie took a beat to choose her words. She didn't want to say too much, but needed to say something. "I'm concerned that you're moving too fast with Jordan, and I've noticed some behaviors in him that concern me," she said softly, her voice tinged with worry. "I'm worried that he's crossing some boundaries and not treating you with the respect you deserve." Julie chewed on her lip waiting for Ashley's response.

"He's just a passionate guy and sometimes his emotions get the best of him, that's all," Ashley tried to justify.

"I know it's hard to see sometimes when you're in the middle of it, but I want you to know that I'm here for you, no matter what."

Ashley was quiet as Julie held her breath, afraid that she had said too much. "I really like him, Mom. I wish you could see the side of him that I get to see. He's so passionate about architecture and design. I think if you got to know him, you'd love him too," explained Ashley.

Julie drew in a deep breath, "Okay, honey."

"Oh, he's here Mom. We're catching a movie tonight at the Tivoli. I love you," said Ashley as she hung up the phone.

Julie's heart was heavy for Ashley and the situation with Jordan. She wiped her eyes and turned her attention back to the drawing. Her grief was changing. She wasn't so much missing her relationship with Jim, but she missed him for her kid's sake. Maybe Carla was right, with some distance, it would get better. She moved her fingers over the drawing, smudging the edges and giving it a blurred look.

***

"Late Night Talking" by Harry Styles

Julie watched the clock as she waited for Marc's call. She made sure her phone had a full charge, and that the ringer was on full volume. The butterflies were active in her stomach, eager with anticipation. Picking up her glass of wine, she took a sip before looking at the time again. Her phone rang promptly at eight pm. Not wanting to seem too anxious, she let it ring three times before answering it.

"Hello?" she said, acting like Marc's number didn't just pop up on her phone. Her heart raced with anticipation.

"Hi Jules, it's Marc," he answered.

"Oh, hi Marc," she said, trying to act cool.

"How was the rest of your day?" he asked.

"Good…well sort of good. Tired, you know jet lag," she rambled, crossing her eyes, mortified at the words that just came out of her mouth. She mouthed, 'What the fuck did I just say,' outside of the phone microphone. Her eyes bulged with embarrassment.

"Okay, that's good, I guess," he responded awkwardly.

"So, how is Lizzy doing?" Julie asked trying to get the topic off herself.

"She's great. She said to tell you hello," Marc said.

"Please tell her hello for me the next time you talk to her," added Julie, as she started to pace in her living room.

"I will," he said, pausing, "What have you been up to since you've gotten back from Cali?"

"Oh, you know, laundry, normal stuff," she rolled her eyes, wondering why this conversation on her part seemed so lame. "What do you do for work, Marc?" she asked, trying desperately to be more engaging.

"I'm in marketing," he answered quickly.

"That seems a little vague," Julie replied with a little laugh.

Marc chuckled, "I'm the VP of Ross Marketing, I oversee three teams of marketing geniuses."

"So, you're a glorified babysitter?" Julie joked.

Marc laughed again, "Uh, I guess you could say that."

Listening to Marc's voice and hearing him laugh made Julie's heart skip a beat. "You have a nice voice," she observed and immediately wished she could take that back.

His voice softened and lowered to a serious tone, "How are you really doing, Jules? You've been on my mind all week. I can't imagine what you've been going through."

Julie was a little taken aback, his voice filled with concern for her. He hadn't seen or thought of her in decades. "I'm…I'm doing fine," she stammered.

"Jules, fine?" he asked.

Julie paused at the fact he was calling her out. She swallowed hard before answering, "To be honest, this week has been better. I think the California sunshine and beach time helped. I still have bad days, but it's slowly getting better." Her mind raced as it tried to figure out why she had the need to be honest with him. Afterall, she really didn't know him as an adult.

"Is there anything you need?"

She inhaled, desperately wanting to say, 'I need you to hold me, kiss me….' She was lost in thought for a few moments.

"You still there Jules?" Marc asked, his voice changing to concern.

"Uh, yeah. Um, I'm fine," she replied.

"Fine again, huh?"

"Sorry," she said with a tinge of sadness to her voice.

"Jules, I know we just reconnected, but I am a good listener and can be a good friend to you."

"Thank you," she squeaked out.

"Do you have a good support system?"

"Yeah, I have Carla and my kids," she answered.

"That's good. Well, you have me too and you can call me anytime you need to talk."

Julie fought back the tears, "I appreciate it, Marc."

Marc paused before responding, "So, what should I tell Lizzy?"

"What do mean?" Julie questioned the abrupt change of subject.

"She wanted me to catch her up on what's been

happening with you for the past forty years," he said with a light laugh.

Julie wiped her eyes and sat down on the sofa before answering, "College, marriage, kids, that about sums it up. I've lived a very dull life, compared to Lizzy moving to Spain."

"Dull? Sounds more like you've been living the dream."

Julie let out a breath that turned into a soft laugh, "I've had a good life, but no one's life is a dream."

"What did you study in college?" he asked.

"Art, specifically painting," she said proudly.

"Now that I think about it, you always carried a sketch book around and were always drawing something," Marc recalled.

She smiled at the memory of her drawings being the most important thing in her life. She was excited for high school because of the art classes. She could almost smell the paint and lacquer that filled the air in the art room. Mr. Barnes told her that she was his favorite student because of her enthusiasm for soaking in anything and everything about art.

"I guess I did," she finally replied.

"Do you still draw and paint?" he asked.

"I didn't for years, no time with raising kids," she lied. "I've reconnected to drawing again, since…" she trailed off.

"That makes sense," he said in a helpful voice. "I'm glad you're drawing again."

"That's what Carla said too. I had a strong connection to three paintings in the house we rented in Venice Beach. It was of the same spot on the beach, but at different times of the day. The line work was amazing, and it made me miss that creative side," Julie replied with a lilt in her voice, thinking back to her time at the cottage in Venice Beach.

"Maybe you need to come back out and do your own paintings of your favorite spot on the beach," Marc suggested.

"I would love that, more than you could imagine. Being at the beach was so freeing. I miss the sounds, the smell, and the sunshine," she said wistfully.

"You don't have sunshine in St. Louis?" he asked jokingly.

Julie chucked, "Of course we do, but it's the trifecta of perfection in Cali."

"Never really thought about it in that way, but you're right. I love living near the beach, but I miss city life too."

"So, you found a job that you could have both. Do you have a place in New York too?"

"Not yet, but I'd like to find one someday." He was quiet for a moment, "I do have another question for you. I promise it's not as personal."

"Sure," Julie said with a smile.

"Would you want to meet up for dinner when I'm in St. Louis next week?" he asked.

"Sure, that sounds fun to catch up in person," she answered before biting her lower lip, a tingle of excitement rushing through her body at the thought of seeing him again.

"Cool. I fly in Wednesday morning, but I can text you once I'm there so we can figure out where and what time, okay?"

"You've given me something to look forward to. Thank you," she said, suddenly feeling comfortable talking to him. He really did have a great voice. It was strong, but kind.

"Great, it's a date," he stated.

Julie's eye grew large hearing him say that phrase, butterflies coming alive in her stomach. "Great," she squeaked out.

"This has been fun, we should talk more often," Marc said slowly.

"Yeah, I've enjoyed it too. Goodnight Marc," she said in almost a whisper.

"Goodnight, Jules. See you soon," he said, his voice wistful, almost matching her whisper.

Julie sat back on the sofa. She held her phone to her chest, and smiled at the thought of a friendship with Marc. Just as quick as the exhilaration arrived, it retreated and left her somehow feeling guilty for making a dinner date with Marc. What would everyone think if she went to a restaurant alone with another man?

Chapter 10

"Dancing with Your Ghost" by Sasha Alex Sloan

Rain splattered on the windshield as Julie drove to meet Carla at the mall. Turning on the wipers, Julie inched forward. Traffic was always worse in the rain, and she hated driving in any precipitation thanks to an accident from college. She was relieved to see the mall parking lot up on the left. She sat quietly in her car after finding a parking spot not too far from the building. Her emotions had been riding high all morning, constantly shifting between grief, anger, and excitement. Julie jumped when Carla knocked on the window of the car.

Opening the door, she laughed, "You scared me."

"Sorry, what were you doing?" asked Carla.

"Talking myself in and out of this dinner with Marc," she answered truthfully.

Once inside, Carla, asked, "Why is that?"

"He said, it's a date, Carla. I'm not ready to date. I never should have agreed to it," explained Julie.

"Are you sure he didn't use that phrase in a more casual manner and you're freaking out over nothing? Don't think of it as a date. Think of it as having dinner with an old friend," suggested Carla, picking up a pair of high-top sneakers in Nordstrom. "Am I too old for high-tops?"

"No. We're GenX, we'll never be too old for concert tees and high-tops," said Julie, giving Carla a nudge. "Dinner with an old friend, huh?"

Carla turned to face Julie, "A friend you want to bang," she said as she stuck her tongue out at Julie.

Julie rolled her eyes, "Must you always be this crass?"

"That's why you love me and keep me around," Carla said with a wink.

Julie picked up a pair of block-heeled, neutral sandals, "What do you think of these?"

"Looks like your style," joked Carla. "You need to tweak your style now that you don't have to worry about…," Carla paused. "Well, you know."

Julie sighed, "You're not wrong, but I have no idea where to even start. My style has been soccer mom for the past thirty-five years," Julie shrugged her shoulders.

Moving away from the shoe department, they moved toward the women's clothing section. Julie picked up a bright blue skirt and held it out to show Carla, "What about this?"

"Do you even like that color?" Carla asked as she pushed blouses on a rounder.

Julie looked at the skirt before placing it back on the rack. "Not really."

"Then don't buy it. Jules, you have to find things that you like," encouraged Carla, picking up a stack of jeans to search for her size.

"I don't know what I like, but it has to be comfortable," Julie picked up a red sweater, holding it up across her chest. "What about this?"

"Now you're talking, you look great in red! You'll figure out your style, just get on Pinterest and search fashion. It's a little overwhelming at first but find one post that you like and then search similar outfits," explained Carla, walking over to Julie.

"I have no idea what you're talking about. You have to remember who you're talking to. I use my phone to text my kids and to actually make phone calls," Julie said with a chuckle.

"Lame. No more excuses. I have to get you into the

21st century, my friend. I'll help you download Pinterest, Instagram, and hmm," Carla said, looking up as if she were thinking about more things to add to the list. "And a dating app, maybe Farmers Only," she said before bending over from laughing so hard.

"Carla! No! I'm not downloading a dating app, let alone a farmer one!" scolded Julie.

"You do like to garden," Carla shrugged her shoulders and held her palms up.

Julie rolled her eyes and started walking away from Carla.

"Where ya going?" asked Carla, following Julie.

"Out into the mall and away from you making fun of me," Julie said turning back to Carla sticking her tongue out at her.

"So, what exactly are we shopping for? Dress, jeans… what exactly is the dress code for this dinner date?" Carla asked as they walked out into the mall.

"I don't have a clue, other than everything that I owned seemed so wrong. Maybe I should just cancel," she said disheartened.

"You are not going to fucking cancel on this hottie. Jules, he wouldn't have asked you to dinner if he didn't want to get to know you better. I'm not saying you have to marry or even date the guy, but he's hot, you're beautiful, it's time to have some fun. Dinner with an old friend. God knows, you don't need any other pressure. Just have fun," Carla said as she grabbed Julie's arm and dragged her into a store that had eighty's band tees in the window. "The 80's are back baby!"

Julie smiled as they walked into the store. "They have a David Bowie tee!" she exclaimed.

"Look at this Stone's shirt. It looks vintage, not like a cheap knock-off. This store is legit," she said picking up a Pet Shop Boys tee. "Oh my god, I saw them back in, I think '86."

"Where was I? I don't remember seeing them," said Julie.

"You were knee deep involved with…" Carla paused, not sure if she should mention Jim's name since Julie was having a good day. She quickly looked back at the rack of tees.

Julie sighed, "It's okay to say his name."

Carla looked up with a worried look on her face. "Sorry, you're having a good day, and I don't want to bring you down."

Julie put her hand on Carla's shoulder, "It's fine. I'm not going to crumble at the mention of his name."

"But aren't you? You've just been in such a dark place for months, but since we went to Cali, you've been better. I don't want to be the one that makes you…I don't know, backslide?"

"He wasn't a religion, Car. I get what you mean, but I'm going to be okay. Today is a good day, we're having a good day, aren't we?" Julie asked.

"Yeah, but I don't want to be the cause of you going home and crying yourself to sleep."

"It's ok, Carla. He was a huge part of my life for over thirty-five years. It was never perfect, but I can't go back and change any of it. I have to move forward."

Carla reached out and hugged Julie. "You're a better person than me, Jules."

Julie just smiled and leaned into the hug. Pulling back, she said, "I love you, bitch."

"Love you more, bitch," Carla said as she smiled at Julie.

After making a couple of purchases, the girls walked back toward Nordstrom feeling good about their selections. "I still need shoes. I liked the sandals I saw earlier," Julie made her way to the shoe department but stopped dead in her tracks as she stared straight ahead.

Carla looked around, "What's happening? What

did we stop for?"

Julie just continued to stare straight ahead, her breathing becoming shallow. It was as if she saw a ghost. "Um…Andrea," she stammered.

"What the fuck?" Carla asked. "This city is big enough; you shouldn't have to even see that slut."

Julie couldn't move, so she stood there trying to catch her breath. Andrea looked their way and started walking toward them.

"Hi Julie," she said in an empathetic voice, "How are you holding up?"

Julie just stared at her, so Carla chimed in, "She found your letter," seething with anger.

"Uh, what letter?" responded Andrea, trying to look confused.

Julie's brain finally kicked in, "The letter you gave my husband before he got sick and died." She stated it so matter-of-factly that Carla looked at her in awe.

Andrea stammered, "Uh, I…I don't know what you're talking about."

Carla interjected, "We know about the affair. Let's see, how did the phrase go? Oh yeah, 'I miss your touch, your kiss, my love.' Wasn't that what you wrote?" Carla looked between Andrea and Julie.

Andrea had a look of shock on her face. "I'm, I'm so…"

Julie cocked her head to the side, "Sorry? You're sorry for sleeping with my husband or sorry that you got caught?"

"I…I, it happened before he got sick," Andrea tried to explain.

Carla asked, "So, why didn't you offer to help take care of your boyfriend? I'm sure Julie would have appreciated the break. Hell, you two could have tag teamed his care in the last months of his life."

Julie looked at Carla, "That's enough." Turning

her attention to Andrea, "I spent thirty-five years with him, and you spent what, a fun, few months with him? What exactly did you expect to happen? For him to leave me and our two children, to what? Run away with you?" her voice calm but strong. "He lied to you, just like he lied to me." Julie's attention was drawn to the small child that was holding Andrea's hand. Her mind spinning about who this child belonged to and if it could be Jim's child.

Andrea's eyes welled with tears, "I'm so sorry. I knew it was wrong, but I got caught up in the moment with him, believing the lies he told me about you. He made it so easy to fall in love with him."

Julie looked at Andrea crying, her anger softening, "He fooled all of us."

"All of us? Were there others?" Andrea asked with a shocked look on her face.

"Yeah," Julie said softly. "I was just the last one standing." Julie composed herself and turned to walk away.

Carla followed Julie, leaving Andrea teary-eyed and alone. "Jules, are you ok?"

Julie didn't say a word, she just walked toward the bathroom. Once inside, she stood at the sink and looked in the mirror.

Carla stood beside Julie and watched her every move. "Let it out, Jules. It's not good to keep it pent up. Scream, cry, whatever, just get it out."

Julie continued to stare into the mirror, her hands shaking as she held onto the countertop. Closing her eyes, she inhaled as tears streamed down her face.

"You are strong, Jules. Let it out," Carla encouraged. Julie finally spoke, "Not here," shaking her head no. Taking a deep breath, she composed herself. Looking down at the sink, she motioned under the faucet and held her hands below the cool water. She patted the water on her face and stared in the mirror again.

Carla waved her hand in front of the paper towel dispenser and handed the towel to Julie.

"Thank you," said Julie quietly.

"What do you need right now? A drink? I'm not going to let you be alone right now, so don't even try to push me away. I'll be damned if he wins again, and you're passed out in bed over this."

Julie straightened her top, not looking away from the mirror, she replied, "I'm fine."

"You are not fine, Jules. Be real. I will take you home, we can pick your car up later, but I'm not leaving you alone," said Carla forcefully.

"Okay," Julie agreed.

Together they grabbed their bags and walked out and directly to the parking lot. The rain had temporarily stopped. Julie slumped into the passenger side of Carla's car, not saying a word. They drove in silence back to Julie's house. Julie immediately hopped out of the car and walked toward the front door. Her hands shook as she dug for her keys and tried to fit the it inside the lock. Carla watched and after two failed attempts, she took the key from Julie's hand and unlocked the door. Julie dropped her bags as soon as she passed the threshold of the door, heading into her marriage bedroom. Carla followed, not saying a word. Julie picked up a box and walked into the closet that she had been avoiding. She picked up a pile of Jim's jeans and threw them haphazardly into the box. Next, she grabbed a stack of sweaters, throwing them into the box on top of the jeans. She saw the letter from Andrea. Closing her eyes, Julie let out the loudest guttural scream before collapsing on the floor of the closet. "Why wasn't I enough?" she screamed next.

Carla sat down beside Julie, wrapping her arms around her friend. They sat on the floor of the closet just rocking back and forth, until Carla broke the silence. "You're staying with me tonight. I've got everything you could need. Let's just go." She stood up, trying to help Julie stand up. "Come on, let's just go." Julie followed Carla to her car.

The car ride was quiet until Julie finally spoke. "I'm going on that dinner date with Marc," she said with a sniff. "I deserve a chance at happiness."

"Hell yeah, you do!" Carla chimed in.

Julie took her phone out of her pocket, looking at her texts. Finding Marc's number, she texted him.

Julie: Looking forward to dinner Wednesday night.

It only took a few minutes for Marc to respond.

Marc: Me too. You, okay?
Julie: Hard day, but I'm....

She started to type the word fine, but she made a different choice today. I'm okay.

Marc: Wanna talk?
Julie: I'm staying at Carla's tonight. We can talk tomorrow.
Marc: I look forward to it. Goodnight Jules.

Julie looked over at Carla and tried to smile but fell short. "I'm going to be okay."

Chapter 11

"Who I Am Without You" by Blu Eyes

Julie lay in bed, her gaze fixed on the slow rotation of the ceiling fan above her. Thoughts swirled in her mind like the blades above. The image of Andrea's child flashed before her eyes, igniting a spark of doubt. Could it be Jim's child? She knew of four other women Jim had cheated with in their thirty-five years of marriage, but how many other women had there been? How old was that child? Was it Andrea's? The questions echoed in the silence of the room, leaving Julie grappling with uncertainty and a deep sense of betrayal. She replayed Andrea's words in her head. 'I got caught up in the moment with him, believing the lies he told me about you. He made it so easy to fall in love with him.' Jim did make it easy to fall in love with him.

The sun was bright as Julie sat under a tree, trying to read and not be distracted by the shirtless boys tossing the football back and forth. She smiled as one of them ran close to her, making her scoot over to avoid being stepped on. She let out a little shriek.

The boy said, "Sorry," and moved back to his friends.

Jim was walking by and ran over to her. "You, okay?" he asked. "Those guys have no respect for anyone else around them."

Julie squinted her eyes up at him, "It's no big deal. They didn't do it on purpose."

"It's nice to see you again...Julie, right?" Jim asked. "I'm headed to grab some pizza, wanna go?"

"Sure," she said smiling up at him. He stood there, waiting for her to get to her feet.

It never occurred to her that he didn't extend his hand to help her get up. Probably because she had a different perspective now. She was older, wiser, and had the knowledge that she was never enough for him. But damn, he was a handsome boy, and he knew exactly how to make her fall in love with him. Andrea was correct about that.

Carla knocked on the door, but Julie didn't answer. She opened the door just a crack to check on Julie. "Did you sleep at all?" Carla moved toward the bed and sat down.

Julie just shrugged her shoulders, not even moving her eyes to look at Carla.

"I took a half day off, so we don't have to rush to get you home," Carla said as she reached out to rub Julie's arm. "You're going to get through this, Jules."

"What if I'm not enough for Marc?" Julie asked softly.

"Oh honey, I'm so sorry that Jim hurt you, but Marc is not Jim. You can't go into a relationship expecting pain."

"Why would he even want me? I'm ten years older than him, he's gorgeous, and I'm damaged, like, really damaged."

"Not gonna pull punches with you, Jules. I'm angry at Jim for what he did to you, but I'm also angry with you for keeping this to yourself for so many years."

Julie turned her head and looked at Carla. "I'm sorry. I knew you'd just tell me to leave him, but I hoped it would eventually stop and we'd be okay."

"The eternal optimist. It's one reason I love you, but it also frustrates the shit out of me. Sometimes life is just dark, for no particular reason. I think you're finally realizing that, or maybe you've always known that, but you chose to…I don't know, rise above or shove it so far down that you eventually forgot. You are so strong, Jules. You will get through this, but you might seriously want to think about therapy. He really played some wicked mind games on you."

"Maybe," was all Julie said as she looked back up at the fan.

Carla laid down on the bed, scooting her head next to Julie's. "We will get through this."

Julie looked over and smiled. "Love you, Bitch."

"Love you more, Bitch," said Carla.

***

"Running Low on Things to Love" by I Shiver

Julie sat on the porch swing, sipping coffee from her World's Best Mom mug that Ben and Ashley had given her one Mother's Day many years ago. Pushing off, she made the swing move faster and closed her eyes, picturing her dad behind her while reminiscing about a time when she adored him and didn't feel like a disappointment to him. She smiled as she opened her eyes. Thinking back to her earlier memory of how innocent she was, were there other red flags that she ignored? Could she have saved herself a lifetime of loneliness? The swing slowed and she took another sip of coffee.

If she hadn't met Jim, how different would her life have turned out? Her mind shifted to Ben and Ashley. They were the best thing that came out of her marriage to Jim. They had been created in a loving relationship, or had they? They represented her and Jim's love, or that's what she always believed. It had to true. It just had to be true. She didn't imagine their love over the years. He had loved her, but in his own way. She just hadn't been enough. Julie wished that she had discovered these memories while Jim was alive. She wanted to hear Jim explain himself, to make her understand his point of view. A wave of anger coursed through her body. Shaking her head, she thought about what life would be like if she had been stronger. She would have left him and created a better life for herself and the kids. She chose to honor their vows, while he stomped all over them. Holding onto the letter from Andrea, Julie set fire to any good memory that she had about him.

Andrea…he had kept her letter, but not any other cards, notes, or letters from any of the other women. Jim was not a sentimental man, so why had he kept her card? It was from at least two years ago, before he got sick. This train of thought only angered her more.

"Was he in love with Andrea?" she whispered aloud. She thought about the funeral, and how she noticed Andrea crying, no, sobbing, which she thought was odd at the time. Julie was stoic at the funeral, keeping the tears to minimum. It was what Jim's expectation would have been. He wasn't a fan of expressing one's feelings in private, let alone in public. Jim left her in the dark most of their marriage and now that he was gone, he haunted her mind and made her question moving on with Marc, or whoever. Her emotion shifted from anger, to sadness, and landed on indifference. She thought about Brian, the dad from Ashley's class. She wondered where he was now, knowing that they moved a few months after she broke the emotional bond with him.

Julie could feel the warmth of Brian's hand as they explored the art gallery where his pieces were displayed. She loved the ways his eyes would light up as he told her about his inspiration for each piece. The way his laughter echoed through the small gallery, as if they were the only two people in the room, surrounded by a symphony of colors and emotions. Their bond was based on their love of creating art, both wanting more than friendship, but neither willing to make the first move.

"You really like it?" Brian asked excitedly.

"I love it," she assured him before walking to the next sculpture. "I am a little jealous," she admitted.

"You'll figure out the balance. You need to talk to Jim about how important it is to you, especially if you're wanting to use your talents and degree to teach at the community center," he encouraged.

"I wish...," Julie paused.

Julie smiled at the sweet memory, but felt sad that Brian was just one more friend pushed from her life because of Jim. Taking a deep breath in and letting it out slowly, she kicked off the railing to push the swing back.

Her mind drifted to Marc, causing a big cheesy grin to appear on her face. She thought about him touching her arm, immediately making her body blush with warmth. What if she was too broken for him? He deserved someone that wasn't so messed up. Rubbing her face, she closed her eyes and rested her palms on either side of her nose.

Her phone buzzed next to her. It was Marc. Smiling, she clicked it open. "Hi Marc."

"Hey Jules, how are you doing?"

"Umm," she hesitated.

"Rough day? Wanna talk about it?"

"Not really," she sighed. "How are you?"

"Good, just avoiding going back to the office," he said with a slight laugh.

"I'm sitting on my porch swing, drinking coffee," she replied, pushing the swing back again.

"I think I can imagine that. Sounds fun. Didn't your parents have a porch swing?" he asked.

"It's the same swing," she smiled.

"That's awesome. Mementos like that are important," Marc said.

"Sounds like you're driving," she observed.

"I am. More like stuck in traffic."

"I'm looking forward to our dinner," she said biting her finger as the swing continued to drift back and forth.

"Me too. Wednesday can't get here fast enough." Julie smiled, thinking about how this seemed so vastly different from the beginning of her relationship with Jim. "I feel the same way."

"Are you sure you're, okay?" he asked again.

"I am. Taking it day by day. Thank you for checking on me."

The street lights began to turn on as the last of the sunset disappeared. Julie realized that she had been sitting on the porch swing most of the day. She was alone, but she wasn't lonely, like she had felt most of her life. Jim doesn't get to steal her joy anymore, well, at least not tonight.

Chapter 12

"Better Late Than Never – Stripped" by Ryan Kinder

Julie anxiously watched the cars drive by her house as she sat swinging on the front porch. Marc was on his way from the airport. He had insisted on picking her up for their first dinner date. He wouldn't tell her what restaurant he had chosen, so she was nervous that she could be underdressed in her white and pink sundress and nude sandals. She pulled the little cardigan sweater close, covering her chest. Looking at her phone, she checked the time for what felt like the one hundredth time.

Jim was coming home from his first business trip. Julie was filled with excitement to see him. It was their first time apart since getting married and three days seemed like a lifetime. Checking the time on the kitchen clock, she surmised that his flight would have landed almost an hour ago, which meant that he should be on the train and headed home. She continued to stir the homemade spaghetti sauce that she had made for dinner. Walking into the living room, she put on Jim's favorite record when she finally heard the doorknob jiggle. Turning around, a huge smile spread across her face, she saw him come through the door.

He dropped his bag, swept her up into a big hug and lifted her feet off the floor. "I missed you so much," he twirled her around.

"I missed you too. I counted the hours today until you would be home," she replied with a shriek of joy. He picked her up, carrying her toward the tiny bedroom. "I have sauce on the stove," she said.

"I don't care about sauce, only you and me, making up for three days apart."

Julie smiled endearingly at the precious memory. She missed that part of her life with Jim. It was such a sweet and innocent time in her life, before things got so complicated. She loved spending every moment she could with him, and at that time, she was sure he felt the same way about her. They were inseparable when he wasn't at work.

Marc pulled up in front of the house. He waved as he got out the car and started walking toward the her. He smiled at the sight of Julie sitting on the porch swing in her sundress and little pink cardigan, her hair put up in a clip. She looked radiant.

"Hey there," she said, standing up greet him. "Did you have a good flight?"

He reached out to give her a hug. "It was uneventful, which was great."

"So, what's the plan?" she asked. "Am I dressed alright?"

"You look perfect. Are you ready to go?" he asked.

"Let me grab my bag," she said turning around to pick up her purse.

He took her hand, walking beside her to the car and opened the door for her. "I hope you like picnics," he said after putting his seat belt on.

"I love picnics," chimed Julie. "Do we need to stop to pick up food?"

"It's all covered, we just have to show up," he said pulling out onto the street.

The gazebo was decorated with twinkle lights around the columns. Fresh flower arrangements and candles were artfully placed around the circle. A beautiful, colorful round quilt lay on the floor, with thick pillows for sitting. A large wicker picnic basket laid to one side, with an elaborate charcuterie board and a bottle of Veuve chilling in a silver champagne bucket.

"Is this for us?" Julie asked as she put her hand over her mouth in surprise.

"I told you it was taken care of," he said smoothly. There was a young man who had set everything up. He nodded at Marc, who then handed him cash. "Thank you, man. You can come back in a couple of hours," he said shaking his hand.

Julie took it all in, the fragrant flowers and the romantic candlelight. She felt a little overwhelmed by it all. She looked out at the other park goers, craning their necks to see what was going on in the gazebo. Feeling a little self-conscience, she took a seat on the dark red pillow. Julie was careful to keep her dress down as she positioned her legs to one side.

Marc moved the other pillow closer to Julie. "They did a great job setting this up."

"Who is, they? I didn't even know that something like this was possible around here."

"You just have to know who to call and what to ask for. I asked my new St. Louis client for recommendations. They were happy to help."

"They signed with you?" Julie asked.

"Yep! Now, I have two reasons to come back to St. Louis," he said with a wink. Grabbing the bottle of champagne, he popped it open and poured each of them a flute full of bubbly. "Cheers to finding each other again," he said holding his glass up to her.

"Cheers," she responded as she clinked her flute to his.

Marc wiped his bottom lip with his thumb after taking a sip of champagne.

'Good god, why is that so sexy?' she thought to herself. He continued talking as she considered what it would be like to kiss Marc. Would it be better than her first kiss with Jim? She looked at his face, noticing the

small lines that crinkled when he smiled. His big, brown eyes were so expressive when he spoke. They were the kind of eyes you could get lost in. She was so smitten that she wasn't listening, just staring and smiling.

"So…," he said, drawing the "o" out.

Julie blinked quickly, realizing she didn't hear his question. "I'm sorry, I didn't hear your question," she said fast.

Marc smiled as he cocked his head, "What were you thinking about just then?"

Julie smiled, suddenly feeling sheepish. "I was thinking about how much you look like Lizzy," she fibbed before taking a bite of prosciutto on a cracker.

"I was asking about your day," he raised his eyebrows, as if he had just caught her in a little lie.

"Oh, it's been a good day. I signed up for a watercolor class at the community college. I figured a refresher course wouldn't hurt," she said with excitement in her voice.

"Don't you have an art degree?" he asked before taking a drink.

"Yes, but it's been so long. I feel like I need to get my sea legs back, ya know?"

"Sea legs?" he asked taking a bite of a cheese and cracker with fig jam.

Julie blushed, "It's something my dad used to say."

"It's cute," he said as Julie rolled her eyes. "At least it is when you say it. I would love to see your work sometime."

"Really?" Julie asked, surprised. "I've been doing a lot of sketches and a few abstract pieces, but my favorite medium is watercolor." She was beaming as she talked about her upcoming class. She was coming alive again.

"Could I ask, why did you stop making art to begin with?" Marc asked.

Julie took a deep breath, trying to decide just how

much to divulge at the dinner. "Oh, you know, we moved and then started a family. Life happened, I guess you could say."

Jim followed Julie into the bedroom of their small apartment. "I agree with your dad. I think that would make you happy. Most men hate their fathers-in-law!"

"Why did I get a degree if I was just going to stay home all day and do nothing?" Julie said exasperated.

Jim grabbed her arm and twisted her around, "You should be proud that your husband makes enough money that you don't have to work."

"At least let me volunteer at the community center and teach art," she bargained.

"My wife will not work, for free or for pay. I make the money!" he said through gritted teeth. "Besides, we're starting a family soon, so you'll be too busy raising our kids."

"I want to work, Jim," she pleaded.

Marc asked, "You, okay?"

Julie snapped back into the present, "Yeah, just thinking about my class."

Marc squinted his eyes at her, "Hmmm, not sure I believe you. You didn't exactly have a happy look on your face. What were you really thinking about?"

"The past," she said with a melancholy to her voice.

Marc cocked his head to the side, "Wanna talk about it?"

"Not really, but…" she paused, taking a breath. "I'm okay now," she said with resilience in her tone.

"I'm glad you're investing in yourself," Marc said with a grin.

Julie smiled, "I like that. I'm investing in myself."

Abruptly and with a sly smile on his face, Marc

stood up before helping Julie stand up, steading her by holding onto her waist. Julie made a mental note of his chivalry.

"Let's go swing," he pointed towards a nearby swing set. He didn't let go of her hand as they walked toward the playground. "Are you up for a game?"

Julie had a confused look on her face. "Game? I'm not very good at playing games."

Ignoring her protest, he continued, "Okay, so here are the rules."

"Rules? I thought we were just coming to swing." Julie asked confused.

Marc explained, "It's a fun game, I promise."

"I'm not exactly dressed to be playing games," she protested lightly.

"It's not that kind of game. You'll swing for 3 minutes and, while I push you, I will talk and you have to listen, then we'll switch."

"Talk? About what?" Julie asked.

"You can talk about anything. It's about listening to the other person, it's a fun way to get to know each other better," Marc explained.

Julie smiled as she took a seat on the swing. Drawing the swing back, Marc gave her a solid push to start. As she came back to him, he began speaking, "I like you, Jules." She smiled back at him and started to speak but he stopped her, "You're just supposed to listen. You'll get a turn." He smiled as she came back, giving her another push, "Mom and Dad's divorce really messed me up as a kid."

Julie turned her head, "Oh Marc, I had no idea they divorced."

Marc held his finger up to his lips, giving her another push with his free hand. "It's okay, it happened a long time ago." He pushed again, his hand brushed her exposed shoulder, making her blush as the swing moved forward into the darkness. "They had a messy divorce. Lizzy was away at college, so mom leaned on me because she didn't have anyone else." He cleared his throat before continuing, "I don't know if you know this, but I had a crush on you when I was a kid." He pushed her again before she had a chance to speak. "I was so taken by you when I saw you at Archie's. I knew it was you as soon as I saw you." Julie looked into his eyes as the swing moved back again and she smiled warmly.

"I kicked myself for the rest of the day, when we met at the café, for not getting your number."

Julie tried to drag her feet to make the swing stop, but Marc grabbed the swing, pulling her close to him.

"Thank you," she said. "You're turn." Hoping off the swing, she motioned for him to take a seat and walked behind to give him a push. "I knew you had a crush on me. Lizzy told me," Julie said as he moved back to her. Pushing him again, "I thought it was sweet. I'm glad you talked to me at the café. I also kicked myself for not exchanging numbers." He looked over his shoulder at her as she pushed him again. "I'm lonely," she admitted. Marc started to speak, but she shook her head no, and continued, "I've been lonely for thirty-five years." Her confession shocked her. The combination of the darkness of the park and the easiness of talking to Marc this way, it just came out naturally. "I'm scared to be on my own."

Marc stopped the swing, stood up, and pulled Julie close as he wrapped his arms around her. "I'm so sorry, Jules." Rubbing her back he added, "You are stronger than you think, and you'll get through this. I know you will be alright."

Julie inhaled his scent, closing her eyes she savored his embrace.

Pulling away, he pulled her chin up so that she was looking at him. "I'm here for you now."

"Thank you," she replied. This time it wasn't the

butterflies that fluttered in her stomach, it was a wave of peace. Something about being in his arms just felt right.

"Your turn to swing," reminded Marc.

Julie took a seat, pushing back with her feet until Marc grabbed the chains of the swing to pull her back farther. Giving her a solid push, he was quiet at first. Julie turned around to see why he wasn't speaking.

"Everything okay?" she asked as she flew backwards toward him.

"Yeah, just lost in thought for a moment," he said as he gave her another big push. She moved forward, her feet in the air as she leaned back. "I sought out a client here in St. Louis to have an excuse to come visit you," Marc confessed.

Julie turned her head as she swung back toward him, "You did?"

Putting his finger to his mouth, "Shh, my turn. I haven't been able to get you out of my mind since that night at Archie's." Julie smiled as he gave her another push. "I want you in my life, Jules, even if it's just friendship. But I'm hoping for more, if I'm being honest. I'm willing to wait until you are ready."

Julie dug her feet to slow down again and jumped off the swing. Walking back to Marc, she looked him in the face and said, "I've only ever loved Jim, so all of this is so new to me. I'm in a foreign country and everything is so different from the last time I visited. I don't know what I'm doing or if I'm doing any of it right, but I'm glad that we met again and I'm excited to see where our friendship takes us. I can't promise anything though," she said, putting her hand on Marc's chest. "Can we take it slow?"

Marc furrows his brow with a serious look on his face. "We can take it as slow or as fast as you want. I only care about having you in my life. You take the lead on this, Jules."

Julie looked up at him, there was a tenderness in his face. She tilted up, intending to give Marc a kiss on the cheek, but he turned his head at that exact moment, making her lips graze his. Julie immediately felt a flush of red across her face, flustered she pulled away, "Sorry."

Marc looked at her with an endearing smile, "No need to apologize. Ready to head home? I'm sure you're getting cold with a dress on, and I have an early flight to catch."

Julie nodded her head, still feeling embarrassed. They walked hand in hand to the car.

Marc dropped her off at her home before saying their goodbyes. As she unlocked the door to walk in, her thoughts replayed every detail of the evening. Julie tried to cement everything she felt, heard, saw and the way he made her feel. Closing her eyes, she took a deep breath, her mind drifted to that kiss, or almost kiss. His mustache tickled her lip, she remembered, as she reached up to touch her lips.

Her mind shifted to Jim, causing her to feel guilty about her date with Marc. Dropping her bag on the kitchen island, she mindlessly walked toward the bedroom, but stopped short of going through the doorway. The room was dark, uninviting, and cold. Her breathing became shallow as she tried to force herself to walk in. She couldn't move, stuck holding onto the doorjamb. She tried to force her mind to focus on her evening with Marc, but it was drawn to the comfort of what she knew in this room. The sadness and despair she had been living with for months. She was jolted out of her thoughts when she felt the buzz of her phone in her hand. Looking down, she saw it was a message from Marc.

Marc: Thank you again for a wonderful evening. I'll call you this weekend.

Her face lit up as she read the text. It arrived at the perfect time. She moved away from the bedroom and turned toward the hallway that led to the spare bedroom. Removing her clothes, she laid down under the covers, pulling her phone up to read the message again. A smile broke across her face as she texted him back.

Julie: I had a wonderful evening and look forward to seeing you when you're back again. Talk to you soon.

Lying in bed, she kept thinking about how she was caught between two worlds. One wanting to move on, to choose happiness, and embrace the chaos while the other was filled with a sadness that rocked her soul, but was comfortable and familiar. Tears filled her eyes, dripping down into her hair. She hadn't done anything wrong, but the guilt still remained.

Chapter 13

"My, My, My" by Rob Thomas

The sunlight streaked through the trees, making a disco ball effect on the ground as the wind blew through the leaves. Julie stepped off the back porch, lazily walking toward her flower garden area. It looked like an overgrown mess right now, neglected for the past two years. She walked through the front of the garden, holding her hand out to graze the tangled weeds and dead sunflower stalks. She thought back to three years ago, when she relished having a cut flower garden. It gave her a creative outlet, designing which flowers were planted in which area of the garden. She smiled and remembered how beautiful the colors of the flowers looked, just like she thought her life was a beautiful, loving masterpiece. Throwing herself into everything at home, she gave up any sense of independence and sacrificed herself for her family.

Now, she was left with a longing for a life that she never had. One she had dreamed about but never truly forgot. She thought about the truth throughout the past thirty-five years, feeling her temperature rise with the anger bubbling up. Tears filled her eyes as she started grabbing the dead plants, ripping the tops at first and throwing them behind her in the yard. Falling to the ground, she pulled at the base of the dead sunflowers, trying desperately to pull the root out of the hardened dirt. Wiping her hand across her forehead, she looked up and gave a scream as she gave it one more tug. Her body jerked when the dirt finally gave up the fight. Rocking back and forth, she gave into the sadness that was overtaking her mind. Standing up, she stumbled to get her footing and brushed the debris from her jeans.

"I can't do this anymore," she said under her breath. She looked around the yard before taking a seat on the patio. She sniffed as she put her hands over her face. Taking a few deep breaths, she tried to get her mind under control by concentrating on the pinkish-orange glow of her eyelids from the sunlight. It wasn't the darkness she was used to from the bedroom. Putting her hands down, she looked up and the darkness changed in the sunlight. Feeling a shift in her mind, she went inside to grab her sketchbook. She plopped down in the middle of the yard, opening a fresh page, and began to draw the dismal reflection of the dead garden. Her hand moved around, making dark streaks representing the dead stalks, moving on to the lighter colored weeds, the dried sunflower heads, and smearing the lines. She began shading the mess until it finally resembled what she saw. She looked back and forth between the page and the garden, adding in small details until she was finished. Julie smiled as she held the book up, taking in what she had created. Taking pride in the drawing, she said, "I should send a photo of this to Marc." It surprised her that he was the first person she thought to send the photo to. Maybe it was because he seemed to be supportive of her diving back into her artwork. Picking up her phone, she snapped a photo of the drawing and one of the garden, to text both to Marc. Looking down at the mess she had made on herself, she could only imagine the dirt that must be streaked across her face. She smiled at the mess, both in the yard and her body, and she felt alive.

***

In the shower, her mind drifted back to her date with Marc. She wasn't sure how he came up with the idea of going to the park to swing and talk, but it was magical. The entire scene of being alone with him in the darkness of the park and only hearing his voice as she swung back and forth. Running her fingers through her hair, she imagined that she was running them through Marc's curls. The water cascaded over her body, warming her to the core, and she grinned, wondering if he had responded to her text yet. Wrapping the towel around her, she moved toward the pile of clothes on the bed in the spare bedroom, relishing in the anticipation of Marc's response. Sitting on the bed, she brushed out her hair and hummed to herself. When she reached for her phone, joy spread across her face as she saw his name on the locked screen.

Marc: Damn, Jules. Your attention to detail is amazing. How long did that take you to draw?

Julie: Not too long, maybe 20 minutes. I'm glad you liked it.

Marc: I'll be back next Thursday, still want to get together?

Julie: Yes, but why don't you come here and let me cook for you?

Marc: Home cooked meal? Yes, please.

Julie: Cool, it's a date.

***

The walls were covered in student's artwork from the previous semester. Julie took her time examining each one, studying the brush strokes. She thought back to the paintings in the Venice Beach house. Opening the photos on her phone, she admired one of the pictures, smiling as she continued to walk around the room.

A young man approached her, "Hi, are you Professor Williams?"

Julie chuckled, "No, I'm actually a student." Holding out her hand to shake, "I'm Julie."

He shook her hand, "I'm Mike."

"Nice to meet you, Mike," she said as the actual instructor walked into the room, followed by a group of young people. After introductions and expectations for the class, Julie removed a piece of watercolor paper from her pad and clipped it to the flat easel where she was seated. Professor Williams allowed the students to pick any photo from their phones to recreate as the painting for this first session. Julie chose to recreate the photo that depicted the beach sunset. She grinned as she thought about how excited she was to get started. Beginning with a pale blue for the sky, she moved the brush across the page, leaving some areas darker than others. Moving on to the beach and the sea grass, she swirled her brush in the water to make it turn a paler blue. She mixed some water with the brown to make it a sand-colored tan, sweeping her brush across the bottom of the paper and added pale green streaks of sea grass in the small dune. She sat back and looked at what she had so far, smiling at how much joy she felt.

Julie sat nervously in her mentor's office, awaiting his critique of her final art project. She had put her heart and soul into it. She rubbed her finger over her thumb until a red spot appeared.

"Julie, thank you for waiting," Professor Anton said.

"So, what do you think? Is it worthy as a final piece?"

Professor Anton looked up at her, smiling, "Julie, it's your best work to date. It is my opinion that you have the potential to be one of the best artists that ever came out of this school."

"Really?" Julie asked with excitement in her voice, smiling from ear to ear.

"Really. You've expressed interest in art therapy, and I would like to recommend you for the Master's program at NYU."

Julie was stunned and her heart leapt. "Oh my gosh! That would be wonderful!" As soon as the words escaped her mouth, she looked down at the engagement ring on her left hand. The high turned into a pit in her stomach. Looking up at Professor Anton, she said, "I appreciate it, really I do, but I'm engaged to be married and my fiancé has already accepted a job here in Chicago."

"That's disappointing. I wish we had a program like that here. Please let me know if you change your mind. Talk to your fiancé and see if you two can work something out."

When class was dismissed, Mike walked over to Julie to see her painting. "Wow! You're really good. I take it, you've been painting a long time."

Julie smiled while she gathered her supplies. "Thank you, Mike. I painted a long time ago, but just rediscovered how much I love it."

"Are you an art major?" he asked.

"I actually have an art degree, so this is just a refresher for me," Julie scrunched up her nose and looked at the painting again.

"You should have your work in a gallery. You're really good. I've got to get to my next class. See you next week, Julie."

"See you," she said back as he turned to walk away.

Julie heard her phone ping with a text, as she climbed into her car.

Marc: How was class?

Julie: Amazing. I recreated a painting that I saw at the rental house in Venice

Beach.

Marc: Send me a photo. I'd love to see it.

Julie: I will when I get home.

Marc: How's your day?

Julie: It started a little rough, but class really helped.

Marc: Good. I'll call you tonight after I'm done with work, if that's okay.

Julie: I look forward to it.

Julie looked out the kitchen window to the mess she made in the yard during her fit of rage. She decided to hire someone to come in to clean up the garden and yard. She could do it, she had the time, but all she really wanted to do was to paint. Turning around, she set up the small easel on the island. The light in the kitchen was the best in the house. Dipping her brush in water before setting it down in the dark paint, she moved her hand across the page to recreate the drawing she had made earlier that day. She was surprised at the muscle memory in her hand as she swiped across the paper. She smiled at the fact that she was genuinely happy. The peace she felt when she was being creative was a salve to her soul. She thought about Mike's words, saying that her art should be in a gallery, and felt a rush of excitement. "I still have time, don't I?" she asked herself out loud. Julie cleared her mind and focused on the details of the dried sunflower. She chuckled as she realized that she still stuck her tongue out of the corner of her mouth when she focused on painting, just like she did when she was younger. The anger she felt this morning seemed like a distant memory.

***

Julie climbed into bed after her phone call with Marc. He was so sweet to offer to stay on the phone with her until she fell asleep, but she was exhausted and didn't anticipate having any issues. It had truly turned into a good day, and her heart felt warm and full. Lying her head down on the pillow, she yawned, closed her eyes, and drifted into slumber.

Julie was walking down the beach, her fingers intertwined with Marc's. Her eyes shifted from the ocean and up to him. His curls moved in the breeze, and his dark eyes so expressive as he talked. She couldn't hear what he was saying, but she felt so full, so happy, so in love with him. He pointed out at a large rock in the water. When Julie looked at where he was pointing, her heart skipped a beat. He had found the spot where the painting from the rental house had been done. The sky was lit up in pinks, oranges, and yellows, just like the painting. Julie jumped for joy.

"This is it!" she exclaimed.

"The paintings?" he asked.

She smiled at the fact that he knew exactly what she was excited about without explanation "Yes!"

Marc took her in his arms, swaying back and forth as they watched the sun set, sinking down into the Pacific Ocean. "I love you, Jules."

Julie looked into Marc eyes, "I love you too," she said before leaning up to kiss him.

Waking up from such a sweet dream, she didn't want to open her eyes hoping it would help her return to the dream. Rolling over, she pulled the covers up to her neck, smiling as she drifted back to sleep.

Chapter 14

"Little Bit More" by Suriel Hess

The kitchen was filled with the scent of lemon as Julie made her favorite Chicken Piccata for Marc. She hummed along to the music playing. He sat nearby, flipping through her sketchbook with a glass of wine in hand. She swayed her hips to the beat of the music as she hummed along.

"Jules, these are all amazing," Marc said, looking up at her.

Julie twirled around smiling, "Thank you. Which is your favorite?"

Marc thumbed through the book again, "Is this me?" He was looking at the smeared drawing she had done of him.

Julie spun back around, her face a flush of red, "Maybe," she said, sounding like she'd just been caught writing the name of her crush on her notebook.

Marc smiled at her blushing, "It's good. Can I snap a photo of it?"

Julie nodded yes, "Sure." Turning back around, she put the final touches on dinner, before plating it and placing it in front of Marc. "I hope you like capers."

"Oh, yeah. It smells delicious, Jules," he said before taking another sip of wine, waiting for her to sit down next to him.

"Let's take this out back. I hired someone to do some clean up and I installed the café lights by myself," she said proudly.

Marc grabbed his plate and wine glass following

her outside. "Cute," he said as he looked around the backyard. "Love the lights. Great job!"

Julie was quiet as she looked back on her now empty flower garden, thinking back to last week when she had a meltdown in that spot. It was a turning point though, and she was thankful for that. Returning her attention to Marc, she realized that he was staring at her. "Did I miss something again?"

"Nope, just wondering what you're thinking about," he said as he took a bite of chicken. "This is delicious, by the way."

"Thank you. It's just this house and yard are filled with so many memories," she took a deep breath.

"Good memories, I hope."

"Yeah," Julie said softly, "Some."

Marc got up, taking Julie's hand to help her up. They could hear the music from inside the house. He took her in his arms, swaying back and forth to the beat of the music. "It's in the past and it can't hurt you now," he whispered in her ear. "I'm here, and I won't let anyone hurt you again."

Julie put her head on his chest as they swayed. Her heart and body felt a flood of warmth rush through. Closing her eyes, she pictured every moment up to this, not wanting to forget the details. Looking up at Marc, she smiled as he leaned down to tip her face up to his. He gently pressed his lips to hers. She melted into a puddle of mush. His hand slipped down to the small of her back as he pulled her closer to his body. Wrapping her arms around his neck, she kissed him back, giving into the desire she'd been feeling all evening.

When Marc pulled away, he leaned back and whispered, "I've been wanting to do that for a long time."

Julie smiled bashfully, "Me too."

Sitting back down, they finished dinner. The conversation turned to memories of growing up in Austin.

"Tell me about Lizzy's family," Julie said.

"Her boys are the kindest, craziest kids. I really miss them. I never pictured having kids of my own, but when they lived in San Diego, I visited a few weekends a month. Taught them to surf."

"A doting uncle, huh?" Julie asked with a smile.

"Oh yeah, spoiled them rotten. That's probably the real reason they moved to Spain," he said with a chuckle.

"I wish I had kept in touch with her over the years," Julie said wistfully.

Marc put his glass up to his mouth, but hesitated, "She has the same regret."

The evening air enveloped Julie and Marc as they sat on the patio, a soft breeze gently rustling the leaves above them. Their plates, now nearly empty, bore the remnants of the delicious meal she had prepared. As they savored the last bites, their gazes lingered on each other, still basking in the euphoria of their impromptu dance and their first tender kiss. The glow of the string lights above them cast a warm ambiance, illuminating their faces as they shared a quiet contentment amidst the tranquil night.

Julie considered how relaxed she felt around Marc, as if he had been a part of her life all along. Even when the conversation lagged, she didn't feel rushed to fill the air with unnecessary words. She cherished the natural feeling she had when she was with him. He was so different from Jim; Marc didn't force his opinion on her. He was thoughtful and considerate of her feelings.

'His eyes are so expressive, even when he's not talking,' she thought with a smile. 'He's too handsome and young for you,' the intrusive thought crept over her positive thoughts. 'Age doesn't matter,' she told herself as she wiggled in her seat. Marc looked up and smiled at her. 'He just wants sex, that's all men ever want. He'll just hurt me like Jim did.' She shifted her eyes down to her lap, not looking to see if Marc noticed or not. 'You'll become invisible to him too.'

Marc noticed the uncomfortable look on Julie's face. "Everything okay?"

Julie looked up, sheepishly forcing a smile. "Yeah, just lost in thought," she swallowed hard. She placed her left hand on the table, exposing her wedding rings.

Marc didn't miss a beat, reaching across the small table, placing his hand on top of hers. "This is nice. It feels so natural."

Julie smiled and looked into his dark brown eyes, "It really does," she agreed. She heard her phone buzz, glancing over she saw that it was Ben calling.

She said, "Excuse me," as she picked up her phone. Walking inside, she answered.

"Hey Benny, what's up?"

"Just calling to check on you. How's your class going?" Ben asked.

"Um," she said, turning around to look out the kitchen window. "It's going well, I'm enjoying it." Just as the words left her mouth, Marc walked into the kitchen.

"Another bottle of wine?" Marc asked.

Without thinking, she said, "Over by the fridge in the wine rack."

Marc leaned in, giving her a peck on the forehead, which made her blush.

"Who's there?" asked Ben.

His voice jerked her back into the conversation, "Uh…it's a friend. I made dinner."

"Since when did Carla's voice drop?"

"I didn't say it was Carla, I said a friend," she said sternly.

"Who is there, Mom? I don't recall you having any male friends. Is this someone from your class?" Ben asked.

Julie rolled her eyes. She wasn't prepared to bring her kids into this part of her life because she wasn't even sure what this part of her life was yet. Taking a deep breath, she said, "No, it isn't someone from class. It's my friend, Marc, he used to live down the street from Gamma's and Gampa's house."

"He just showed up? Mom, I don't understand," Ben inquired.

"His sister, Lizzy, was my best friend growing up. We grew apart in college, but I ran into Marc when Carla and I were in LA." Julie explained.

"Older brother?" Ben asked.

Julie sighed, "Younger, he's ten years younger."

"Mom! You can't date a younger man like that. He's probably trying to take advantage of you!"

"Ben, it's ok, we're just friends. He is in town on business, and I invited him for dinner. That's all," she assured her son.

Marc stood there opening the bottle of wine, looking over at her when she mentioned only being friends. She noticed and smiled at him, mouthing 'I'm sorry.'

"Well, it's after nine pm there, he needs to be going back to wherever he came from," said Ben.

"Okay, well, I'm fine, honey. Thank you for calling to check on me. Did you need anything else?" she asked, trying to get him off the phone.

"Nope, just called to see how you're doing. We will talk tomorrow, Mom." Ben said before hanging up.

Julie looked stressed and Marc noticed. Walking over to her, he wrapped his arms around her waist. "One of your kids?"

Julie forced a smile, "Yeah. That was my son, Ben."

"Hmmm," responded Marc, before kissing her on the cheek.

Julie still distracted, "Yeah."

"Hey, we don't have to do anything you're not comfortable with. No pressure," he said taking her hand leading her to the back yard. He took her in his arms, "I'm sorry that I put you in an uncomfortable position with your son."

Julie looked up at Marc, "It's not your fault. I haven't told my kids about you yet, because I'm not sure what this is, if I'm being honest."

He stroked the back of her head, "It's okay. We'll take things as slow as you need."

"Thank you," she said, laying her head against his chest, feeling it rise and fall with every breath. She wasn't sure if it was the wine talking or the fact that she had been so lonely, but having Marc hold her was a little slice of pure heaven. She felt comfortable with him, but Ben's comment about Marc being so much younger than her bothered her. Closing her eyes, she held Marc a little tighter. He rubbed her back as their bodies swayed back and forth.

They finished the second bottle of wine as they reminisced about their shenanigans growing up in the old neighborhood. Moving the party inside, Julie led Marc to the living room, plopping down on the sofa and patting it for him to sit next to her. She was buzzed and that liquid courage kicked in as she leaned in for another kiss. He complied, slipping his tongue into her mouth, as she felt a bolt of electricity run through her. She let out a faint moan with that kiss.

Marc pulled back, "I should get going back to the hotel."

"We've had two bottles of wine, you should just stay here," she suggested.

"I don't know if that's a good idea, Jules," Marc responded.

"No, I mean, you can stay in the spare bedroom," she replied.

"Are you sure?" he asked.

"Yes, it wouldn't be right to let you drive after drinking."

"Okay," he conceded as he leaned forward to kiss her again.

Drawing back, she held her hand up to her head. "I need

to change the sheets on that bed." She started to stand up but stumbled a bit.

Catching her, Marc, said, "I can take care of it, just show me where they are."

Julie pointed to the hallway, taking Marc's hand as they walked toward the linen closet. She opened the door, grabbing the first set of sheets that she saw, but stopped, staring at how organized the closet was. She intentionally reached inside and started messing up a stack of sheets and another stack of towels. Julie turned to look at Marc as she felt a wave of embarrassment come over her. Shaking her head, she walked toward the spare bedroom. Marc followed not saying a word. He watched as she stripped the bed. She laid the sheets on the bed, as she felt his hand on her back.

Turning around, he pulled her close, holding her. "I don't know what you've been through, but you are safe with me. I promise not to hurt you, Jules."

"I know. You're a good guy, Marc. It's just a lot right now. We need to slow down."

"Whatever you want. I'm here for whatever you need," he said softly.

"Good night," she said. "Let me know if you need anything."

"Good night, Jules. Thank you for a wonderful evening," he said as she turned to walk away.

Julie walked towards her bedroom, turning off lights as she went. When she entered, she stood for a moment and looked at the closet before grabbing some shorts and a t-shirt from the bed. But she couldn't make herself sleep in that room. She walked back into the living room, picked up a blanket, and laid down on the sofa. She took a deep breath as she stared at the ceiling.

Julie was sitting with Brian at the all-school talent show. They were chatting to themselves when Jim walked into gymnasium. Neither Julie nor Brian noticed him, being wrapped up in their own private conversation. Brian's eyes moved up as Jim towered over them, Julie noticed and turned around.

"Oh, you made it?" she said, motioning for him to take a seat.

"Julie, what are you doing?" Jim asked in a stern voice as he sat down.

"I'm waiting for the talent show to start. I wasn't sure if you were going to make it or not," she said genuinely confused.

Jim leaned in and whispered in her ear, "It looks like I made it just in time to see my wife fawning all over some jock dad."

His expression was bland, but she could see the fire in his eyes. She whispered back, "I'm not fawning over anyone. We were just talking."

Jim grabbed her arm, making her stand up with him. With gritted teeth he looked at Brian and said, "No need to save our seats." He pulled on Julie, making her walk in front of him until they were outside. He forced her to face him, "Are you sleeping with him?"

Julie was taken aback and embarrassment flushed her face, "No! I don't sleep around, that's your thing." She couldn't believe that she was standing up for herself.

He snarled, "You better stay the fuck away from him!" He turned to walk toward his car before spinning around to say, "See what you made me do? Tell the kids that I showed up but had to leave because of you and your boyfriend. We will discuss this further when I get home."

"Where are you going, if not home right now?" Julie asked.

"Don't worry about it. It's just another thing you've forced me to do," he scoffed before storming toward his car.

Chapter 15

"Everything Everywhere Always," by Elijah Woods

The smell of fresh coffee wafted through the air into the living room. Julie opened one eye, realizing that she had slept on the sofa. She yawned, stretching before sitting up. She hazily stood up and walked toward the kitchen, expecting to see Jim. Stopping short when she reached the doorway, she realized it was Marc who was making coffee. Glancing down at the short shorts and oversized tee she had on, she started to back up, hit the doorframe, and yelped. Marc turned around before she could duck out of the way.

"Hey there, sleepyhead," he said with a little laugh.

"Uh…I'll be right back," she said as she turned to walk quickly back to the bedroom. She quickly threw on a pair of black leggings and a sweatshirt before returning to the kitchen. Marc was sitting at the island with a cup in hand and a second cup of coffee next to him.

"Thank you," she said, taking a seat. He was wearing a grey tee, jeans, bare feet, his hair was a mess of brown curls, and his scruff was a little shaggier than the day before. She bit her lip and stared at him until he looked over, catching her. A pink flush came over her cheeks as she smiled nervously.

"You didn't have to change for me," he said teasingly.

"Yeah, I did," she said in a quiet voice. "Thanks for making coffee," she rubbed the back of her neck.

Nodding as he took a sip of coffee, he said, "That's why I should have slept on the sofa."

"It's fine. You're my guest, so you get the good bed." Julie insisted.

"I could have gone back to the hotel. You didn't sleep well because of me," he said looking over at her.

"Don't be silly. We drank a lot of wine, and you were in no condition to drive."

Marc took a deep breath, "So, what's the plan for today?"

"I thought I would take you to my favorite place in all of St. Louis, SLAM."

"SLAM?" he asked with one raised eyebrow.

"St. Louis Art Museum," she explained.

"Ahh, that makes sense," he said nodding his head. "I need a shower. Are the towels in the same closet as the sheets?" asked Marc.

The thought of him being naked in her house made her pulse increase. "Yeah, help yourself to anything you need," she squeaked out. Standing up she added, "I'll go get ready."

Marc handed her a cup of coffee, "You might need this."

Julie took the cup from Marc, grazing his hand as she accepted it. "Thank you."
She smiled as she walked toward the bedroom, turning back to get another look at the handsome man in her kitchen.

***

Forest Park was busy as they drove toward the art museum. Budding trees and multi-colored tulips lined the drive up to the hill to the three-story stone building with statues on each side of the steps. Marc opened the car door for Julie, taking her hand as they walked. Joy spread across Julie's face as they walked inside. They were greeted by the docent, who recognized Julie, giving her a tip of his hat.

"This way," guided Julie. Marc followed without saying a word. Walking past some of the ornate sculptures and artifacts, she led him to the abstract painting room. Julie stopped in front of her favorite painting, Twilight Sounds by Norman Lewis. Marc looked over at Julie instead of the painting. She had a glow to her presence.

"Isn't it beautiful?" she asked, not taking her eyes off the painting. "It's my favorite piece here."

"It's so chaotic yet beautiful," he replied, moving his gaze to the painting.

"I agree. I think it represents life, especially my life the past year. So much chaos but small touches of beauty woven into hard moments."

This was a side of her that he hadn't seen. She was getting lost in the painting as she let go of his hand and moved around to get a different perspective from another angle. He patiently watched her, lost in her element. Sitting on the bench in front of the painting, she looked up at Marc, patting the seat next to her. He quietly sat down, putting his arm around her waist and pulling her closer to him. She looked over at him, pure bliss across her face.
He smiled back at her. "I can see why it's your favorite."

"It was painted in 1947. Norman compared his process to the creativity of jazz music. I've been coming here for years. The entire museum is amazing," she paused, "I have stood in this spot just diving into this painting. That's why they put the bench here," she said with a giggle.

Mr. Dawson approached Julie standing at the Twilight Sound painting. "Here again?"

Julie looked at him, "Yes, it draws me in every time."

"Are you new to the area?" he asked.

"Yes, my husband and I moved here from Chicago two years ago," she said as she rubbed her large belly. She smiled when Ben kicked inside of her.

"When are you due?" he asked.

"In just over a month," she replied.

Mr. Dawson nodded his head, "Next time you come in, I'll make sure you have something to sit on, so you don't have to stand in your condition."

"That's sweet of you, but you don't have to go to that trouble. I won't be able to visit for a while after he's born," Julie said with a smile.

"Nonsense, I'll take care of it. Can't have our favorite patron standing around, when we have plenty of benches that we can move," he assured her. "You can call me Bob, by the way."

She smiled feeling overwhelmed by such unexpected kindness. "Thank you, Bob."

Marc pulled Julie a little closer, looking up at the painting again. "It's beautiful, Jules," he said before leaning over to give her a kiss on her cheek. She turned to him, giving him a wide grin.

"Let's go explore some of the other areas," she suggested.

"I'm along for the ride," he said as he stood up. He held out his hand to her.

Taking his hand, Julie stood up, but he didn't let go. She intertwined their fingers as they walked around the rest of the abstract room.

"Have you ever been to the MoMA in New York?" he asked.

"Yes, Carla and I went many years ago when we were in college," she said with a sad tone to her voice.

"I have an idea," he said with a smirk.

"What's that?" she asked looking up at him as they passed a group of children,

"I have to go to New York for work in two weeks, why don't you come with me?"

"Um, I don't know if I can do that," she responded.

He held her hand a little tighter, "What's keeping you from saying yes?"

"I don't know, it's just sudden. If you're working the whole time, what would I do by myself?" she asked.

"I'll take a couple of extra days off, and when I'm working, you can explore MoMA or visit galleries. Whatever you want to do."

"I don't know, Marc," she hesitated.

"Why don't you invite Carla?" he suggested.

"Hmm, I can ask her," Julie mused.

Walking toward the sculpture area, she led him around a group of teenagers that were goofing off, much to the chagrin of the adults around them. He sidestepped a young girl, who was staring up at him. Julie gave him a little shove in the shoulder as they walked.

"You're popular," she teased.

Marc laughed as he rolled his eyes.

As they moved from room to room, Julie began to watch Marc, taking note to the paintings, sculptures, and multi-media art he was attracted to.

Ben and Ashley followed Julie into the art museum, which was a weekly visit during the summer months. They always began their visit at the Twilight Song painting. Walking room by room, floor by floor, she was amazed at their reactions or awareness of a statue or painting for the first time. She was stunned that Ashley was drawn to the classics and the columns, while Ben was fascinated by the modern sculptures that used steel and other metals. She was eager to see if their preference to art would change over time, as their understanding of the world expanded.

Julie was quiet, giving Marc room to do the talking. She loved hearing his ideas and the feelings that stirred inside of him as he gazed at the beautiful pieces of art and history. It was like seeing it all for the first time. She took a deep breath, holding it for a second before releasing as they walked out into the sunshine.

Marc turned to look at Julie, "You, alright?"

Julie had a wide grin as she looked up at Marc, "Happy."

Marc shook his head, "Happy, hmm…, yep, that sums up today. I'm happy too."

***

The coffee shop had a cozy vibe as light jazz music played over the speakers. Couches, chairs, and poofs were situated in small groups with tables. Julie picked a corner that had two big, grey comfy chairs, and a small table with a red tablecloth. Marc stood at the counter to order their drinks. Julie watched him, smiling the whole time. Setting the white diner style mugs on the table, he took a seat.

"What was your favorite piece?" She looked toward him, putting her elbow on the table.

"The moonlight painting with the boats, by that French artist," he replied, with a shrug.

"Camaret, Moonlight & Fishing Boats, by Maximillien Luce. It's a gorgeous painting," she agreed. "What drew you to that one?"

"The moonlight on the water, the darkness surrounding the boats, the shades of blue with the reflection of the moon." He took a breath before continuing, "I know what your favorite painting is, but what is your favorite besides that one?" he asked, leaning forward.

"Hmm….," she took a moment before continuing. "My favorite was watching you go through the entire museum for the first time. I could see it from your eyes and relive seeing it all for the first time." She lifted one shoulder to her ear, with a little smirk on her face.

Marc smiled as he stared into her grey eyes. "You win for best answer, but in my defense, I didn't know my favorite thing could have been watching you absorb your favorite painting. You've viewed it hundreds of times, but you still look for something new in it."

Julie smiled warmly, feeling a rush of blood as she looked over at him. "Anything else catch your eye?"

"I liked the Chihuly chandelier, it was so much bigger than I cxpected."

"I love how it looks like a bunch of grapes. I never got into blown glass art, but I'm fascinated with it. Ash would find videos on YouTube for me to watch," said Julie. She smiled thinking about Ashley.

Marc noticed how Julie's expression glowed when she mentioned her daughter, "I'm sure she's a lot like you."

"Yeah, she really is. Ben is just like his dad," feeling her heart sink when the words left her mouth. "I mean, work wise," she stammered looking down at her lap.

Marc reached across the table, putting his hand on Julie's, rubbing her thumb with his. "It's okay. I can't wait to meet them…, of course, whenever you're ready."

Julie slowly blinked her eyes. She wanted to slow this day down. It was all going by too fast. "I wish you didn't have to leave tomorrow."

"Believe me, I wish I didn't have to. Promise me you'll think about New York," he asked looking into her eyes.

"I promise," she gazed back at him as a warm wave of desire washed over her.

With a playful glint in his eyes, he asked "Wanna get out of here?"

"Really?" she laughed. "That's your pick-up line?"

Marc smirked, "I'm pulling out the best lines for you, what can I say?" he joked.

Julie lips tuned into a big smile. "Okay, we can go."

***

"Cherry" by Jungle

Marc pulled Julie to him as people exited the elevator, and he rested his hand on the small of her back. Julie smiled at his touch. Her breath became shallow as his hand lingered. Inside the elevator, Marc pushed the button for the doors to close quickly, wrapping his arms around Julie, kissing her lustfully and dipping her back slightly. Taking her hand, he led her down the hall to his suite. Julie took a deep breath. She was so caught up in the moment, and nothing mattered except for him. He swung the door open, kissing her as they walked into the living room. The room was dark and they bumped into a chair, making Julie laugh. Marc turned on a small lamp, still not taking his eyes from her.

Pulling her closely, he began kissing her neck and cupping her face with one hand while moving the other hand to her ass. Julie was drunk in her desire for him. They continued to move toward the bedroom. He was alternating between kissing her neck and her lips. She couldn't have stopped herself if she wanted to, caught up in this moment and caught up in him. In the bedroom he began to unbutton her blouse, never taking his lips off her. She started to unbutton his shirt as he carefully laid her back onto the bed, kissing her neck the entire time. He moved his hands down to remove her skirt as she kissed his chest. Picking her up, he placed her in the middle of the bed. It had been so long since she had a connection with someone. Feeling his hand between her legs, she gasped, and arched her back as he pulled her close. His kisses were tender at times and passionate at others. She kissed his neck and chest until he pushed inside of her, making her moan with pleasure. Together they moved in sync as they had sex for the first time. She moaned softly as she gripped the comforter in her fists. Grabbing her by the waist, he rolled over so that she was on top of him, leaning up he kissed her as she continued to move her hips in a rhythmic fashion until she screamed out his name. Julie looked back down and it was as if he was looking into her soul. Collapsing next to him on the bed, neither of them uttered a word as she laid in his arms in total silence. It felt as if either of them spoke, it would tarnish what had just happened. She looked over at him, completely immersed in his brown eyes. He just held her, stroking her hair, afraid to speak. She didn't want this night to ever end. Leaning down, he kissed her on the forehead.

Chapter 16

"Fine Line" by Harry Styles

As the soft light of dawn filtered through the hotel curtains, Julie lay awake in bed, tangled in the sheets beside Marc. The remnants of their passionate lovemaking lingered in the air, mingling with a sense of guilt that weighed heavy on her chest. She stole a glance at Marc, still peacefully asleep beside her. His gentle snores filled the room, a stark contrast to the turmoil churning within her. She couldn't shake the feeling of betraying Jim, whose memory seemed to loom over her like a specter. Closing her eyes, Julie replayed the intimate moments from the night before. With the memory of Marc's warm touch, she could almost feel his hands on her body. Despite the overwhelming guilt, she couldn't deny the raw desire that had drew her and Marc together last night.

The morning light grew brighter, and so did Julie's sense of unease. She shifted in bed, trying to shake off the conflicting emotions that threatened to consume her. How could she move on with her life while still holding onto the past? With a heavy sigh, Julie removed herself from Marc's embrace, careful not to wake him. She walked quietly across the plush carpet, muffling her footsteps toward the living room area of the suite. Leaning against the windowsill, she gazed out at the tranquil morning to seek solace in the stillness. The weight of her guilt lingered, but so did the memory of the loving moments that she shared with Jim.

Jim pushed her hair behind her ear and leaned down, "I think I'm falling in love with you, Julia Marie Koffman." Julie started to speak, but he put his finger over her mouth, "Shh, you don't have to say it back to me. I know it's early in our relationship," he said with a twinkle in his eye.

Julie smiled as she gazed up at the tall boy standing in front of her. "I love you, too," she said softly. They made love for the first time that night.

Looking out the window at the sun rising in the distance, she thought about how tender and gentle Jim was back in the beginning of their relationship. She considered how he changed over the years, with their lovemaking becoming more demanding and rougher at times. She thought of Marc and how he made her feel desired, something that she hadn't felt in a long time. She smiled as she pictured him in the throes of passion, tuned into her expressions and movements, being careful with her and not push her too far. She could feel the rising sunlight on her face. She took a deep breath, entranced with the view, not noticing that Marc had walked into the room.

He made his way quietly toward her, putting his hand on the small of her back. She drew in a sharp breath at his touch. "Good morning, Jules," he whispered in her ear.

Julie turned her head, leaning it against his. "Good morning. Isn't the view spectacular?"

Marc breathed in her scent as he nuzzled her neck, "I could wake up to this view every morning."

Julie turned to look at him and noticed he was looking at her and not the sunrise. "You're not even looking out the window," she chided.

"It's still the best view," he said before kissing her neck.

She felt a rush of warmth come over her from the

touch of his lips. Turning around, she put her arms around his neck and pulled him into her. "Do you have to go back today?"

He stroked the back of her head, "Believe me, I wish I didn't have to."

"How much time do we have?" she asked with a smirk.

Marc cocked his head to the side, raising an eyebrow. "Oh, we'll make time for that." He said with a lightness in his voice. Picking her up, he headed back to the bedroom.

***

"Where You Belong" by Matt Hensen

Marc pulled Julie into a big hug in the hotel lobby. "It's only goodbye for two weeks and then we'll be in New York together." Stepping back, he looked her in the face, brushing a single tear from her face.

Julie smiled while taking a deep breath. "I'm still going to miss you."

He walked to her car. She leaned back against it, reaching up she pulled him against her. Marc took Julie's face in his hands, gently kissing her. He pushed back, taking her hands in his, kissing them, he said, "I can't wait to show you around New York."

"I'll check with Carla, and let you know," she said with a half-smile. She was concerned that a trip together was happening too fast. They shared another kiss before she watched him walk away toward the valet to pick up his rental car.

She sat in silence; a mix of emotions flooded her mind. Relief mingled with guilt, as if by moving on she was betraying Jim's memory. Yet, beneath it all, a spark of hope flickered as a reminder that life, in its complexity, still held moments of connection and pleasure…so much pleasure. She smiled as she looked in the rear-view mirror, seeing the flush of desire still splashed across her face. Driving home, she drove by the park where she and Marc played on the swings, their first date. Her heart warmed at the memories of that night. Opening the garage door, her heart sank when she saw Jim's beloved, black truck. The sight of it sent a pang of guilt coursing through her, overshadowing the past two days with Marc. Sitting in the car, the engine still running, grappling with the conflicting emotions. How could she enjoy herself with Marc when Jim's presence loomed over her. The guilt washed over her like a tidal wave, threatening to drown out any semblance of happiness she had felt the past two days.

With trembling hands, she turned the engine off and stepped out of the car, her shoulders felt heavy with betrayal. As she entered the house, memories began to flood her mind, his laughter echoing in the empty rooms. Tears stung her eyes as she struggled to figure out why she was still missing him, even after all she knew now. Walking into the bedroom she shared with Jim, she stood staring at the mostly empty closet, surrounded by partially filled boxes. She whispered to Jim, asking for his release of her.

Julie sat on the porch swing, picking up the bright blue pillow, and held it to her chest. She could feel herself retreating into the darkness, caught between falling in love with Marc and the guilt that plagued her about moving on from the life she led with Jim.

"I need to unlearn what I thought love was, or is," she said softly. "If I want to move forward, I have to let the pain of loving Jim go, so that I can find out what love really is," she said as she wiped the tears streaming down her face. "I can't keep living in the past, our story is over and I owe it to myself to live the life that I choose."

She looked to see if anyone had heard her exclamation of independence for her life, but she only saw the birds flittering around.

***

The watercolor paint tin laid open; brushes sat in a jar nearby. Julie removed one brush, dipping it slightly in the glass of water and setting it into the light blue color. She moved her hand across the paper in long strokes to make waves across the skyline. Picking up a darker color, she added depth to the painting before blotting up some of the excess water and creating white spots of clouds. Standing up, she walked over to her kitchen speaker to flip it on. Sitting back down at the island, she chose the song, *"Lost on You" by Ryan Kinder.*

She took a moment to sway back and forth to the song, before returning to her painting. Rinsing her brush, she dipped it into the water to swirl it around, then picked up a light tan color to create a sandy beach on the painting before adding some birds flying in the distance. She glanced at the mess that she had made on the island and it brought a smile to her face.

She was interrupted by Ashley walking into the kitchen. "Hey Mom," she said.

"Hi honey, what are you doing here?" Julie asked.

"I just wanted to stop by and see how you're doing. Oh, you're painting," said Ashley as she looked over Julie's shoulder at the beach painting.

"Yeah, I signed up for a watercolor class at the college."

"Ben said you had some man at the house the other night. Is that true?" Ashley asked.

Julie took a deep breath, not sure how much she should disclose. "Yes. My friend, Marc Diaz, was in St.

Louis for business and I invited him over for dinner so we could catch up."

"Ben said he's ten years younger than you. Are you dating him?" Ashley asked with an attitude in her voice as she grabbed an apple from the bowl on the counter.

"Marc is ten years younger than me, but I grew up with him and his sister, Lizzy," Julie explained.

"But are you dating him?" Ashley demanded.

"Ash, we are just friends at this point. He lives in California and I'm here," Julie justified, knowing that after last night they were more than friends.

"Mom, ten years younger makes you a cougar," Ashley said with a raised voice. "What about Dad?"

"What about him?" Julie asked, taken aback.

"Mom, it's only been a few months since he died and you're already moving on?"

Julie took a beat to consider her words. She wanted to lash out, telling her daughter the truth about what kind of husband her father was, but she held her tongue. "Ash, we are just friends," she lied. "I'm well aware of how long your dad has been gone and how young Marc is. I would like to think you would want me to be happy."

"I think it's gross and so does Ben," Ashley said with anger in her tone.

"You're just going to have to trust me, Ash."

"Ben thinks he's after your money."

"He is not after my money, Ashley," Julie informed her.

"I'm sorry Mom, but it's just so weird. It's like you don't love dad any more," Ashley said getting choked up.

"I will always love your dad, Ash. You know that and no one can replace what he meant to me, to us," Julie said compassionately, walking over to hug Ashley.

"I just miss him and it's hard to see you move on," Ashley choked back the tears.

"Oh honey, I miss him too. You trust me, don't you?" Julie asked.

"Yeah, but I don't trust this guy."

"I think you'll like him once you meet him. He's becoming a good friend to me."

"I don't want to meet him, and neither does Ben"

"Ash, don't be like that," shushed Julie.

"Be like what? I don't need a fake dad hanging around," said Ashley, as she walked toward the front door.

Sitting down, she rested her head in her hands in pure exasperation. Her mind drifted back to the amazing night she had with Marc in his hotel room. Was it a mistake? It didn't feel like a mistake at the time, but now that she's faced with reality of her kid's words, she was having second thoughts. It felt like her night with Marc was a dream, but now she's left with the reality of stitching her life back together. Leaving the mess of an unfinished painting, she made her way to the spare bedroom. Stripping her clothes off, she laid down in the bed that Marc had slept in and where his scent still lingered. Pulling the pillow close to her chest, she breathed in the smell of his cologne.

Julie smiled at the thought of falling in love with Marc, but that smile swirled with tears to grieve the life she knew and loved.

Chapter 17

"Where You Are" by A R I Z O N A

The taxi drove across the bridge into the bustling streets of Manhattan. Carla's excitement was palpable, her eyes wide as she took in the towering skyscrapers and the vibrant energy of the city. Julie fidgeted nervously; her gaze fixed on her phone screen as she scrolled through the messages from Marc. She sighed with disappointment as they pulled up in front of The Bowery Hotel.

"What's happening?" Carla asked, noticing Julie's sigh.

Julie smiled, "I was just hoping to hear from Marc. He's probably just busy with work."

"Jules, he knows we're here. Relax, we'll see him tonight. I only have 2 days here with you, so let's just enjoy our girl time, do some shopping, and have fun."

"You're right," Julie sighed.

"Is there something else going on?" Carla asked, tipping the taxi driver.

"Just a little nervous, that's all," said Julie as she grabbed her bags.

"That's to be expected, Jules," assured Carla as they walked into the hotel.

***

Julie heard a knock at the door, rushing to open it expecting it to be Marc, but it was a man with a room service cart and the most beautiful arrangement of roses.

"Room service for two, Mam," he said as he rolled

the cart into their room.

"We didn't order room service. We just checked in," Julie said confused.

The man produced a card and said, "It's been taken care of, Mam, tip included. Have a good day," he said as he put the covered plates of food onto the small table in the room.

"Thank you," Julie replied as she shut the door behind him. She opened the card to see it was from Marc.

Welcome to New York! I wish I could be there with you right now, but
I will see you tonight. Enjoy lunch and stop to smell the roses before
you two hit the town.
Love, Marc

Carla walked into the room and saw the food, "You must be starving if you ordered food and had them put a rush on it."

"It's from Marc, food and flowers," Julie replied with a huge smile on her face. "Let's eat."

Carla sat across from Julie, her gaze gentle yet probing. "Jules, I know it's not an easy thing to consider, but have you thought about removing your wedding rings?"

Julie's eyes flickered with a mixture of surprise and discomfort. "Remove them? It's…it's."

Carla interrupted her thoughts by saying, "I don't mean to be a dick, but how would you feel if the roles were reversed and Marc was still wearing his wedding band?" She looked up at her friend with empathetic eyes. "You don't have to take it off if you don't want to, but how can you start a new relationship with Marc while holding onto the one from past?"

Julie sighed, her fingers absently tracing the side

of the wedding set. "I know you're right."

Carla leaned forward her voice soft yet firm. "Jules, removing the rings doesn't diminish the love you shared or the good memories. It's about giving yourself permission to open up to new possibilities, including a new relationship with Marc. You found a great guy, Jules."

Julie took a deep breath, thinking about how to say what she was feeling in a way that would make sense. "He is a great guy, but...," she paused.

"But, what?" asked Carla.

"The kids are concerned because of the age difference, making them not trust him," Julie said, picking at the food on her plate.

Carla got up from the chair and joined Julie on the sofa, placing her hand onto Julie's arm. "I know this won't be easy, but if you want a relationship with Marc, you're going to have to stand your ground with your kids."

"I know you're right, but they just lost their dad. Maybe Marc and I are moving too fast," Julie said lying her head on Carla's shoulder.

"Jules," Carla said taking Julie's hand in hers. "You deserve to live the rest of your life with whomever you want, however you want. You went through some hellish times in the past with Jim, but it's your turn to be and do whatever you want."

"How do I know for sure, Car?" Julie looked up.

"You don't, but that's the exciting part. Enjoying the journey and figuring it all out. Take your time, and if it's Marc you want, then stand up to your kids and make it happen," Carla explained.

Julie's phone chimed. Looking down at it with a knowing smile, she opened the screen.

Marc: Having fun?
Julie: Yes, thank you for lunch and the bouquet

of flowers.

Marc: My pleasure. I can't wait to see you. Time is dragging today.

Julie: I'm sorry. What's our plan for tonight?

Marc: Dance club. I'll send a car to pick you two up at eight.

***

"Put some music on," yelled Julie from the bathroom. "Something to get us pumped up for a night on the town."

"Old school or something from this decade?" yelled Carla back.

"Your choice. Surprise me," answered Julie. After she finished her hair, she walked toward the living room area of their suite where Carla was.

When she entered the room, Carla queued the music and started laughing. Simon and Garfunkel's 'Mrs. Robison' blared over the little speaker.
Julie looked over at her with a furrowed brow, squinted eyes, and pursed lips, but then surprised Carla by cocking her head to the side and raising her shoulders before saying, "Hey, if I robbed the cradle, at least he's hot!" She fell onto the sofa, laughing hysterically. Carla dropped onto the sofa beside her friend and the two giggled like they were back in college. A few minutes later, Marc texted Julie to see if they were ready yet.

Carla grabbed Julie's phone, "Boyfriend said the car is downstairs."

Julie responded, "Tell him to give us 10 more minutes." She jumped up to get dressed.

"I don't think you've ever moved that fast when I've texted you," said Carla as she nodded her head then continued, "Oh wait...I'm not Boyfriend," she laughed.

"Get dressed, it's time to paint the town!" Julie threw Carla's dress at her.

"Bossy, bossy. Can't disappoint Boyfriend," she responded teasingly.

The club was lit up with neon lights like a bar right out of Sex and the City. They followed the host to a private suite above the dance floor.

Marc stood up and smiled when he saw Julie. She smiled back at him. He kissed her cheek and whispered, "You look stunning." Looking over at Carla, he said, "Hey Carla, I'm glad you could be here with us." He looked back at Julie, his eyes glancing up and down as he smiled the whole time. Marc finally looked away and motioned to his coworker who had stood up when the ladies entered the room. "Ladies, this is Paul. We work together. He's in town just for tonight, so I asked him to join us. I've got a great night planned."

"Nice to meet you, Paul," said Julie as she put her hand out to shake his. "This is my friend, Carla."

"Very nice to meet you both," he said as put his hand out to shake their hands. Turning his attention to Carla, he added, "Can I buy you a drink?"

"My six favorite words," she chuckled. "Lead the way, Paul," Carla said, before looking back at Julie, "You good?"

Julie smiled as Marc wrapped his arm around her waist, "Better than good."

Marc pulled Julie close, "I'm so happy that you came on this trip."

Julie looked into Marc's eyes, her breath catching at how expressive they were when he looked at her. "Me too," was all she said, blinking slowly.

He proceeded to twirl her around, dancing in their private suite. Julie laughed as he caught her in his arms and gave her a little dip backwards before leaning down to kiss her. Bringing her back up straight, she bit her bottom lip, thinking about how their bodies moved together the night they made love in his hotel room. She was falling in love, and she could only hope he felt the same way.

As the night unfolded, the music enveloped them, creating a magical atmosphere where time seemed to stand still and the only thing that mattered was the connection they shared in this intimate space. They danced, laughed, and drank, cheering to anything and everything. It had been way too long since Julie had felt this free.

Marc looked at his phone. "Hey, I have to take care of something. I'll be back in a few minutes."

Julie nodded as she watched him walk away. Paul and Carla were having their own conversation as Julie joined them at the bar. Carla ordered a drink, but the bartender explained that she would have to go down to the main bar to get that drink made as he only had a limited selection of alcohol in the private suites.

"Come with me to the bar downstairs," Carla said with a hint of frustration in her voice. Julie followed Carla, leaving Paul alone in the suite. Walking down the stairs, they made their way to the main bar. Carla turned toward the dance floor while the bartender made her drink, as Julie stood leaning on the bar, swaying to the music.

Carla noticed Marc talking to a brunette young woman, his hand on her arm. Carla's voice trembled with emotion as she said, "We need to go, now!"

Julie, oblivious to the betrayal, looked puzzled until she followed Carla's gaze and saw Marc's lips graze the woman's cheek. Her wide eyes filled with tears, as she watched Marc make his way toward them.

Marc noticed the look on Julie's face as he approached them. "What's wrong?" he asked reaching for Julie's hand.

Julie jerked her hand away, wiping the tears falling down her face.

Carla unleashed her anger onto Marc, screaming, "Go back to your fucking brunette. Julie deserves better than you, ass hole!" Grabbing Julie's hand, they made a swift exit from the club.

The taxi ride back to the hotel was silent, other than a few sobs coming from Julie.

***

"No More" by Nick Moore

"I'm so sorry, Jules. Men are pigs," Carla said when they got back to the hotel.

Julie's phone rang. It was Marc. She ignored it but Carla grabbed it and turned it off. "He won't be bothering you anymore tonight. Go get a shower and I'll look at getting your flight changed so you can leave with me tomorrow. No sense staying in town by yourself."

"Okay," said Julie as she moved toward the bathroom.

Carla turned Julie's phone on and listened to Marc's voicemail:

"I don't know what happened. The girl I was talking to is my sister, Gabby. I would have introduced you and Carla to her, but she just needed my advice before heading back to her friends. Please call me. You know that I would never cheat on you. Just call me. I need to see you."

Julie collapsed on the bed next to Carla.

"I listened to the message Marc left," confessed Carla.

Julie took a beat before asking, "What did he say?"

"The girl he was with is his younger sister, Gabby. You know his family. Does he even have a younger sister? I've only heard you mention Lizzy."

"I don't know. I guess it's possible that Mrs. Diaz

had another baby after Lizzy and I graduated and left for college. Marc would have been eight," explained Julie, recalling Marc saying that his parents divorced after Lizzy went to college. "I guess it's possible. Gabby could even be a half-sister; he did say his parents were divorced." Julie heard the phone buzz on the side of the bed.

Marc: Jules, we need to talk about this. The girl I was with was my younger sister. It's a long story, which I can tell you, but I have to see you. Please don't leave with Carla tomorrow before we have a moment to talk.

Julie didn't respond, she just laid the phone back on the table and closed her eyes as she rolled over. Carla scooted closer, wrapping her arm around Julie and comforting her friend.

Julie heard the garage door open, knowing that Jim would be walking in the door any moment. Their fight at the school talent show was still fresh in her mind. The kids were in bed, fast asleep. She steadied herself, knowing that the conversation was going to be anything but pleasant.

"What are you still doing up?" Jim asked as he entered the kitchen.

She could smell the scent of alcohol on him from across the room. "We need to talk about what happened earlier."

"Nothing to talk about," he slurred. "You fucked some random dad, so I fucked a random woman. No big deal, right?" he laughed, swaying as he walked toward her.

She drew in a breath, steadying herself for what was coming next. She quietly said, "I didn't cheat on you. I've never cheated on you."

Grabbing her arm, he twisted it as she gasped in

pain, "But you wanted to. I could see it in your eyes when you spoke to him."

"Stop, you're hurting me," Julie demanded.

Dropping her arm, he moved his face close to hers. She could feel the vomit rising in her throat as he blew his hot, alcohol-scented breath into her face. "You are mine, not his. Stay away from him," he growled.

"I could say the same thing to you, but I know you won't listen. You'll always find someone else, won't you?" she said, her chin trembling as she fought back the tears.

"What I do is none of your business. I'm the man. I make the money. What would you be without me? A fucking starving artist, that's all you would have been," he smirked, knowing that his words cut her more deeply that anything he could do physically to her. The tears gave way, streaming down her face. He smiled, "Sleep in the other room. I don't want a whore in my bed tonight."

Chapter 18

"Anything 4 U" by LANY

Julie opened the curtains as Carla threw the last few items into her suitcase. Julie sat down on the edge of the bed; her eyes swollen from the tears shed during the long night. She reached up to gently massage them, the skin around her eyes pink and tender. She let out a breath when she heard her phone buzz.

Marc: I'm downstairs, if I can have just 10 minutes of your time before you leave.

Julie: Headed down now. You have 10 minutes, not a minute more.

The elevator ride was quiet until Carla asked, "What are you going to say?"

"I'm going to let him apologize in person and hear what he has to say. I don't have a canned speech prepared."

"Flying by the seat of your pants. I like it. Do you want me there with you or should I just sit within earshot?"

Julie didn't answer because the elevator door opened. Wiping away the remnants of tears, she straightened her shoulders, determined to put on a brave face despite the ache in her chest. Marc was sitting on one of the sofas, so Julie headed that direction.

Standing up as she approached, he offered a seat next to him on the sofa, but she chose a chair next to the sofa. She wanted to make sure that he knew where she stood at this time. He obviously didn't sleep last night. His eyes didn't twinkle when he saw her, but instead, they were filled with sadness.

"What do you want to say?" Julie stared blankly at him.

"First of all. I am so sorry. I assumed that you knew about Gabby," he started.

"You just told me two weeks ago that your parents had divorced, but you never mentioned a younger sister. I would have remembered that."

"You're right. I should have told you and not assumed. Dad cheated on Mom, which led to Gabby being born. They divorced so that Dad could be with Jeannie and they could raise Gabby together. I stayed with Mom, and didn't find out about Gabby until her first birthday." He reached for Julie's hand, that rested on her knee.

"Jules, I would never cheat on you. You have to believe me. I wouldn't hurt you like that. You know me."

"How did she even know you were there?" Julie asked, moving her leg and causing Marc's hand to drop.

"She texted me earlier and asked if she could drop my name to get into the place. I had already made plans to take you and Carla there, so it was no big deal," Marc explained as he studied Julie's facial expression. "I should have brought her over to meet you. I'm so sorry."

Julie took a deep breath before speaking, "I believe you. I just need you to know that if you want a relationship with me, you have to be honest. I know everyone thinks I'm fragile, but I can take the truth. I'm stronger than you think."

"I know you are. It was just a misunderstanding, that's all. If you stay, I can arrange a dinner for you to meet Gabby and get to know her." A chuckle escaped from him as he said, "It's funny, she's a lot like Lizzy and they have rarely been together. Lizzy didn't speak to Dad for about 5 years after the divorce. I was so young that Mom made me continue to see him, even if it wasn't very often."

Julie looked over at Carla, who was sitting nearby within earshot of her and Marc. Carla gave her a knowing look and a nod. Julie stood and walked over to her and gave her a big hug.

"Have a safe flight home. I love you."

Carla hugged her back and then said, "Are you sure you want to stay?"

"Yeah, I need to see this through. I'll keep in touch, and we'll get together when I get back."

Carla grabbed her luggage and walked over to where Marc was sitting, "Don't make her cry again. She's cried enough the past few months to fill a river. Don't make me hate you."

Marc stood up and said, "I promise, I won't make her cry. Can I give you a hug?"

Carla rolled her eyes, "I guess."

She leaned in and gave him a hug before walking over to hug Julie again. "I'm a phone call away, if you need me."

"I love you and thank you for taking care of me last night."

"Bitch, that's what besties do!"

"Let me know when you land."

"Will do." Then looking over at Marc she said, "Take care of our girl."

Marc arranged for Julie's luggage to be taken to her room, which was adjacent to his suite. Turning to Julie he said, "Let's take a walk," he took her hand as they walked out of the hotel. "I want to say this as delicately as possible. After what happened last night, we might be moving a bit fast. I don't want to do anything to scare you off and I feel like I am the one moving too fast. I don't want to push you into a relationship that you're not ready for."

"I realize that you've been very patient with me," Julie said looking down. "It has been hard navigating all of the feelings and emotions that I've gone through in the past few months."

"Losing Jim was hard on you. I don't know exactly what you're going through, but I can still empathize and give you whatever amount of space you need," said Marc as he caressed her shoulder.

"There are times when I wonder if this will fade. That you'll become disillusioned with me and want to move on to someone your own age or younger," Julie said while looking up at Marc, searching his face for reassurance.

Marc put his arm around her waist and pulled her close. "I want you, only you. If that means I have to wait until you are ready for a romantic relationship, then I'll wait." Marc stopped, pulling Julie close to him and kissed her softly.

The crowds scooted past the two, caught in a special embrace, but Marc and Julie didn't even notice as if they were the only two people on the sidewalk at Bowery and Bleeker.

Pulling back, Julie looked up into Marc's eyes, "I'm falling for you Marc Diaz." The sounds of the city melting away as their eyes locked in an intense gaze.

Marc smiled, rubbing her back, "I've been in love with you for almost forty years, Jules." The love they felt for each other was palpable in the air.

Julie's eyes grew large as she realized the impact of what she just heard. "Marc," she started to say, before he interrupted her.

"I'm willing to wait or do whatever I have to do to keep you in my life," he continued.

The people on the sidewalk continued to walk around them as they stood, mesmerized by

each other with the backdrop of the city that never sleeps. They both realized that their lives will never be the same now that they found each other.

"I took the day off, should we visit MoMA?' he asked with a smirk.

Julie took a moment to consider his question. "I think we should save that for another day. I want to take my time there, but we could find a small gallery nearby, if that's okay?"

"Whatever you want to do is fine with me," he said squeezing her hand.

They strolled along, holding hands with their fingers intertwined together. Marc's footsteps seamed heavier. Julie sensed his unease, glancing at him with concern.

"Is everything alright, Marc?" she asked, her voice filled with worry.

Marc took a deep breath, his expression somber. "We agreed to be honest with each other, right?"

Julie sucked in a breath, afraid of what he's going to confess to her. "Yes, we did."

"There's something that I need to tell you." he started his words measured. "I flew to St. Louis to find you after I graduated college."

"You did?' asked Julie as she looked over at him, her eyes wide with surprise. "Why?"

"I wanted to surprise you," Marc explained, his voice tinged with sadness. "But when I got to your house, you weren't there. Instead, I found Jim."

Julie stopped in her tracks, turning to Marc, "Oh, I'm so sorry. I hope he wasn't rude to you. He could be very jealous at times."

"Um," Marc stammered, trying to find the words to tell her the rest. "He was…with another woman."

Julie's heart sank as she processed Marc's words. A wave of shock and disbelief washed over her. Tears welled up in her eyes as she struggled to comprehend the revelation. The color drained from her face, and Marc noticed. He reached out to steady her.

"I'm so sorry, Julie," Marc continued, his voice filled with remorse. "I didn't know how to tell you."

"Thank you for telling me, Marc," Julie whispered, her voice barely above a whisper. "I don't know what to say."

"You knew he was cheating?" he asked. Finally making sense of Julie and Carla's intense reaction to seeing him with his sister last night. "Of course, you knew," he whispered. "Jules, I understand now and I'm so, so sorry that last night was triggering for you. I didn't put the pieces together until now." He stepped toward her, taking her in his arms. "I'm so sorry."

They stood for what seemed like a lifetime, just holding each other on the sidewalk until Julie was ready to move. Pulling back, she wiped her eyes and inhaled a deep breath before letting it out slowly.

"Don't tell Carla that I made you cry," he said, trying to lighten the mood, while cracking a wonky smile.

Julie smiled as she sniffed, "I won't."

"She's scary sometimes," he joked.

"She's amazing, and I don't know what I would do without her," replied Julie.

"I'm glad you have her. Should we continue walking toward the gallery?" he asked.

Julie took his hand, nodding her head yes.

As Julie and Marc stepped into the small art gallery, they were immediately enveloped in a world of vibrant colors and abstract shapes. The walls were adorned with paintings in every hue imaginable, each one bursting with energy and emotion. Sculptures of all sizes dotted the space, their intricate forms captivating the eye.

Julie's gaze swept across the room, taking in the kaleidoscope of artwork before her. She felt a sense of wonder wash over her as she marveled at the creativity and talent on display.

"Wow, this place is incredible," Julie's voice filled with awe, she temporarily forgot the seriousness of their earlier conversation.

Marc nodded in agreement, his eyes alight with excitement. "It's like stepping into another dimension," he remarked, his voice hushed with reverence.

They wandered through the gallery, pausing to admire each piece with Julie examining the tiniest details. Some paintings seemed to dance with movement, while others drew them in with their mysterious allure. The sculptures, crafted from a variety of materials, stood as silent sentinels with each one telling its own unique story. They continued to explore, and Julie found herself drawn to a particularly striking painting filled with a vibrant swirl of colors that seemed to leap off the canvas. She couldn't break her eyes away from it, feeling a strange sense of connection to the artist's vision.

"It's like the colors are alive," Marc murmured, his voice low but filled with wonder.

Julie smiled, watching him with fondness. "That's the beauty of abstract art," she replied. "It's open to interpretation, allowing each viewer to find their own meaning within the canvas." Julie felt a sense of peace wash over her, grateful for the opportunity to experience this with Marc. Taking his hand in hers, she laid her head on his shoulder.

"I love seeing it through your eyes. You're so in tuned to the process and meaning of the paintings. It's so intriguing to hear your take," said Marc softly as he rubbed his thumb over hers.

"Art is subjective, which is why I love it and connect to it so much. Our world turns on absolutes, but art is its own beast to be admired and reckoned with. It stirs within your soul to figure it out. It's a feast for your eyes while nourishing your soul at the same time," explained Julie.

"God, that's deep, but I like it," Marc exclaims.

Julie just shrugged her shoulders and said, "It feels so good to discuss art with someone that has a genuine interest."

"Jim wasn't interest in art?" Marc asked.

"No," she took a deep breath, "He never got the

gist of it, not seeing the value. As an engineer, he dealt with absolutes, not the perspectives of art," she said with a sadness to her voice.

Marc reached out, taking her hand and lifting it to his lips, "Well, you make me want to learn more about art."

Julie smiled, tilting her head and asking, "Really?"

"Absolutely, you make it fascinating. Your enthusiasm is contagious," Marc said before kissing her hands. "What is something you've always dreamed about doing with your artwork?"

"I always dreamed of having my work in a gallery or museum, but I really wanted to work with kids at a community center and teach them about art," she replied as she walked to another painting.

Marc followed her, "You can still do that," he said reassuringly. "What was your first memory about art?"

"Hmmm, probably when my mother took me to the Blanton Museum of Art, back home in Austin."

"Isn't that on the UT campus?" Marc asked.

"Yeah, it is. My mother actually served on their board for a year, but daddy's view of art as frivolous, limited her time there. He felt like she should be at home." Julie scrunched up her face in thought. It had never occurred to her that Jim was a lot like her father.

Marc noticed her change in demeanor and asked, "Penny for your thoughts."

Julie smiled, "Just lost in thought about when I was a kid."

"Have you been back home lately?" he asked.

"Not since my parents both passed. The last time I was there, it was to empty the house and put it on the market. Have you been back lately?" she asked turning around to look at Marc.

She walked over to a bright colored painting with broad brush strokes. Julie moved her right hand in front of it, mimicking the brush strokes.

Marc watched her before answering, "No. Dad and Jeannie moved to Dallas, and mom followed Lizzy and me to California. She still lives in Santa Barbara."

"I'm sure it's nice having her close," Julie said turning around to face Marc.

"Yeah, it is," Marc said as he brushed a strand of Julie's hair behind her ear, not being able to resist the magnetic pull he felt towards her. With a tender gaze, he leaned in and pressed his lips against hers in a gentle, yet passionate kiss. The moment hung in the air like a suspended note in a symphony of emotions.

Julie, momentarily surprised, melted into his embrace, feeling the warmth of his affection enveloping her. In that intimate exchange amidst the art, they both knew that some connections were too powerful to resist, even when trying to slow down their relationship.

Julie and Marc strolled back towards the hotel; the warmth of their intertwined fingers echoed the growing intensity of their connection. With each step, the anticipation heightened and the air thickened with unspoken desires. As they reached the hotel entrance, a shared glance ignited a silent agreement, and without a word, they embraced in a passionate kiss, lost in the moment. Julie could hear her heart beating faster as they entered the elevator.

Together, they moved their bodies in sync to the rhythm of their hearts, leaving behind the outside world as they immersed themselves in the intimacy of making love. Julie curled up into Marc's arms as they laid breathless. She gently circled his chest as if she were painting a masterpiece, using broad motions.

Chapter 19

"This is How You Fall in Love" by Jeremy Zucker & Chelsea Cutler

Julie slowly opened her eyes to the soft morning light filtering through the curtains in Marc's hotel room. Stretching lazily, she realized that she was alone in bed. She sat up and noticed a tray on the bedside table, laden with a carafe of coffee, a spread of fresh fruit, and croissants. The aroma of freshly brewed coffee filled the room, mingling with the scent of the pastries and fruit. With a smile, Julie reached for a cup and saucer to pour herself a cup of coffee and savor its warmth as she took a sip. She looked over at the beautiful plate of food, touched by Marc's thoughtful gesture. She indulged in a pastry, feeling grateful for having him in her life. Despite his early departure for work, his care and affection were evident in every detail of the scene before her.

She lazily lounged in bed for a while. Her phone buzzed on the side table, and as she reached over expecting to see a call from Marc, instead, it was Ashley.

"Hi Ash,"

"Mom, I just saw Carla driving on Manchester. I thought she was with you in New York," Ashley said with an accusing attitude. "I know you're not home, because Jordan and I are at the house."

"Carla was here with me, but she had to get back early and I stayed," Julie said.

"Who is there with you?" Ashley demanded. "You're not there with that guy, are you?"

"Ash, I…," Julie stammered, searching for the right words to say.

"Mom! Why are you lying to me?"

"I didn't lie to you, Ash. You and Ben made it clear how you feel about me moving on, but I…." Julie stopped short.

"It's not about moving on. We don't know this guy and Ben thinks he's just after your money. Mom, he is ten years younger than you. Why would he want to be with an older woman?"

Julie drew in a deep breath, "Ashley, that is hurtful. You haven't even met him yet. You will love him, I promise," Julie assured her.

"Ben and I don't want to meet him. The three of us can discuss it when you get home," Ashley said before hanging up.

Julie slammed her phone down on the bed, frustration etched into every line of her face. She took a deep breath, trying to calm the storm raging inside of her. The conversation with Ashley was maddening, filled with assumptions she and Ben had made about Marc. Julie was left feeling a mix of anger, worry, and helplessness inside her. Closing her eyes, she tried to gather her thoughts and decide how to handle this situation when she got home. How dare her kids treat her like she was the child? Flopping back on the bed, she let out a soft scream to get rid of the tension welling up inside.

***

"Wanderer – Disco Cowboy Remix" by A R I Z O N A

Julie exited the car, looking up at the beautiful building that housed The New York Library. Inside, she looked to the right to see the staircase that Carrie walked down in the Sex and the City movie when she was supposed to marry Big. She smiled before going down the stairs to the gift shop, wanting something new to read while she hung out in Central Park. Her watercolors and a pad of watercolor paper were in her bag, but she wanted something to read as well. Checking out, she walked toward Central Park and grabbed 2 bottles of water as she passed a street vendor.

She placed her jacket on the ground to sit on. Opening a bottle of water, she took a long drink before pouring some in the cap for her painting. She pulled out her supplies and looked around for something to paint. She focused in on a group of girls, who were laughing and singing. They were about Ashley's age, and she sat and watched them for a bit before deciding to paint the tree-covered walkway. She loved how the benches lined the sides of the path and the way the trees bent over each other to provide shade to visitors. Sitting back after finishing her painting, she looked for the group of girls, but they had left.

She sat quietly for a while, just thinking about the past few months, and how much her life had changed. A small part of her was ready to be back at home, in her quiet sanctuary of monotony, but the rest of her was soaking up every crazy moment of this magical city and Marc. She was in love with him. He made her feel young, and helped her enjoy life again.

Checking her phone, she saw a text from Marc:

Marc: I hope you are having an amazing morning. If you don't mind, I made plans to meet Gabby for dinner tonight. She's excited to meet you.

Julie: I'm hanging out in Central Park, painting and reading. What time should I be ready for dinner?

Marc: I'll be back at the hotel around six, we're meeting Gabs at seven.

Julie: (smiley face emoji)

A wave of nervousness washed over her. It was one thing to know Lizzy because they grew up together, but meeting Gabby made this all seem so real. Was she ready for this kind of commitment to Marc? It made her feel sad just thinking about the alternative of not having Marc in her life. She was head over heels in love with him, which scared her. This all happened so fast.

Getting up, she packed her jacket and stuff back into her backpack. Walking north in the park, she looked for the Bethesda Fountain. Walking through the Bethesda Terrace building, she gasped when she saw the famous fountain. It was more breathtaking in person than it was in the movies. Walking over to the fountain, she pulled out her phone and took a selfie with the fountain in the background. She quickly sent it to Carla.

Carla: How's it going?

Julie: Good. Ashley saw you driving this morning, so she knows I'm here with Marc.

Carla: Oh shit! What did she say?

Julie: She said I was too old to date Marc.

Carla: She did not!

Julie: Yep. She and Ben think Marc is out to steal all my money.

Carla: I'll call her.

Julie: Please don't. I'll sort it all out when I get home.

Carla: Don't let it ruin your time with Boyfriend. Fuck that boy silly! LOL

Julie: (eye roll emoji) Talk to you later.

Carla: Love you, Bitch.

Julie: Love you more, bitch. (heart emoji)

Julie watched the families with kids running around the fountain. She smiled as she thought about how much she missed her kids being younger. They were so much nicer, she thought to herself. Walking north again, she set out to find Belvedere Castle. Looking at the map on her phone, it was a ten-minute walk. Finding a spot on the grounds of the castle, she pulled out her sketch pad and a charcoal pencil. Starting with the outline of the building, she sketched it out before going back to add detail and shading. Stopping periodically, she held the pad up to look between the castle and her drawing, smiling at the progress. She noticed a little blonde girl holding her mother's hand as they walked up the steps. She thought about how she should have brought Ashley to New York to see all of the architecture. Missed opportunities because of Jim and his constant control. Wiping a tear from her face, she packed up her belongings and started the walk toward The Met. It would be easier to get a cab or Uber from there back to the hotel.

***

"What is it to Love" by Ruxley

That evening they were meeting Gabby at a restaurant near her apartment. Julie was quiet as she walked in following Marc. He walked right over to a beautiful brunette with his same dark brown eyes. He excitedly introduced Gabby to Julie, who immediately gave her a big hug.

"You're already family," said Gabby when she stood back after the hug.

Julie smiled and said, "It's a pleasure to meet you, Gabby."

They sat down at the table and ordered a bottle of wine and an appetizer.

Other than the eyes, Julie noticed that Gabby

looked nothing like Lizzy or Marc. As Gabby kept talking, Julie saw exactly what Marc meant when he said that Gabby was a younger version of Lizzy. They had the same mannerisms from the way she spoke to the phrases she used. It was crazy to think Gabby and Lizzy had only met a few times, yet were so much alike. Julie sat back, listening to the two siblings catch up. Marc had his hand on Julie's knee for the first part of the evening before moving it to her back once they had finished eating. Julie smiled but remained quiet. Gabby seemed much younger than 35 years old. She had the energy of an excited twenty-something. Julie kept looking at Marc as he was laughing and enjoying the conversation with his little sister. Julie noticed he looked completely at peace and so happy at this moment. It was obvious by the conversation that Marc hadn't told Gabby about the incident that happened at the club a few nights ago. Julie appreciated that he kept that to himself, but immediately felt bad that he didn't have anyone to support him during that time. She at least had Carla in her corner for support.

After goodbye hugs and kisses, Julie and Marc walked back toward the hotel, hand in hand.

"Penny for your thoughts?" asked Marc.

Julie smiled, "Just thinking about how you and Gabby have such a deep connection, despite the circumstances surrounding your family. It's beautiful." She didn't want to tell Marc about her conversation with Ashley, she knew it could hurt his feelings.

Marc looked over at Julie as they continued to walk, "Yeah, it didn't happen at first, but once I got out of my teen angst phase, I forgave my dad and decided to be a part of Gabby's life. She didn't have the same upbringing as Lizzy and I. Her Mom worked a lot, and she was left alone at home quite often. She needed a big brother. Mom always encouraged me to have a relationship with Dad and his new family, but she didn't push it. I wish that Lizzy had been more open to being a part of Gabby's life."

"I always wished for a sibling, but it wasn't in the cards. Mom said she was lucky to have me," said Julie.

Marc asked, "When did your parents pass?"

"Mom passed right after I had Ashley, and Dad passed away three years later."

They continued to walk in silence, until they reached the hotel. Before walking in, Marc turned to Julie and said, "I love you so much. Thank you for being open to meeting Gabs tonight."

"She's really nice. I'm glad that I met her."

"I noticed that you were quiet throughout dinner. Everything okay?"

"I was just taking it in. It was fun to watch the two of you interact, laughing, telling stories. It was wonderful."

Marc took her by the hand as they walked to the elevator, where they shared a short kiss. "Do you want to stay in my room tonight?"

Julie smiled and looked into his eyes. "Of course, I do."

He quietly led her to his room and opened the door for her to walk through. As she passed him, he took in a deep breath, inhaling the scent of her perfume. "Damn, you smell great." Julie smiled and motioned for him to follow her into the bedroom.

Chapter 20

"Little Bit More" by Suriel Hess

As Julie stepped into the Museum of Modern Art, she was greeted by a wave of creativity. The grand atrium echoed with the hushed whispers of visitors and the occasional click of a camera capturing the essence of each masterpiece. Julie wandered through the galleries, her eyes dancing from one vibrant painting to another as each one told its own unique story. She paused in front of a bold abstract expressionist piece, feeling the raw emotion radiating from its chaotic swirls of color. Moving on, she marveled at the intricate sculptures and the way their forms defied gravity and challenged her perception of space. Julie felt herself being transported to different worlds, each artwork inviting her to see the world through a new lens. As she rounded a corner, she was greeted by the breathtaking view of the city skyline through the museum's expansive windows. A reminder that even amidst the hustle and bustle of New York, there was always a moment of serenity to be found in the beauty of art.

Setting her bag down, she pulled out a sketchpad and pencil before taking a seat on the floor. Gazing up at the Norman Lewis painting, Phantasy II, she began to sketch the perimeter lines before moving into the center of the drawing. Pulling out her phone, she snapped a photo of the painting for reference. Julie moved her hand back and forth to create the bold shapes and lines, before moving to fine lines. Looking up and down she kept adding, erasing, and smudging the drawing, mimicking the painting as close as possible. Feeling at ease, she stretched her arms and moved her head around in circles before working on the drawing again. Suddenly, she felt like she was being watched. Turning her head to look over her shoulder, she noticed a young woman standing behind her.

"You're good," said the young lady.

Julie turned toward the woman, "Thank you. Am I in your way?"

"No, I was just curious," the lady said, with a light chuckle. "I'm Vivian"

Julie stood up, holding her hand out to the woman, "Hi Vivian, I'm Julie." Noticing Vivian's uniform, she added, "Is it okay that I'm sketching?"

"Oh yeah, we have a lot of art students that come in to draw, but mostly the sculptures. You should check out our art classes," offered Vivian.

"You hold classes here? What kind of classes?" asked Julie, with a quizzical look on her face.

"We rotate out classes. You can check out the schedule online or you could pick up a calendar and brochure downstairs before you leave," said Vivian.

"It was so nice to meet you, Julie. I hope to see you again."

"Thank you for the information. It was a pleasure to meet you," said Julie.

Sitting back down, she finished her drawing. Packing up her art supplies, she smiled at the drawing before snapping a photo of it. Strolling through the halls, she couldn't help but feel a sense of wonder and introspection wash over her. Each artwork seemed to beckon her imagination and stir her emotions. Lost in a world of colors, shapes, and textures, she moved from one exhibit to the next, letting the art speak to her in ways that words never could. With each step, she felt a deeper connection to the creative spirit that flowed through the walls of the museum, reminding her of the beauty and complexity of the human experience.

Stopping at the front desk, she asked for a calendar of the upcoming classes. Taking a seat, she scoured over the details. There were sculpture classes, oil painting, acrylic, multi-medium, and watercolor classes listed. She smiled at the thought of spending a week here taking these courses and wandering around New York.

Julie emerged from the grand halls of MoMA, and the frantic energy of New York City enveloped her once again. The bustling streets teemed with life, each corner revealing a new slice of the city's kaleidoscopic charm. With a contented smile, she began her leisurely stroll back to the Bowery Hotel, savoring every moment of solitude amidst the urban symphony.

Passing by iconic landmarks and quaint cafes, Julie indulged in some people-watching, marveling at the diverse tapestry of humanity that populated the city. From stylish fashionistas strutting their stuff to hurried commuters lost in thought, each passerby added a layer of richness to the cityscape. The rhythmic pulse of the city served as her soundtrack, accompanied by the occasional honk of a taxi or the distant melody of a street musician. Julie relished in the sensory feast, letting the sights, sounds, and smells of the city wash over her like a warm embrace.

As she approached the Bowery Hotel, a sense of tranquility settled upon her. The familiar façade welcomed her back with open arms and offered a sanctuary amidst the chaos. With a grateful heart, Julie stepped through the doors, carrying with her the memories of her enchanting journey through the streets of New York City.

***

"Waiting for a Girl like You" by Foreigner

Sitting at the hotel bar, she looked down at her watch. 'He's running late,' she thought to herself. Her mind shifted to what life with Marc would be like. She would volunteer at a local community center teaching art, while Marc ran the New York office. In the evenings they would go to Broadway plays or gallery openings, and on the weekends, they would stroll Central Park hand in hand. She would read to him, while he teased her about the romance books she loved. She would paint while he watched his favorite sports teams, they would make love in a loft apartment while listening to rain splatter against the window. She stirred the last of her martini, lost in the daydream of a life together.

The bartender approached and asked, "Would you like another martini?"

"Yes, please," she replied.

Marc came up behind her and said, "Make it extra dirty."

Turning around, she smiled at him. He took her in his arms and said, "God, it was awful being without you today. I hope you missed me."

Julie made a half smile and held her finger and thumb up to show a small amount, "Maybe just a little bit."

"Anything for you, Sir?" asked the bartender.

"I'll have the same."

"Right away," replied the bartender.

Marc turned his attention back to Julie, "Anything special you want to do tonight?"

She knew that her time in New York was coming to an end, but she wanted to savor every moment she could with him. "I just want to be with you."

"How about a quiet little bar in the Village? I know the perfect place, it's one of my favorites."

She responded, "That sounds magical."

As they sipped on their martinis, Julie told Marc of her adventures of the day, alone in New York. "I'm sorry you had to spend the day alone. I wish I could have been with you more," said Marc.

"It's been fun exploring this city alone," she leaned forward, close enough that she could smell his cologne.

"Tomorrow is our last full day here and I get to spend the day with you." he pulled her closer, not taking his eyes from her as he grazed her lips with his.

They finished their drinks, paid the tab, and walked with their fingers intertwined, toward their next destination.

When they arrived at the bar, it was early enough that it wasn't crowded. They found a small round table in the corner. Marc looked around and said, "I'll go up to the bar to order. Dirty martini?"

"Yes, please and a glass of water."

Marc disappeared towards the bar. Julie sat quietly to take it all in. 'How did I get here, to this place with this man? Liz's little brother. What would she think of this relationship?' she thought to herself. A few minutes later, she heard a song come on over the speakers. She recognized the song immediately. It was one of her favorite songs from her teen years, "Waiting for a Girl like You" by Foreigner. She couldn't help herself but to sway to the music.

Then she saw Marc walking toward her without their drinks. He held his hand out to her, "Dance with me?"

Julie looked around the bar and didn't see anyone else getting up to dance, "Of course," she said as she grabbed his hand to stand.

"I picked this song for you," Marc said as he moved her to the middle of the floor.

"I don't remember telling you it was my favorite song growing up."

"You didn't," he said as looked deep into her eyes. "I remember my mom playing it when she and my dad would dance in the kitchen. I always hoped that I would find someone to dance in the kitchen with. I wasn't sure if I ever would, until I found you again." He paused as he turned Julie around, and then whispered in her ear, "I've been waiting for you. I love you, Jules." He pulled her close and gave her the most passionate kiss she had ever experienced. She was mesmerized and didn't care if anyone was watching them. She loved being in this bubble with him.

"I am falling in love with you, Marc Diaz," she said before kissing him again.

He continued to sway back and forth with her in his arms, and it was as if the world disappeared. When the song ended, he took her by the hand and said, "Let's get out of here."

***

"Like That" by Bea Miller

The next morning when Julie woke up, Marc wasn't in bed with her. She looked around the bedroom but didn't see him. She wrapped the sheet around her and walked into the living area of the suite. A man in uniform stood next to a cart with all kinds of pastries. Marc was standing next to him, dressed only in jeans and bare chested with no shoes. His hair was messy, and he was wearing his glasses. 'Damn,' she thought to herself, biting her bottom lip.

Marc was getting cash out of his wallet and hadn't noticed that she had walked into the room. The man in uniform looked up at Julie and nodded.

"Good morning," she said. Marc turned around and smiled. He handed the man the cash and closed the door behind him.

"Good morning," he said, as he walked over to kiss her. "I ordered a variety of breakfast options. I woke up famished, for some reason," he said with a wink.

"I've got an appetite too this morning," she said as she kissed him. "Coffee?"

"Ah yes, I have enough coffee to satisfy any caffeine addict," he laughed.

Looking down at the sheet wrapped around herself, "Maybe I should go put on a robe."

"Don't do it on my part. I would have you walk around naked all the time, if it were up to me."

He smiled a devilish grin and grabbed her around the waist, making them both fall on the sofa. They laughed and kissed, then made love again before ending up on the floor. This time there was no silence afterwards. This was really happening, and they were both completely and fully on board with this new part of their relationship. She laid with her head on his chest, listening to him breathe and made circles with her finger on his chest.

"So, what are you lost in thought about?" Marc asked with that twinkle in his eye.

"You. Us. Last night. Just now."

"It was good, right? I know it was for me, but I want you to be satisfied too."

"Oh Marc, I was more than satisfied. You were perfect."

"Perfect, huh?" he asked, moving his head around, making a silly face.

"Don't get cocky," she laughed.

He reached down and tickled her side. "There's no cockiness, only my love for you."

She stretched up to kiss him. "Less talking, more kissing, please."

"That I can do," he said as he leaned forward to continue kissing her.

Coming up for air, Marc got up to grab a croissant and a cup of coffee for Julie. She was the one that couldn't take her eyes off him this time. He was tan, fit, and had the cutest butt that she had ever seen. She pulled the sheet up over her breasts as he returned. He handed her the cup of coffee and sat down beside her.

"Aren't you eating anything? I thought you were famished."

"I don't like to eat after a workout," he said jokingly.

She took a sip of coffee and a bite of the croissant. She didn't say a word, just smiled at him. He smiled back, and it was warm and inviting. His curls were disheveled on his forehead but it somehow complimented his good looks. He was staring at her again. With anyone else this would bother her, but with him, it was as if he was checking to see if she was really in his life again, which was endearing to her. Biting the end of her finger, she stared back at him. She could dive into his deep, brown eyes, getting lost in them.

He broke the silence and said, "Is there is anything you really want to do today?" Marc looked over at her and said, "If you want to stay in and I don't know, stay in bed all day, I'm cool with that too. Just sayin'," he said, as she shot her a playful look and bit his bottom lip.

"How about a little of both? We could stay in all day and go out tonight?" she suggested.

Leaning over, he kissed her on the forehead. "I love you, Jules."

She smiled and gazed into his face as she placed her hand on his cheek, "I love you too."

Chapter 21

"Butterflies" by Abe Parker

Julie sat in the bustling terminal at LaGuardia, lost in thought about the past few days with Marc. Smiling as she twisted her hair, she daydreamed about a life with Marc and living in New York. Opening her phone, she typed in the website for MoMA to look at the classes that Vivian had told her about. Scrolling down the page, she looked at the class schedules. Sitting back, she looked out at the tarmac and then at her watch. She felt someone drop down into the seat next to her. Without even looking up, she scooted her bag over to make room.

"Thanks for making room for me."

Julie turned her head around as she recognized the voice. She smiled and then asked, "What are you doing here? This isn't your terminal."

Marc leaned over and kissed her on the cheek. He then held up his phone and said, "It is now." His eyes lit up as he smiled before kissing her on the lips.

"I'm confused. What's going on? I thought you had to go back to LA."

"I do, but I changed my flight to go with you to St. Louis. I can stay an extra day or two before flying home."

"What an amazing surprise!" Julie squealed as she hugged him. "You can stay with me. No need for a hotel, okay?"

"I was hoping you would say that, but if you're uncomfortable at all with me being there, just say the word and we can go to a hotel. I don't want to push you into anything that you aren't ready for," he said as he held her hand and pulled it up to his lips for a kiss.

"I love you," she said leaning in for another kiss. She felt her phone buzz in her bag. Grabbing it, she saw that it was Carla.

"Hey Carla," said Julie when she answered.

"We have a situation that you need to know about," Carla said frantically.

Julie stood up and walked away from Marc. "What happened?" she asked Carla, matching her frantic tone.

"Ashley is okay, but she and Jordan got into a fight last night. She left to give him time to calm down, but when she came back, he had somehow locked her out," Carla explained.

Julie's hand shot up to her mouth, as she listened. "Is she with you?"

"No, she's at your house," Carla had concern in her voice, "She's pretty sure he has a girl in her apartment."

"He's cheating on her? And locked her out of her own apartment? The apartment that I pay for every month?" Julie's voice became loud as she paced back and forth. "Has she called the police? Or her landlord?"

Marc got up as Julie paced near him. "Come sit down," he whispered.

"She doesn't want to call the police. She wants to wait it out, hoping he'll calm down, and apologize," explained Carla.

Julie nodded her head "no" at Marc as she walked over to the giant window that faced the tarmac. "Thank you for being there with her. I should have been the one she turned to, but she's mad at me," Julie said with a tinge of regret in her voice.

"You know I am here for you, Ash, and Ben. Always…Jules," Carla paused before continuing. "You have to tell Ash about Jim. You know I'm right about this."

Julie rubbed her forehead before settling her thumb and finger on the bridge of her nose. She exhaled before speaking, "I know. I don't want to." Turning her head, she looked over at Marc with his gaze directed at her. "Um, Marc surprised me by changing his flight to come home with me. This is going to be a nightmare, Car," she said rubbing the back of her neck.

"Yeah, it will be, but we'll get through it together, like always," Carla assured her. "Have a good flight. I'll pick you two up at the airport."

"Thanks, Car. Love you," Julie said.

"Love you more," replied Carla before she ended the call.

Julie stared out across the tarmac and watched planes arrive. Holding her phone up to her mouth, she patted it against her lips as she thought about the situation and how grateful she was that Carla was home to comfort and help Ashley. "Ashley…my sweet baby girl," she whispered.

Walking back to Marc with her head hung down, her footsteps felt heavy.

Marc stood up and motioned for her to take a seat. "What happened?" he asked with a concerned voice.

Julie plopped down into the seat next to Marc. Shaking her head, she finally spoke, "We're walking into a bad situation when we get back to my house."

Marc's confused expression turned to worry, "What happened?"

Julie put her hands over her face, lost in thought about how much she should tell Marc. Her thoughts ran rampant. If we are going to be in a relationship, Marc deserved to know what he was walking into. Her kids hate him, her dead husband was abusive, and now Ashley, poor Ashley was in a relationship that mirrored her life with Jim. Julie rocked back and forth as Marc rubbed her back.

"What can I do to help?" he whispered. "Please let me help."

Julie looked over at him, tears in her eyes, "I…I don't know."

"Tell me what happened? Did something happen to Ashley?" he asked.

Biting her upper lip, tears streamed down her face as she said, "Ashley's boyfriend, Jordan, is borderline abusive, definitely mentally, and emotionally abusive." She continued to explain the situation between Ashley and Jordan.

Marc's voice of concern changed to anger, "Why would she put up with someone like that? She deserves someone who loves her."

Julie closed her eyes, "Because she's attracted to someone who reminds her of her father." Opening her eyes, she looked over at Marc. "I'm sorry. This is too much. If you want to just go back to LA, I get it." She sighed, giving him the out that he deserved.

Marc's face softened, "No." He took her hand, kissing it again. "Let me be there to help you. I could even meet with this Jordan character," his voice tinged with anger again.

Julie wiped her tears and leaned into Marc. "Thank you," was all she could squeak out.

They sat in silence, waiting to board the flight. Julie's mind wandered back to dreaming about a life in New York with Marc, and how that seemed like a pipe dream now. Her reality burst the bubble they were in. She glanced over at Marc as he typed on his phone, and she wondered if he was regretting getting involved with her. How could he still want to be with her? Her life was a mess, her kids hate him, and now all of this with Jordan. How was she going to explain how Jim really was to Ashley. She had kept so much of the trauma pushed down for so many years. It was too painful for her to think about, so she knew it was going to devastate Ashley. She was going to be ruining the memory of Jim in her eyes. Carla had pushed for the kids to know, but Julie had her doubts. They were adults, and in light of this new situation, she had no choice but to tell Ashley. She had to come clean about all that she hid from them for so many years.

Marc grabbed her hand, "We can board now." He helped her up, grabbing her bag with one hand and placing his other hand on the small of her back, "Let's get you home."

***

"Ashley?" Julie called out as she walked into the house.

Ashley responded, "In the kitchen."

Julie turned to Marc, "Have a seat here. I'll go check on her." Marc let her take the lead and took a seat on the sofa. She mouthed, "I'm sorry." He motioned for her toward the kitchen.

When Julie entered the kitchen, Ashley turned around and rushed to her mother. "Mom," as she embraced her tightly.

Julie held Ashley, "I'm here. It's going to be okay." They continued to embrace for what seemed like forever. When Ashley pulled back, Julie asked, "What happened?"

Ashley explained the story and how Jordan had been blowing up her phone all day. "I'm just so angry at him. I know that he had a girl in my apartment, I just know it. I could fucking hear her, Mom."

Taking a seat the island, Julie counseled her daughter, "Ash, this is a huge red flag, and you need to really think about what you want and what kind of person you want in your life."

"Momma, I love him. He's not always like this," Ashley defended.

"I know you do," Julie responded, looking down

and taking a deep breath before letting it out slowly. "Ash, there's something I need to tell you about," Julie said, her voice shaking. "It's about your dad."

"Mom, what does Dad have to do with anything? I wish he was here, to set Jordan straight," mused Ashley.

Julie's eyes filled with tears that dripped over the edge and streamed down her face. "Your father was a lot like Jordan."

Ashley was quick to retort that statement, "No! Dad was perfect."

Julie sniffed, wiping the tears, "He was not perfect, Ash. Our marriage wasn't perfect. I'm not perfect."

"What the fuck are you talking about, Mom? Dad loved you. You loved Dad. You both loved me and Ben," Ashley said standing up, starting to pace.

That's when Julie noticed the bruises on Ashley's arms and on the side of her neck. "What the fuck has he done to you, Ash?" Standing up, she grabbed Ashley and forced her to stand still. "You have bruises that look like fingers on your neck and arm."

"He likes it a little rough, that's all. I'm okay," Ashley tried to assure her mom.

"Ashley, that's not a little rough, that's abuse," Julie said sternly.

Ashley jerked free from her mother. "Don't change the subject!" she shouted. "You're deflecting away from disparaging my dad."

Julie shook her head, taking a seat again. "It's not disparaging if I'm telling you the truth. Your dad started cheating on me shortly after we got married and continued until he got sick." She stopped short of spewing her theory about the child with Andrea in the mall, and how that could be a half-sibling. Reaching up to scratch her head, she continued, "I never wanted you and Ben to know. I hid it from you two. I even hid it from Carla, until recently."

Tears streamed down Ashley's face. "You're lying.

You just want us to hate Dad so you can be with that guy," Ashley accused.

"Ashley, that isn't true at all," Julie defended. "I'll be right back." Julie headed out of the kitchen toward the bedroom to get the letter. She passed the living room where Marc sat, looking between the kitchen and his phone.

"Is everything okay?" he asked, but she didn't respond.

Picking up the letter, she marched back into the kitchen and handed it to Ashley. "Here, read this. I wouldn't lie to you."

Ashley opened the letter, reading each word as her face flushed with confusion and hurt. She looked up at Julie, "Where did you get this?"

"I found it tucked away in some of your dad's sweaters. I found it before Carla and I went to California," explained Julie.

"You knew that long ago and never said anything? How do I know this is real?" asked Ashley. Throwing the paper on the island. "No! He loved you. He wouldn't have done this to us!"

Julie took Ashley into her arms. "I know you're in shock. I didn't want to tell you or your brother, but with everything happening with Jordan, I couldn't let you make the same mistake that I made and lived with for thirty-five years."

Ashley pulled back and yelled at her mother, "So Ben and I were mistakes? Is that what you're saying?"

"No, of course not. You and Ben are the best things that ever happened to me. I have zero regrets when it comes to you two. I just wish that I would have been strong enough to stand my ground with your dad, standing up for us. We deserved better. You deserve better, Ash," Julie consoled. Her attention was drawn to Marc standing at the doorway.

Ashley turned her head to see where her mother

was looking. "What the fuck, Mom? You brought your boytoy home with you?"

"It's not like that, Ash," defended Julie.

"So, what's it like Mom? You couldn't fuck him enough in New York, so you're moving him in here?" Ashley spewed, knowing her words were like daggers to her mother's heart. Spinning around, "I can't stay here." Ashley stomped out of the kitchen and walked toward her childhood bedroom, slamming the door.

Julie burst into tears as Marc rushed toward her, wrapping his arms around her. "It's okay," he said as he held her.

Julie pushed him away, "It's not okay. I'm sorry, but you need to go. I have to get her to see the truth about Jim…I mean Jordan."

Marc stepped back, "I know you're upset. Tell me what to do to make this better."

"There's nothing you can do Marc. This is a family matter and as much as I love you, you're not family. I need you to go," said Julie as she turned her back to him. "Just go."

Chapter 22

"I'm Fine" by Van Andrew

Julie sat at the dining room table, her hands trembling slightly as she clutched a worn photograph of her and Jim on their wedding day. She knows she can't keep the truth from Ashley any longer. With a heavy heart, she takes a deep breath and prepares herself for the conversation that lies ahead.

As she crossed the threshold of Ashley's room, she sees her daughter's tear-stained face and knows that the time has come to reveal the painful truth about Jim, their troubled marriage, and the demons he battled before his passing.

With a mixture of sorrow and determination, Julie begins to speak with a voice that trembled with emotion, "I sent Marc away so that we could talk. Just me and you."

Ashley didn't respond or even look up.

Julie knew that she had to share the secrets that have haunted their family for far too long. "It all started just a few months after we got married. It was like a switch flipped," Julie sniffed as Ashley looked up at her. "He, um…he started out making sharp jabs with his words, making fun of my love of art. He was an expert in making me feel small. The late nights at the office started happening, drinks with co-workers…" Julie looked off in thought. Saying this out loud rattled her mind. "The first time I caught him cheating was during one of those late-night work sessions. I missed him so much during that time, he always worked late back then. I brought him dinner as a surprise, only to find him walking out of the building with his arm wrapped around a blonde intern. I started to call out to him, but stopped short because they stopped, he turned her towards him and pulled her in for a kiss." Julie recounted with tears streaming down her face, still struggling with just how much to tell Ashley. As Julie paused, there was a moment of silence between them as the gravity of her revelation sunk in. A heaviness hung over them, as if the air in the room had been sucked out.

Ashley looked over at her mother, noticing the pain written on her face. "I don't understand, dad adored you."

"I'm not sure if adored is the right word," Julie said looking over at Ashley. "I think I provided the wife that he wanted at first, but then got bored with. We never discussed if he was unhappy or if he would have rather had a divorce."

"Did you confront him about what you saw?" asked Ashley, through tear-stained eyes.

"I did. He denied it, of course, saying it was someone else that looked like him. But I knew the truth in what I saw."

Ashley didn't want to believe what her mother was saying, "Maybe he was telling the truth, and you were just a suspicious wife. Did you ever think about that?" Not caring that her words would cut her mother deeply.

Julie hung her head down, "Believe me, he was a pro at gaslighting, and I constantly questioned what I saw. I wasn't the perfect wife, but I tried. I did the best that I could, but he was so mean at times. Always controlling the narrative, controlling me, controlling us." Her voice softened, "I loved him, with all my heart. I sacrificed myself, molding myself into the wife he wanted."

Ashley realized how hurt her mom was by her words, "I'm sorry, Mom," she whispered. "Why did you stay with him?"

"Each time, I thought it would be the last time.

Maybe I was afraid to be alone, or I didn't want to disappoint my parents," Julie said, thinking deeply about Ashley's question. "I eventually stayed for you and Ben. You both deserved having two parents that loved you dearly and lived in the same home. I know I was afraid to be a single mom and not be able to give you all that you needed."

They sat in silence for a while before Ashley spoke up, "Why didn't you tell me and Ben?"

Julie looked at Ashley and smiled through her tears, "Because you both adored your father, and I didn't want to tarnish your memories of him. I had no intention to tell you any of this, but this situation with Jordan scared me. I want to spare you the pain of being with someone who doesn't care about your happiness. You deserve someone that wants to be your partner in life, who wants you to succeed, to be overjoyed about a lifetime together, not someone who's always ready to jump ship for a fling."

"Is that why you cried so much when we were little?" Ashley asked, quietly.

Julie looked at Ashley with her mouth agape, "You knew about that?"

"Yeah, I remember when Dad would travel, you always seemed worried and you cried at night," Ashley said softly.

"Did Ben know that too?" Julie asked.

Ashley let out a sigh, "I don't know. I never talked to him about it. I just assumed that you missed dad so much that it made you sad. I had no idea that you were worried he was with someone else. How many were there?"

Julie's breath hitched, "There were more women over the years, I don't know how many. The last one was Andrea, which was before your dad got diagnosed."

"Andrea," mused Ashley. "Why does that name sound familiar?"

"She worked with your dad and was at the funeral.

Blonde, petite…" Julie recalled.

Ashley's eyes grew wide, "The chick that wouldn't stop crying? Is that Andrea?"

"That's her," Julie said with a sigh.

"Ben and I talked about how she was acting at dad's funeral. She cried more than any of us. It was so weird," Ashley recalled.

"I thought the same thing, but it all clicked when I found the letter. Then Carla and I ran into her at The Galleria," Julie said. Her face contorted at the memory and she began to sob uncontrollably. Putting her hands over her face in embarrassment.

"Mom, it's okay," Ashley tried to comfort her mother. "You don't have to tell me if it's too painful." Ashley said, putting on a brave face.

"She tried to act like nothing had happened. Carla started quoting the letter back to her. It was awful, Ash. To stand there knowing that he was going to choose her, but then he got sick and stayed because he needed me."

"Isn't she, my age?" Ashley asked.

"Close enough," replied Julie. "I think she's a year or two older."

They sat in the quietness of all that had been shared, both pondering the information. Julie worried that she said too much. She wondered if any of her confessions had sunk into Ashley about Jordan. Julie reached over and stroked Ashley's long, blonde hair.

"If you continue with your relationship with Jordan, I can guarantee that you'll have a lot of nights crying yourself to sleep, wondering if he's with someone else. He will make you feel small, just to pump up his own ego. You'll never have peace and you'll always second guess yourself. Does that sound like a good life to you?"

"No, it doesn't, but I love him, Mom. I really love him. What do I do with that?" Ashley asked.

"Heartbreak is never easy, but it's better to figure

out what you are willing to put up with, in a relationship now, rather than months or years down the road. You don't want a life filled with trauma and the duress of feeling beat down, emotionally, verbally and physically. You are a smart girl, Ash. Losing your dad was so hard on you, but it's better to wait for the right person to come along than to put up with less than you deserve. Please don't be like me, and mold yourself into something that you are not, just to appease a man," explained Julie, as she pulled Ashley into a hug.

Pulling away, Ashley asked, "Is Marc different than dad? Is that why you're attracted to him?"

The mere mention of Marc's name made Julie smile. "He is very different. He's kind, attentive, and encouraging, but we're still getting to know each other."

"Don't you worry about him cheating on you?" Ashley asked as she rubbed on the bruised spots on her arm.

"Honestly, I don't know. There was a night in New York when I questioned if he would cheat on me, but Carla and I had the situation all wrong. I don't think he would now, but I second guess myself a lot. A bad habit I've had for many years," Julie said, as her gaze turned toward the bedroom window. She stared at the darkness, barely making out the swing set in the back yard that Jim built. Continuing she said, "Your dad loved you and Ben so much. Please never doubt that."

"You just wish that he loved you like that too," said Ashley as she wiped her eye and put her head on Julie's shoulder.

Julie wrapped her arm around Ashley's face and patted her cheek, "I should let you get some sleep. We have some decisions to make in the morning."

"Decisions?" Ashley asked pulling away from her mother's touch.

"What we need to do about this Jordan situation,

and…," Julie's mind drifted.

Ashley looked at the expression on her mother's face, recognizing the sadness from the past. "Marc?" she asked quietly.

Julie looked at Ashley. "Yeah."

Shutting the door behind her, Julie reached into her pocket and pulled out her phone. No calls from Marc, which caused a pit in her stomach. Had she been too abrupt with him about leaving? Where did he even go? Her head was spinning. As she walked through the house and turned the lights out, she heard a voice from outside. Quietly, she walked toward the front door and peeked out the sidelight, surprised to see a dark figure out in the porch swing. She put her ear to the front door to see if she recognized the voice. Was it Jordan? He knew where she lived, and it's obvious that Ashley would come here if she was upset. She slowly cracked the front door open to get a clearer sound of the voice. She smiled as she opened the door and walked out onto the porch.

"Hey, I've gotta go. Talk to you tomorrow, Paul," Marc said as he saw Julie. Scooting over on the swing, he patted the cushion for her to sit down. "How is she?" he asked with a tenderness to his voice.

Julie sat down on the swing and looked into Marc's brown eyes. "I've given her something to seriously think about."

Marc paused before asking, "But how is she doing?"

"She's sad, angry, and confused," Julie stared straight ahead to the streetlight beaming down in the darkness. She thought about how it mirrored her life right now. The darkness was Jim, his death, his wandering, his cruelness, and Marc was the beacon of hope, the light exposing some of darkness for what it really is…the past.

"What can I do to help her, and to help you?" Marc asked.

"There isn't anything you can do," Julie said in

monotone. "I think you need to go to a hotel tonight. I can pay you back for it," she said looking over at him. He stayed. He could have taken off, caught a last-minute flight back to LA, but he stayed. He didn't crowd us, or express his opinions, force his demands, or pout when things didn't go as planned. He's a good guy, a great guy. She looked over at him, smiling and said, "I'm really tired."

"It's okay, I'll get a hotel nearby. Do we need to be worried that Jordan will try to see Ashley tonight? If so, I can hang out here for a while," Marc offered.

Julie nodded her head, "We'll be fine."

They sat in silence on the porch swing until Marc's Ubcr arrived.

"I'll call you in the morning," said Marc, before standing up. He leaned down and kissed Julie on the forehead. "I love you, Jules."

Julie looked up, forcing a smile, "Love you too." She sat watching Marc, walk away from her. Standing up, she moved inside and secured the lock behind her. Julie walked in toward Ashley's bedroom, listening for any sounds on the other side of the door. Not hearing anything, she quietly opened the door and peeked inside the dark room. Ashley was curled up in the bed, making Julie's smile spread far and wide across her face.

Walking back toward the living room, Julie thought about the months immediately following Jim's death. Ashley was the one that stayed and cared for her as she mourned her husband. "Was she able to grieve losing her dad?" Julie whispered as she walked into the bedroom that she shared with Jim. Had she been so selfish that she didn't notice her daughter grieving him?

Her phone pinged, pulling it out of her back pocket, she opened the message:

Carla: How's Ash doing?
Julie: She's sad and angry.
Cara: Did you tell her?
Julie: Yeah, but not everything.
Carla: Is Marc still there?

Julie: No, I sent him to a hotel. He stayed out on the front porch, wanting to protect us, in case Jordan showed up.

Carla: He did? Wow.

Julie: I know. Talk tomorrow? I'm exhausted.

Carla: For sure. Love you, Jules.

Julie: Love you more.

Julie stood in front of the mirror; the weight of her thoughts seemed to pull at her shoulders. She ran a brush through her hair mechanically, her mind preoccupied with the decision she knew she had to make. Her life was a mess right now, and Marc deserved better. He shouldn't have to put up with the drama that is unfolding in her life. She resolved to let go of Marc, the man who had been a constant presence in her life the past few months. Someone who always wanted what was best for her. Removing her makeup, each stroke of the cotton pad felt like a small act of liberation as she wiped away the layers of uncertainty and doubt that had clouded her mind since finding the letter from Andrea. She stared at her reflection, searching for strength to follow through with her decision.

Julie slipped into her pajamas with a sigh, the soft fabric a comforting embrace against her skin. She climbed into bed, pulling the covers up to her chin, and feeling the heaviness of her heart settle in for the night.

Chapter 23

"Another Day" by Michele Morrone

Ashley walked into the living room, to find Julie sitting and waiting on Marc. "Good morning," she said, rubbing her eyes. "Did you make coffee?"

Julie turned and smiled at Ashley, noticing the dark circles under her eyes, "Yeah. Did you sleep much last night?"

"Not really. Let's talk after I get coffee. Do you need a refill?" Ashley asked nodding at Julie's mug.

"Sure. Thank you," Julie said, as she handed Ashley the mug. She was thankful that Ashley was at least making an effort and wasn't mad any longer. Picking up her phone, she opened the Pinterest App and started scrolling as she noticed a few new recipes to try and a couple of cute outfits. Her mind drifted back to Marc and wondered what his mindset was this morning. Looking back at her phone, she typed 'bedroom makeover' in the search bar. The results were almost overwhelming, but the bold color palettes excited her. Jim always liked things bland with his favorite shade of blue, but Julie was ready to add some color back into her life. Starting with the bedroom seemed like the perfect place to start.

Ashley handed Julie the mug of coffee. "Did you get any sleep last night?"

"A couple of hours, maybe," replied Julie, taking a sip of her coffee. "Let me know when you're ready to talk more. I don't want you to feel rushed into continuing," Julie looked out the window before looking back at Ashley, who was now curled up on the sofa with a plush throw blanket wrapped around her.

"Have you heard from Marc this morning?" Ashley asked.

"No, and I don't know if that's a good thing or a bad thing," Julie said taking a deep breath.

"I thought about what you said, and I want to try one more time to talk to Jordan before giving up on him," Ashley said as she looked down at her mug of hot coffee.

"Hmm," said Julie. "How many chances have you given him so far?"

"Probably too many," Ashley sighed.

"Well, if that's the case, do you think he really deserves one more chance?" Julie asked as she stared directly at Ashley. Her mind was screaming for Ashley to stop and think about what a future with Jordan would be like. She could never go to work and not worry about who Jordan was with, or if she would come home to find herself locked out again, or God forbid if she had a child with this boy. Julie's heart was heavy because the warning signs were lit up in neon, she just needed Ashley to look up and see them.

Ashley looked down at her cup of coffee, "Don't start again, please."

"I'm not trying to start anything, Ash. I just want you to think about your future and what the rest of your life would be like, if you…" she paused, the burning taste of vomit rising in her throat. "Married him," she choked out.

"God, Mom! Don't be so dramatic. We're just dating," Ashley spewed.

"Ash, you said that you loved him. Love means more than your favorite kind of cupcake or rock band. Love is a serious word and it's thrown around like it's nothing nowadays," Julie explained. Her mind thinking of the first time she told Marc that she loved him. Her heart sank, because she wondered if she threw that word around nonchalantly herself. After all, she was ending it with him today. Did she truly love Marc, or just the idea of being really cared for by someone? Closing her eyes, she thought about the way he made her feel. It was intoxicating to experience that kind of attention. She had craved that for so many years from Jim, but never really received that unconditional love like she felt from Marc. Maybe it really was love that she felt for him. If that was the case, why was she pushing him away?

Ashley interrupted Julie's thoughts, "Mom, I'm old enough to know what love is." Her tone had a bratty edge to it.

"Okay, you're right. You are an adult and it's your life, but while I am paying for your apartment, I don't want Jordan living or staying there. Once you are done with your Master's degree, you can move in with whomever you want. For now, I don't want this situation to happen again where you can't even sleep in your own apartment because he's taken another girl to your bed and locked you out!" Julie said, as she watched Ashley for a reaction.

Ashley looked up at her mother, shocked by her statement. She eventually looked back down at the cup of coffee that had started to get cold. They sat in silence for what seemed like an eternity before Ashley got up and walked into the other room, leaving her mother alone.

***

Julie took a seat by the window; the ticking of the clock seemed to echo her racing heartbeat. As she fidgeted with the hem of her sweater, her gaze flitted nervously to the door every few seconds. Outside, the rain tapped gently against the glass, mirroring the storm brewing within her. Each passing minute felt like an eternity as she anxiously waited for Marc to arrive. She rehearsed the words she needed to say in her mind, but they felt heavy and foreign on her tongue. How do you tell someone you love that it's time to let go? She thought about Ashley and Ben's issues with Marc, and while she knew that none were valid, she didn't think it was right to keep stringing Marc along while she got her life and her kid's lives together. Her time with Marc was magical, freeing, and so satisfying, but they had moved forward in their relationship too fast. She didn't have the stomach to fight with her kids about him, when all they really needed was time to heal from the death of Jim and the trauma that surrounded their family.

Julie's mind raced with conflicting emotions. She couldn't take the knowledge of his infidelity, yet the thought of leaving him weighed heavily on her heart. She had rehearsed the conversation countless times in her mind, but now, faced with the reality that he would be walking through the door any minute, uncertainty gripped her. She saw him with the blonde intern and this sudden work trip seemed highly suspicious. What if she stayed? Would starting a family save her marriage and make him faithful? He wanted a big family, so would that even matter now that he had someone else?

Her phone lay silently beside her, the screen mocking her with its empty notifications. She longed for a distraction, something to ease the tension coiling in her chest, but there was only the deafening silence of the empty room. As the minutes stretched into what felt like hours, doubts crept in. What if he didn't understand why she wanted to take a break? What if he tried to convince her to give their relationship another chance? He lived in Los Angeles, so it wasn't like they spent every waking moment together. Why should they halt their relationship? She loved him, that she knew for sure, but did she love him enough to put him before her kids? Deep down,

Julie knew that she needed to let Marc go. Holding on wouldn't be easy, but allowing her kids to slowly erode the relationship would be too heartbreaking for them both. She would just be prolonging the inevitable pain. A knock at the door interrupted Julie's thoughts.

Julie met Marc at the door. Her nerves were in overdrive, the pit in her stomach seemed to be growing at an exponential rate.

He greeted her with a kiss and a hug. "How are things with Ashley this morning?" he asked, taking her hand and intertwining their fingers together.

Julie felt like she was melting inside from his touch. "She's hiding out in her room," she answered honestly.

Pulling her close, he wrapped his arm around her waist, "I missed you last night."

"I missed you too," she replied, relishing his embrace, and knowing it would be the last one for a long time… if not forever.

"How did the talk go last night?" Marc said pulling back and looking at Julie's face for any indicators.

"It was rough," Julie said, leaning into Marc for another hug. "I haven't really talked to her this morning to know how she's feeling, but she mentioned giving Jordan one more chance."

Marc wrapped his arms around her back, "Why would she do that? The guy is obviously a jerk. She deserves better."

"She says that she loves him. Love can make people do stupid things," she gave a little laugh, "I should know, I put up with a lot of…bullshit because of love."

"You were young and you didn't know any better, but you can set her straight. Just tell her the truth, making her see that it's not worth it," he encouraged.

"It's not that easy when your heart is involved. It's not a business transaction," Julie explained.

"I didn't say it was a business transaction. She has

to know her worth, and he is definitely not deserving of her love," Marc said matter-of-factly.

Julie pulled back, looking up at Marc. "I know my child, and I know how amazing she is. I know Jordan is not the right person for her, but she is an adult and I only have so much control over what she does."

Marc's phone buzzed in his pocket. Pulling it out, he noticed it was Paul calling. "I have to take this. I'll be right back," he said, making his way out onto the front porch for some privacy.

Julie took a seat on the sofa, watching Marc pace back and forth on the porch. She nervously chewed on her cuticles, waiting for Marc to finish and come back inside. The look on his face when he entered the house again was anything but pleasant.

"I have to get back to LA. I'm so sorry," said Marc.

"Uh, what's going on?" Julie asked, dumbfounded by the rush.

"We have a major client that is being poached and they'll only speak to me," he explained.

"So, call them," Julie suggested.

"It's not that easy. They've requested a meeting tomorrow morning and I'm expected to be there. I've got to check flights," he said kissing her on the forehead before going back to the porch.

Julie followed him out, "So that's it?"

"What's it?" Marc looked up from his phone.

"Things get rough and you're just out?" she asked, realizing that she's picking a fight to make the breakup easier on herself.

Marc stood up from the porch swing, "I'm not leaving because of a rough patch, Jules. It's my job. A job that I love." He walked toward her, grabbing her hand in his.

Julie pulled away from his touch, "It just seems very convenient, don't you think?" She stared up at him, her face flushed. "My life isn't all perfect like yours, Marc. I'm a mess, my daughter is a mess, and my son doesn't trust you."

Marc had a look of shock on his face, "I never said my life was perfect. I'm sorry you're having a rough time with Ashley, and I have no idea what Ben's problem is with me. It sounds like you need to let your kids be the adults they are, stand up to them, and do whatever you have to do to be happy. I thought that I made you happy. What's this really about, Jules?"

Julie crossed her arms, anger boiling underneath the surface. "It's about us, Marc. We're moving too fast, and I can't deal with my kids hating me because I chose a man over them."

Marc shook his head, "I've never asked you to choose me over your kids. They've never met me, so why are they the judge and jury over who I am to you? They are adults, Jules."

Julie stepped toward Marc, "You need to leave. I've given you a way out, Marc. Take it. Runaway back to your perfect life in California."

Marc dropped his gaze down to Julie's face, "What is happening? This isn't you right now."

Julie wiped at the tears running down her cheeks. "That's the problem, you don't really know me, Marc," she looked up at him, her heart racing. "I'm broken, and you deserve someone that has their shit together, and that's not me," she whispered.

Marc took a step toward Julie, but she took a step back. "Jules, I have loved you since I was a kid. I know you better than you think I do. I don't understand why you are doing this."

Julie hung her head down, "Just go. Please just leave. I can't do this. My heart is breaking and I...," she paused.

"You what, Jules? Talk to me. Just fucking talk to

me!" he said as his phone started ringing. "God damn it! I have to answer this." Not taking his eyes off Julie, he answered, "Paul, I'm in the middle of something."

Julie turned around, entered the house, and closed the door behind her. Turning the deadbolt, she walked toward her bedroom. From her bed, she could hear Marc knocking on the front door and begging to be let in. She ignored it, rolled over, and began sobbing into her pillow. He continued to knock, call and text, but she couldn't bring herself to speak to him. She knew in her heart that letting him go was for the best. She laid in bed for what seemed like hours before she heard Ashley open the door to the bedroom.

"Mom?" she asked, before walking into the room. Seeing her mother lying in bed, crying, brought back all the memories of the first few months after her dad died. She inhaled and held her breath, the trauma of losing him and feeling like she was losing her mom came rushing back. Sitting on the bed, she said, "I can't do this again, Mom. What happened?"

Julie rolled over, "Is he gone?"

Ashley said, "Yeah. Are you going to tell me what happened?"

"I told Marc that we are done. The timing isn't right. I need to concentrate on healing our family," said Julie, sitting up wiping her eyes.

Ashley was quiet for a few minutes, looking down at her hands. "Mom," she paused. "Do you think all guys are like dad?"

Julie sniffed, wiped her nose with a tissue, and scooted closer to Ashley. "No, I don't think all guys are like your dad. What made you even think to ask that?"

Ashley looked up at her mother with tears in her eyes, "Why do we attract men like that, then?"

Julie's expression softened, trying to find the right words to explain something she herself struggled to understand. "Sweetheart," she said brushing a tear from Ashley's face. "It's not because we attract them intentionally. Sometimes, certain people can be drawn to individuals who are kind, caring, and empathetic like us. They see those qualities as vulnerabilities to exploit."

Ashley frowned, trying to make sense of it all. "But why us, Mom?"

Julie reached out to gently hold Ashley's hand. "It's not something we can control darling. But what we can control is how we respond to it. We can learn to recognize the signs early on and prioritize our own well-being above all else. Most importantly, we can break the cycle together."

"I thought you said Marc was different than dad," Ashley looked at her mother, searching for a sign that there was hope in finding someone who would be a good partner. "If he was a good guy, like you said, why did you break it off with him?"

Julie nodded her head, "Sometimes, you have to do what is best for the other person. It wasn't fair to Marc to wait around while I figured things out."

"You pushed him away before he could hurt you?" whispered Ashley.

"Something like that," Julie responded looking up at the ceiling. The same ceiling that she stared at for months as she laid in bed mourning Jim. Her thoughts drifted to Ashley's words, *'You pushed him away before he could hurt you.'* She was exactly right; she was pushing Marc away before he could disappoint or hurt her. Her mind silenced for just a moment before she pondered, when did my baby girl grow up to be giving me advice?

They laid there as mother and daughter, facing a harsh reality. They were determined to overcome it, and they found solace in each other's strength and resilience.

Chapter 24

"LA is Lonely" by Ricky Manning

She could hear Ben and Ashley gleefully giggling as Ben pretended to be a dinosaur and chased Ashley around the backyard. Their small figures darting around, so full of boundless energy. Meanwhile, Jim diligently assembled the big wooden play set, his focused expression softened by occasional smiles as he stole glances at their joyful antics. It was a snapshot of pure familial bliss, a moment etched in her memory forever. Julie stood at the kitchen sink, watching them as she filled up the lemonade pitcher with water. Moving outside, she carried a white wicker tray filled with the lemonade, cookies, and cups. The kid's eyes lit up when they saw her, running over and ready for a snack.

As she set the tray down, she called out to Jim, "Honey, take a break and come have a glass of lemonade."

He looked up and nodded at her, "Just a minute. I need to finish tightening this bolt."

When he turned the wrench one last time, he tossed it on the ground and walked over to his family. Leaning toward Julie, he gave her a quick peck on the cheek. "Thanks, babe."

Julie smiled warmly at him. Today is a good day, which meant the world to her, after their heated exchange three days ago. She watched him walk back to his project, noticing his cute butt in the beige shorts he was wearing. This was the man she fell in love with.

When Jim was finished and the kids were tired from being outside and running around all day, he walked into the kitchen to find Julie cleaning up the kid's favorite dinner, hot dogs and Macaroni and Cheese.

He walked over to the sink, wrapping his arms around her waist. "Wanna just order some pizza for dinner so you don't have to cook?" he whispered in her ear, giving her a tight squeeze, before kissing her neck.

"Gross!" screamed the kids before busting out into laughter.

Jim let go, turning around to the kids, "Finish up and get ready for a bath. You're going to bed early tonight." Turning back around to Julie, he whispered, "I've got plans for us after the kids are in bed." He gave her a little smack on her butt, which made her squeal.

"You heard your dad," Julie said following the kids out of the kitchen. "Ben, you can shower in our bathroom and Ashley, you can hop in the shower in your bathroom. Scoot."

After the kids were tucked into bed, Julie and Jim sat on the sofa, indulging in slices of pepperoni pizza and savoring each bite as they laughed about the antics of their favorite television characters. The aroma of the melted cheese and savory toppings filled the room, creating a cozy atmosphere as they relaxed together and enjoyed each other's company. It was simple and nice; however, Julie secretly was waiting for the other shoe to drop. Today had been too perfect. Her mind drifted back to three days ago, when Jim had to work late yet again and came home with the scent of another woman's perfume lingering on him. She knew better than to ask him about it, knowing that it would cause friction between them, and he would end up gaslighting her into thinking she was the crazy one. She couldn't help but wonder why he made himself available for his family today. Was the woman he was seeing busy? Did she have a family that she was spending time with? No, that couldn't be it. He liked the young interns.

Jim put his plate down on the coffee table and

turned the television off, which jolted Julie out of her thoughts and back to the present. He bit his lower lip and said, "Should we take this into the bedroom?"

"Uh, sure. Just let me clean up first," she replied as she stood up, stacking the plates on top of the pizza box. "Can you grab the bottle of wine and the glasses?"

Jim shook his head back and forth, "No, that's your job. I put the play set together."

Julie turned around and said, "You're joking, right?"

"Why would I joke about that? I make the money and put together a fucking wooden play set for our children. I've done enough today. You made lemonade and hot dogs. Make two trips, it's easy."

"Why are you ruining a wonderful day by being rude?" Julie asked as she raised her shoulders.

"Why are you being a bitch to me right now? Just clean up so we can have sex," he smirked, thinking he was being funny.

Julie turned back toward the kitchen and almost ran into Ben. Neither she nor Jim realized that he was standing there, seeing and hearing their heated conversation. He looked like he was about to cry.

"Oh, honey, let's get you back to bed," she said following Ben to his room.

Julie stirred in bed, waking from the dream as her mind still tried to cling to the fragments of warmth and joy. Yet, as consciousness seeped in, the dream morphed into something unsettling, like shadows creeping into a sunlit room. The warmth dissipated, replaced by a chill that danced along her skin. As she blinked away the remnants of sleep, the dream's discordant notes lingered, casting a pall over her waking thoughts. Rubbing her eyes, she looked over at her phone on the nightstand for the time. It was 9am, and she felt defeated already. What had started off as a beautiful memory quickly turned sour, just like her marriage to Jim. Without thinking, she opened her text messages to see if Marc had texted her, but the memory of their breakup a week ago settled into her mind. Forcing herself out of bed, she moved toward the shower when she heard a familiar voice call out to her from the other room.

"Mom!" Ben called out to her as he walked toward her bedroom. "Are you up?" he said as he tapped on the door.

Julie grabbed her robe, swinging it around her and tying it as she said, "Yeah, Benny, I'll be right out." Opening the door, she pulled Ben into a big hug. "What are you doing here?"

"You wouldn't respond to my text messages or calls. Ash said she hadn't been over all week. You had us worried," he said as if he were scolding a child.

Stepping back, Julie looked up at her tall son, reached up, and straightened his messy brown hair, "I'm fine, Benny. I remember when you were shorter than me and it was easier to reach the top of your head."

"Why haven't you responded to anyone? Carla was even worried about you," he said, again in a scolding tone.

"Hey, I'm still your mother. Watch how you talk to me," she scolded back to him, wagging her finger in his face.

"Then stop acting like a child that didn't get her way," he retorted back, giving his head a shake to undo the straightening that Julie had done to his locks.

Julie rolled her eyes, "Can I make you something for breakfast?"

"I ate at the airport before my flight. I would take some coffee, if you're making some," he conceded.

They walked toward the kitchen. Julie realized just how stubborn Ben was and how much he reminded her of his father. She filled up the coffee pot before dumping coffee grounds into the machine and turning it on. Julie paused a moment to take a few deep breaths, before turning around to face Ben. He was seated at the island, drumming on the countertop. He did the same thing as a child, the memory turning her frown into a small smile.

"How long are you in town for?" she asked, pulling two white coffee mugs down from the cabinet and setting them on the island.

"Just a couple of days. What is going on, Mom? Is this about that guy?" he asked, looking at her to confirm his suspicions.

"His name is Marc. I broke it off with him, so there's no need to worry about your inheritance," she said jokingly.

Ben rolled his eyes, "That's not what I was worried about. I just didn't want some sleaze bag trying to take all YOUR money, leaving you to come live with me."

"Oh, so it was about you being inconvenienced, not the money. I would stay with Ashley anyway, so I wouldn't have to move far," she said as she stuck her tongue out at him before shifting to a slight smile.

"Yeah, right. She can barely take care of herself, let alone take care of you," he said with a chuckle. "Did she tell you that she broke up with Jordan?"

"No, she didn't tell me that. When did that happen?" Julie asked as she walked back toward the coffee pot, picking it up and pouring the hot black coffee into the cups on the island. "I'm surprised she didn't call me."

"She did Mom. You just didn't pick up. I can't believe that you are so hung up on some dude that you stop communicating with your own family," he said before taking a sip of his coffee.

"I wasn't hung up on some dude. His name is Marc, and I was in love with him," she said hanging her head down, focusing on the steam of the coffee escaping from her cup. "I still love him," she said in a whisper.

"Mom, he's ten years younger than you. You know what that makes you, don't you? A cougar," he said with disgust in his voice. "My mother is NOT a cougar. Got it?"

Julie quietly said, "Do you remember the day that your dad built the play set in the backyard?"

"Yeah, why are you bringing that up?" Ben asked, with a puzzled look on his face.

She looked over at him, "Do you remember getting up from bed that night and wandering into the living room, where your dad and I were having a conversation?"

Ben stared at her for a moment. The silence was almost deafening as she waited for his response. He looked out the kitchen window to the backyard. "I think so," he said quietly. He sat still for the longest time. "I didn't like the way dad was talking to you."

Julie reached over and rubbed Ben's back. "And to think that was a mild conversation."

Ben looked over at her, "Mild? He called you a bitch, Mom." Tears filled his eyes as he thought about the cutting tone his dad had used that night.

Julie hugged her son like she had done when he was a small child. She continued to hold him until he finally signaled that he was ready to pull away from her embrace.

Ben looked up at her, tears streaming down his face. "Did he talk to you like that when Ash and I weren't around?"

Julie inhaled, choosing her words carefully. "There's a lot you don't know about your father, Ben. The week before he had been with his mistress, we argued when he came home smelling like her," her voice trembled. She hated destroying Ben's vision of his perfect father, but she knew that if she didn't tell him the truth, there was a chance that he would turn out like Jim. He was so much like him in mannerisms, his looks, and his cocky attitude.

Ben sat there quietly processing what he had just

heard. He stared straight ahead as Julie looked over at him, tears streaming down both of their faces. "Mistress?" he asked.

Julie quietly said, "There were many over the years."

Ben said, "I didn't want to believe Ash when she said that dad had cheated, but I know you wouldn't lie to me."

"If I ever lied to you, it was to protect the way you viewed your father, Ben. I never wanted you and Ash to know about that side of him," she pleaded.

"Then why did you tell us now?" he said turning his head over to look at his mom.

"Because of Jordan. I could see that Ashley was headed into a toxic relationship, much like the one your dad and I had. I had to be honest with her to help her see that Jordan wasn't the right man for her. And…because I see so much of your father in you,

I don't want you to hurt your partner the way he hurt me," she explained.

Ben reached over to hug his mom. "I'm sorry, Mom. I'm so sorry."

Julie embraced her son, sitting at the kitchen island for what seemed like forever, before he pulled away. Reaching up, she smoothed his hair into place, like she'd done a million times before. He was and will always be her baby boy. He was the child that made her a mother. She smiled up at him.

Ben wiped his face with his hand, gazing at his mother. "I always wanted to be just like dad. He was always bigger than life, taking us to ballgames, building the goddammed playset. He was there for every game that I pitched. I became an engineer to be like him, you know?"

Julie silently nodded her head up and down, her hand reaching up to stroke Ben's cheek. "I know."

"But I don't want to be like him anymore," he said boldly.

"Just take the good parts, not the bad," she offered.

"I don't want to be like him at all, Mom," he said with a resolve in his voice. "Fuck him."

Julie sighed, knowing that she had destroyed Jim in her son's eyes. She also knew that she had done the right thing in being honest with Ben, even if it was painful for both of them.

Chapter 25

"Malibu Nights" by LANY

Sunlight filtered through the windows of the classroom, casting a warm glow on the easels and colorful palettes scattered around the room. With a determined smile, Julie settled into her seat and was eager to let her imagination flow onto the blank paper before her. Other students chatted amongst themselves as they walked into the room before finding their seats at the easels. Professor Williams entered, setting his portfolio bag onto the desk. Today, he was discussing portfolios and how to put one together.

Julie listened intently, admiring the pieces of art that Professor Williams showed of his collection. She only dreamed about having such an astounding collection to add to her portfolio. It made her think about how much she had sacrificed because of Jim, giving up something that was so near and dear to her, for far too many years. Her gaze drifted over to Mike, the young man she met on her first day of class. He was fidgeting. She wondered why he seemed so nervous today, but dismissed it and instead concentrated on the professor's instructions.

When it was time to do some painting, she leaned toward Mike and asked, "Everything okay?"

Mike looked over to her, giving her a quick smile. "Yeah, I'm just nervous about tonight."

Julie raised her shoulders, giving him a nod, "What's tonight?"

Mike replied with a gleam in his eyes, "I'm asking my girlfriend to marry me."

Julie smiled, "That's awesome. How long have you two been together?"

"Two years. I graduate in the spring. After that we'll move to New York, to work on my Master's," he said excitedly.

Julie felt a tinge of pain in her stomach. Mike was living out her dream. Leaning down, she sorted through her supply bag, looking for nothing in particular, but trying to appease the sadness that traveled from her stomach up to her chest.

"Congratulations, Mike. I'm sure you two will be very happy in New York," she mustered without seeming too envious.

Julie rushed home to tell Jim what Professor Anton said about recommending her for a specialty Master's degree at NYU. When she arrived at his office, she saw him sitting on the desk of a blonde intern. Noticing her, he quickly jumped down and walked over to Julie.

"What are you doing here?" he asked quietly.

"I have news that couldn't wait and I'm dying to talk to you about it. Can you take a quick break and go to the coffee shop around the corner?" she asked with a broad grin.

"Uh, yeah, I guess," he said ushering her past the reception desk. Turning his attention to the lady behind the desk, "I'll be back in 15."

At the coffee shop, Julie couldn't hold it in any longer, "Professor Anton wants to recommend me to a specialty program at NYU." She beamed with excitement, even though she had doubted that it would really happen, but her hopes were still high."

Jim's expression fell at the news, "No. No. No. We are engaged to be married, and my job is here in Chicago. You cannot move to New York for silly degree that you'll never use. Are you kidding me?"

"It would only be for two years, and then we can get married," she tried to bargain.

"Absolutely not. You are my fiancé and you need to stay in here, where my job is. Damnit, Jules. If I had my way, within two years, we'll be married and you'll be pregnant with our first child," Jim said with an authoritative look on his face. "You have to decline. Seriously. I mean, what a waste of money."

Julie's entire body seemed to sink; tears filled her eyes as she looked up at him. "It's a program to teach art to underprivileged kids." Shrugging her shoulders she added, "It's my dream job."

"Dream job? You're not going to need a job, Jules. You're marrying an engineer. I'll make plenty of money, so you won't have to work," he said, rubbing her arms. "Baby, I'm going to take care of you so you don't have to work, ever again."

"But...," she started, before he interrupted her.

"No. You had your fun at college with your silly art classes. We are engaged and I will not be embarrassed to have my wife work. That's it, so go tell your professor, thanks but no thanks."

Julie carefully stowed her brushes and watercolor paints as Professor Williams approached her, a gleam of excitement in his eyes, "Julie, I've been meaning to talk to you," he said, his voice carrying a hint of anticipation. "My friend is one of the owners of Square One Gallery. They have an opening for a show and I think your work would be a perfect fit. Your talent deserves to be showcased beyond these classroom walls."

Julie's heart skipped a beat as she looked up, her eyes wide with surprise and gratitude. "Oh my gosh," Julie moved her hand up over her mouth. She could feel her emotions getting the best of her as her eyes filled with tears of happiness. "Really? I had stopped painting for...," she shook her head. "It doesn't matter. Professor Williams, thank you. Oh my god, thank you."

"Put together your portfolio and bring it by my office. Include some of your earlier work. You can go back as far as including your work from college," he instructed.

Julie's gaze fell as she said, "I'm afraid that all I have are painting and sketches that I've done recently. I don't have any of my artwork from college."

"Hmmm, that's okay. Bring in what you have, and we will make it work," he said as he looked past Julie and smiled. A beautiful older woman approached them. Professor Williams leaned over, giving her a quick peck on the cheek. "Julie, this is my wife, Grace."

Julie smiled warmly, "Nice to meet you, Grace." She couldn't help but notice that Grace was older than her husband. Julie wondered what the age difference was.

"Nice to meet you too. Would you like to join us for lunch?" Grace asked.

"Oh no, I wouldn't want to intrude," Julie said, grabbing her bag. Turning her attention to her professor, "Thank you and I will drop off my portfolio later this week."

Professor Williams looked at Julie, "I look forward to seeing what you've been up to. I'll tell my friend that I found the perfect artist for their show."

***

"I Miss NY"- Acoustic Demo by Fly by Midnight

Julie sat at the kitchen island with her pad of watercolor paper and paint, her mind swirling with thoughts as she absentmindedly sketched out a vase of flowers to paint. Her mind wandered to her professor and his older wife. She wondered how long they had been together and if the age difference ever bothered them or their families. Lost in her thoughts, Julie's mind wandered to Marc. It had been two weeks since she last saw him.

He had tried repeatedly to call and text her, but she never responded or answered his calls. Doubts crept in, mingling with memories of their time together. Was breaking it off with him the right choice?

The room felt suffocating as Julie wrestled with her emotions, the weight of uncertainty pressing down on her. She longed for clarity, for a sign to guide her through the tangled maze of her thoughts. For now, all she could do was sit and contemplate. She hoped that somehow, the answers would reveal themselves in due time. Picking her phone up, she scrolled through photos that she had taken with Marc of their dates and time in New York. A wave of loneliness washed over her as her mind wandered back to the vibrant streets of New York City, where she had once walked hand in hand with Marc. Memories flooded her mind like a rushing tide, each one tinged with a bittersweet longing.

She remembered the laughter they shared, the late-night conversations and the way Marc's eyes sparkled with excitement as they explored the city together. Amidst the recollections, doubt gnawed at her heart like a persistent ache. Had she made a mistake in letting him go? Was it fear that had driven her to end their relationship? She blamed the circumstances that seemed to build a wall, but was the underlying reason her fear? The fear that kept her from another relationship, scared that he would turn into a control freak, like Jim? The loneliness that enveloped her now seemed to whisper the truth; she was still in love with Marc.

The photo of Julie and Marc, taken by Gabby, stayed on the screen as she placed it on the kitchen island. She traced the outline of Marc and murmured, "Marc isn't Jim."

Tears welled up in Julie's eyes as he realized the depth of her feelings. She missed him more than she had ever admitted, and the emptiness in her chest echoed with the absence of his presence. In that solitary moment, amidst the quiet of her kitchen, Julie knew that she needed to find a way to mend what she had broken. She couldn't bear the thought of another day without him in her life.

Picking up her phone, Julie opened her messages and scrolled down to Marc's number. She read the last message he had sent her.

Marc: Jules, please. I'm in the dark, we just need to talk. Please call me.

She could hear him saying those words to her, imagined the pain in his voice as he begged her to respond. Wiping the tears away, she started to text him, but an idea stopped her. What if she flew out to Venice Beach to surprise him? She smiled broadly at the thought of the look on his face when she unexpectedly showed up. He would take her in his arms, twirling her around, grateful that she came to her senses. She couldn't wait to feel his lips on hers, and to have his hands wrap around her, making her feel like she was finally coming home…to him.

Opening a travel app, her fingers couldn't move fast enough to type in the date. She pondered if she should purchase a round-trip ticket. "No, I'll buy a one way. He's going to be so surprised," she smiled as she typed in her credit card information. "Now to tell the kids." she said, as a pit formed in her stomach. She took a deep breath before texting Ashley and Ben.

Julie: Hey Ash, anyway you could stop by tonight at seven? Ben, Ash and I will Facetime you tonight when she gets here.

Ashley: I guess. What's up?

Julie: I'm in a bit of a rush, so I'll catch you up when you get here.

Ben: Yeah, I should be home by then. Everything okay, Mom?

Julie: I'm fine. Talk to you both tonight.

Julie grabbed her carry-on out of the garage, taking it to the bedroom. Dancing around as she packed, a lightness filled her and she felt hopeful for the first time in weeks. She swayed to the music, pretending that she was in Marc's strong arms. She smiled with giddiness.

***

Julie sat Ashley down at the kitchen island, where she had her phone propped up with Ben on facetime.

"I have something important to talk to you both about," she began, her heart racing.

Ashley looked up from her phone with a raised eyebrow, "What's up Mom?"

"I've been thinking a lot lately, and I have decided," she paused, taking a breath to try to calm her pulse. "I've decided to fly out to California to surprise Marc." She looked between Ashley and Ben, trying to gauge their reactions.

Ben spoke first, "I thought we agreed that you weren't going to see him anymore." His tone indicated that his opinion hadn't changed.

Julie nodded, acknowledging Ben's concern. "I understand that you both have your reservations about Marc, and I respect that because it comes from a place of love and concern. I understand, but I have been miserable since I pushed him out of my life. He is important to me, and I want to see him…be with him."

Ashley looked at Ben's image and then to her mother. "If it's important to you, then we will support you."

Ben ran his hand through his hair before speaking. "I still don't like it. We're not his biggest fans, but we do want you to be happy." Ben shook his head as if he couldn't believe he and Ashley were conceding to their mother's wishes. "Will you promise me one thing?"

Julie looked between Ashley and Ben. "Depends on what it is," she said cautiously.

Ben said, "Please talk to dad's attorney to set something up, so that you are protected financially if things go south with Marc."

Julie let out a light laugh, "Of course. If that would ease your mind and allow you to trust Marc, I would be happy to do that." Tears welled up in Julie's eyes as she hugged Ashley. She looked back at the image of Ben on her phone, "Benny, I wish you were here for me to hug. I promise to be careful, and I appreciate your support more than you know."

With her children's understanding and blessing, she felt the excitement and nervousness swirling in her stomach as she thought about the look on Marc's face when she arrived. She was at peace, knowing that she finally knew what she wanted. She was finally working towards an artist's life… with Marc by her side.

Chapter 26

"Losing a Friend" by Elijah Woods

Julie approached Marc's cottage in Venice Beach, her heart raced with excitement at the thought of surprising him. However, as she reached for the door and knocked, there was no answer. Frowning, she decided to wait outside, hoping he would return soon. She opened her phone to text Carla.

Julie: I've been waiting for a while and his car is in the driveway, but he's nowhere to be found. Did Paul by chance buy a red sports car?

Carla: No, he drives a Range Rover.

Julie: Hmmm, there's a red sports car next to Marc's car.

Carla: Maybe you should call him instead of just sitting outside of his house.

Julie: I'll give him a little more time and then call him. I'm just so excited to surprise him!

As minutes turned into an hour, Julie's patience waned. Just as she was about to order an Uber and leave, she heard muffled sounds coming from inside. Curiosity piqued and she tiptoed to the window to peer inside. Her heart sank as she saw Marc, lying in bed with a naked woman. Shock and disbelief washed over her as she realized Marc hadn't been pining away for her as Paul and Carla suggested. The scene before her shattered any hope of reconciliation, leaving Julie feeling betrayed and heartbroken. Backing away from the window, she realized that she was caught in the bush as she fell into it and released a squeal. Quickly jumping up, she made her way to the front of the house to grab her bag and to order an Uber. She was so embarrassed, being heartbroken about their breakup, that she never stopped to consider that Marc might move on quickly. She began to sob about the time that Marc walked out the front door and saw her.

"Jules, what are you doing here?" he said in disbelief, standing in his boxers on his front porch.

Julie wiped her tears, "Surprise," was all she could get out before the anger boiled up over the despair. "Who the fuck was in your bedroom?" she asked looking up at him, noticing the half-naked woman was standing just inside the door and wearing nothing but Marc's t-shirt. Julie wiped her nose and looked back at Marc.

"Why didn't you call me?" he asked.

"How many women are you juggling right now? Were we even real?" she yelled across the yard at him.

Marc shook his head in disbelief, "How could you even ask me that?"

"Stop gaslighting me!" she screamed. "Tell me the goddamn truth. How about we start there?"

"You broke up with me, remember? I tried calling and texting you for days, Jules. You never answered or replied. What was I supposed to do? I was lonely."

"Lonely? You were fucking lonely after two weeks of being apart? How could you even know what loneliness is?" Mimicking him she said, "I've been in love with you for decades. Bullshit! Complete and utter bullshit!" screamed Julie.

"You don't own the term loneliness, Jules. I was heartbroken and yes, lonely. You wouldn't even fight for us. I had to move on. The pain of losing you was more than I could take."

Julie shook her head as she paced back and forth, "I may have broken up with you, but I never stopped loving you. That's why I'm here, you…you motherfucker!"

Julie's Uber driver pulled up. Not wanting to make an even bigger scene, she grabbed her bag and dragged it behind her to the end of the driveway where the driver was parked. As she turned to get into the car, she looked back at Marc. She took a deep breath and said, "Have a nice life, Marc." The tears began to fall as soon as she shut the door to the Uber. She immediately began to shake uncontrollably. Fumbling, she found her phone in her purse and began wiping the tears from her eyes. She was trying to find Carla's number, but everything looked so blurry. Finally, she was able to find Carla's number and hit dial.

"Hey Jules, did Marc make it back yet?" Carla asked, but then she realized that Julie was trying to catch her breath and had been crying. "What happened?"

Julie finally squeaked out. "It's really over. He's moved on and has a new girlfriend."

"What the fuck?" Carla asked. "How do you know this? It's been two fucking weeks!"

After a few more sobs and sniffles, Julie answered, "I heard a noise in the house and I looked into the bedroom window…," she said before sobbing again.

"What exactly did you see Jules?"

"A naked woman was crawling into bed with him," she said. "It's really over. There's no coming back from this. I'm done."

"Fuck that dude!" yelled Carla. "So, what's your plan?"

"I'm in an Uber headed back to the airport. I'm coming home."

"I'm so sorry Jules," was all that Carla could think to say. "Let me know what you need once you get to the airport."

Julie hung up with Carla as she sobbed, not even noticing the Uber driver staring back at her in the rearview mirror. Her phone rang and she couldn't see who was calling through her tears, so she answered it expecting it to be Carla calling her back, but it was Marc.

"Jules, please come back so we can talk," he said with an edge to his tone.

Julie sat quietly for moment, trying to think of what to say.

"Are you there?" Marc asked. "Jules?"

Julie sniffed before saying, "I'm here."

"Why didn't you let me know you were coming?" he asked with a softer tone.

Julie's face scrunched up as she sniffed again, "It would have ruined the surprise."

"Surprise? Hmm, I'm confused, Jules. You say you love me, but the moment something hard happens, you shut down. Why?" Marc asked.

Julie sobbed quietly, not knowing what to say. Drawing in a deep breath, he let it out slowly before choosing his word carefully, "You wouldn't let me inside. You wouldn't take my calls or return my texts, Jules." He paused. "I tried, over and over to talk to you." There was a pain in his voice from reliving those moments.

"I know," Julie said softly. "I wanted to spare you from the mess that my life had become."

"I wanted you, Jules. No matter how big of a mess your life was or is, but you left me with no choice but to move on," Marc said quietly.

Julie sobbed softly before saying, "I…I had to work through some things." She bit the inside of her cheek as she thought about her response, "I was afraid."

"Afraid? Of what?" he asked, concern in his voice.

"That you'd get tired of me, just like Jim did. That our ages would work against us, and my kids would never accept you," her breath trembled as she spoke.

"I don't know how to make it any clearer, Jules. I am not Jim. I would never cheat on you or force you to comply with some version of you that isn't the real you," he said, his voice shook. "I loved you for you, not what you could be or who you used to be."

"It only took you two weeks to get over me, so I guess that's just another lie," she choked out.

"Jules," he started before she interrupted.

"I saw you. I saw her. Naked in your bed," she said in between sobs. "It's over for real, Marc. I can't unsee the betrayal." Looking at her phone, she hit the disconnect button.

***

At the airport, Julie sat down at her gate and reached into her bag for a tissue. Alone with her thoughts, she began questioning her and Marc's entire relationship. Could Ben have been right? Was she losing her ability to read people. How did she miss this about Marc? They had talked daily until the breakup, and she really felt like she knew him. How could she have misread him? The questions and memories scrolled through her mind like short films on a movie screen. She closed her eyes and tried to breathe, her heart was racing and she needed to stop the panic attack that she was on the verge of. She tried to concentrate on her breath and counted between inhales, but Marc returned to her mind each time. She slowly opened her eyes and took a breath before looking down at her phone. Nothing. She could feel the tears forming around her eyes, and she knew even with a blink, the waterfall would start, and she was afraid of not recovering from this one. Picking up the tissue on her lap, she dabbed her eyes to stave off the water works. Her phone lit up and she reached for it.

Marc: I'm sorry.

Perfect timing to trigger the tears. Julie began to weep, which quickly turned into sobs. She hated that people were staring at her. An older woman came over and sat next to her. Julie looked up to her and tried to smile, but immediately went back to crying.

The woman put her arm around Julie and whispered, "There, there, dear, you're going to make it through this. Don't give up, you have a great life ahead of you." This just made Julie sob even harder.

"I'm so stupid," was all that Julie could get out in between sobs.

"Is this about a man?" the woman asked.

"Yes," Julie finally admitted.

"Well, if he made you this upset honey, fuck him," the older woman said.

Julie looked at her in shock but let out a little laugh.

"I hope that wasn't too forward, but men are not worth your tears. I was married to my Harold for sixty years, and anytime he made me cry, I just told him to fuck off," she said with a giggle.

"Thank you," Julie said with a forced smile.

"You'll get through this. That is a guarantee," the woman said as she got up to go back to her family. Turning around, she added, "You're stronger than you think."

Julie's phone vibrated and she looked at it, hoping that it would be Marc saying he was on her way to find her, but it was Carla.

Carla: Marc is a fucking idiot.

Julie: I shouldn't have assumed that he hadn't moved on. This is all my fault. I messed everything up.

Carla: No, you didn't. You only did what you thought was best.

Julie: I know, but I threw it all away. He deserves better than me.

Carla: You're bullshitting yourself, you know that, right?

Julie: Maybe I'm just facing reality. Could you pick me up when I land?

Carla: Absolutely, what time does your flight land?

Julie: 11pm, it was the last direct flight tonight.

Carla: Ok, see you tonight.

Julie: Thank you. See you soon.

Chapter 27

"Memory Lane" by Haley Joelle

Julie sat on the edge of her bed, staring blankly at the wall. Two weeks had passed since her trip to California, and she still missed Marc. Tears welled up in her eyes as she replays the scene in her mind, the image of Marc with another woman etched painfully in her memory. The realization hit her; this short chapter was over, and she had to move on. Hugging her knees to her chest, she tried to hold herself together as waves of sadness washed over her. The future she had envisioned with Marc now seemed like a distant dream, shattered into a million pieces.

Picking up her phone on the nightstand, she opened the email from Professor Williams about her upcoming art show at Square One Gallery. Wiping her eyes, she made her way to the kitchen, a makeshift studio, surrounded by canvases and vibrant tins of watercolor paints. With each brushstroke, she poured her heart and soul onto the canvas, lost in the colors and shapes that danced beneath her fingertips. The gentle strokes of her brush created scenes of beauty and emotion, each a reflection of her innermost thoughts and feelings. As she painted, the outside world faded away to leave her and the canvas in a timeless dance of creation. The soft music played in the background provided a rhythm to her movements, guiding her hand as she brought her imagination to life.

Hours passed in a blur, but Julie hardly noticed. She was in her element, completely immersed in the process of creation. With each completed painting, she felt a sense of accomplishment and anticipation building within her. The upcoming art show loomed on the horizon, but Julie was undaunted. She knew that with each brushstroke, she was one step closer to sharing her passion with the world. As she put the final finishing touches on her latest masterpiece, she couldn't help but feel a thrill of excitement coursing through her veins. She was so enthralled in her work that she didn't hear Carla come into the house.

"You're alive!" Carla said dripping with sarcasm.

Julie turned around, "Very funny. I've just been busy."

"Busy avoiding conversations with your best friend and kids, huh?" Carla said as she leaned in for a hug.

Julie smiled after their embrace, "No, I have the art show coming up and…," she paused. "I booked a flight to New York."

"New York? Is that a good idea?" asked Carla as she picked up one of the canvases leaning against the wall, studying it. "Venice Beach?"

Julie turned her attention back to the painting at hand, "I signed up for a watercolor class at MoMA."

"You're avoiding my question," pressed Carla. "Aren't you afraid that you might run into…," she hesitated, putting the painting back down. "You know who?"

"You can say his name, Carla. I'm not going to melt into a puddle at the mention of his name," said Julie, trying to steady her voice.

"Okay, okay," Carla said with a roll of her eyes. "We haven't talked much since you got back from seeing him, so…," she stammered.

"So, what?" Julie asked, peeking around her easel. "Please don't touch the paintings."

"When do you leave?" Carla asked as she walked over to stand behind Julie. "Damn, Jules, your talent still amazes me, even after years of not painting."

"Thanks," said Julie. "My flight leaves on Sunday morning. The classes are Monday through Thursday, so I'll fly home on Friday," Julie said without looking up from her finished painting.

Carla nodded her head, "Okay. Wanna go grab some dinner?"

"No, thank you. I need to get some more painting done for my show and start packing for my trip," Julie said, as she turned to face Carla. "Yes, I've considered the fact that Marc might be in New York the same time as me, but I know his usual hangouts, so I'll just avoid those areas. Besides, I'll be busy with classes and working on portfolio stuff in the evenings and it's a massively large city."

"I love you, bitch," Carla said with a smirk.

"Love you more," retorted Julie with a grin. "Thank you for checking on me. I really am fine."

"Back to 'fine', huh?" Carla said, making air quotes.

"Just doing the best that I can right now, but I have to start living for me and what I want in my life, ya know?" Julie hugged Carla.

Embracing her friend, Carla whispered, "It's about damn time."

All day, Julie had thrown herself into her artwork, determined to keep busy and maintain a façade of strength. As the sky grew dark, moments of Marc's absence crept into her mind, triggering a dull ache in her chest. The weight of her emotions became too much to bear. Sinking into the sofa, she pulled up the photos of their time in New York. With tears streaming down her face, she mourned the life that she had hoped for, living in New York with the love of her life.

Forcing herself to get up, she walked into the spare bedroom, the room where Marc had slept. She began stripping the bedding off and throwing it into a heap on the floor. Grabbing the mattress, she pushed and wiggled it off the bed to stand against the wall. Running to the garage, she dug through Jim's tool chest, looking for a screwdriver to take the bedframe apart. She didn't care how long it took, but she was determined to turn this room into a studio. Moving this and that to Ashley's and Ben's old rooms, she finally had an almost clear space to work with.

Julie rubbed the back of her neck as she moved her head around in a circle when she was done for the night. Looking at her watch, it was two in the morning. Yawning, she walked toward her bedroom for the night. The heaviness she had felt reliving her memories of Marc were a distant thought now, as she had literally exhausted herself.

***

Waking up, she felt a wave of excitement fall over her at the idea of having a real art studio in her home. Opening Pinterest, she searched "art studio at home." She poured over the pins, clicking on some and saving them to her new Art Studio board. She swooned over the photos trying to figure out what style she would choose.

Making her way into the kitchen, she surveyed the paintings stacked around the room as she made coffee. A sense of awe came over her. She was finally going to be living her dream of being an artist. She smiled and let out a little giggle at the strides she had made in her art, going from doubting herself to booking her first art show in a real gallery. Filling her coffee cup, she walked toward her new studio area, notebook in hand. She made a list as to what furniture she would need to make this into the studio of her dreams. Julie twirled around in the room, smiling and laughing.

***

Walking into the art store still gave Julie a thrill, just like when she was in college. The smells of paint, lacquer, and freshly stretched canvases enveloped her senses as she strolled the aisles, checking out all the items that were new to her or things that had been revamped over the years. As she walked to the paint area, she grazed her hand across the brightly colored tubes of paint. She smiled, like she was a kid in a candy store.

"Is there something in particular that you're looking for?" a male voice asked from behind her.

Julie stopped at the sound of that familiar voice. She slowly turned around to see Brian, the man she had an emotional affair with so many years ago. "Brian?" she asked, not believing her own eyes.

"Julia," he replied, shocked to see her. "Uh, hello."

Walking over to him, she nervously reached out with arms open wide to give him a hug.

"What are you doing here? I thought you moved to…," she paused. "I'm sorry, I forgot where you moved to."

"No need to apologize. Olivia and I moved to Champaign, where I grew up," he said as he released her from the hug.

"That's right. How is Olivia?" she asked with genuine interest.

"She's good, she married her college boyfriend last year and they're expecting their first child. That's why I moved back to St. Louis, you know, to be closer to my first grandchild. How is Ashley?" he asked.

"She's working on her Master's in Architecture. No grandbabies in my near future," she said with a laugh. She couldn't help but be grateful that Ashley had been wise enough to break up with Jordan. "So, you work here?" she asked, looking around the store.

"I actually bought the place a few years ago," he said, looking down. "Actually, it was you that inspired me to get back into my art. It made sense to buy an art store, I guess," he said motioning around the store. His gaze turned back to Julie, "I saw Jim's obituary in the Post. I'm sorry for your loss."

"Thank you," she said as she looked up at him. "He had cancer," she blurted out, not knowing how to respond. Trying to change the subject, she said, "I'm glad I ran into you. I am turning my spare bedroom into a studio and I'm prepping for an art show at the new Square One Gallery in a few weeks."

"Congrats! That's awesome, Julia," he smiled.

She had forgotten that he used to call her by her given name, Julia. It made her smile to hear him say it now. "Looks like I might be your newest customer because I'm basically starting from scratch. Jim didn't really like my art, so picking it up after so many years was a little daunting, but I took a watercolor class at STLCC."

"That's right, you always loved watercolors. I remember that being your favorite medium," he said.

Julie shrugged her shoulders, "I guess habits are hard to change."

"Would you want to go grab a coffee and catch up? My assistant will be here any minute, and there's a coffee shop just down the road. We could even walk there," he suggested.

"Um…," Julie hesitated, looking down at her watch. She quickly mulled over the idea of being with Brian again, even for just a cup of coffee. Shaking her head yes, she said, "Yeah, that would be great to catch up."

***

Julie found a table for two near the window as

Brian ordered their coffee. She looked outside until he set the mug down, taking a seat across from her.

"How are you really doing?" he asked.

"The first few months were rough, but I'm adjusting to my new normal. I mean, you are the one person who knew that my marriage to Jim wasn't perfect, but it was still painful to lose him," she said taking a sip of her coffee.

"Yeah, I'll bet," Brian said, totally distracted, like he had something else to say. He let out the breath he was holding, as his shoulders slumped. "He treated you awful. When I close my eyes and think of you back then, I can still see the pain in your eyes."

Julie's breath hitched. She looked down at her coffee cup before looking back up to Brian's eyes. "I was so surprised by your sudden move to Champaign. I mourned our friendship for a long time."

Brian looked out the window, "He never told you?" The tone in his voice serious.

Julie knitted her brow as she placed her hand across the table onto Brian's hand. "He never told me what?" she asked with trepidation in her voice. She wasn't sure that she really wanted to know what he was going to say next.

Looking at Julie's hand on his, Brian moved his eyes back up to Julie's face. "Jim came to see me one day after school. He was convinced that I had feelings for you. Let's just say, he said to stay away from you."

Julie's mouth was agape in shock, "He threatened you?"

"Not so much of an actual threat, he was too smart to do that Julia, but it was enough that I didn't want to test him," explained Brian.

Julie's hand flew up to cover her mouth, "Is that why you moved?" she asked.

"It wasn't the sole reason, but it definitely played a part in my decision. He wasn't wrong, I did have feelings for you," Brian said with a nod.

Julie sat quietly for a moment, taking this news in. "I'm so sorry Brian. I wish you would have told me. Things may have turned out so different."

Brian reached up and scratched the scruff on his chin, "It was for the best. Mom had a stroke a couple of weeks later, which sealed my fate of moving back home. It was a good move for Olivia, too, to grow up in a smaller city," he said.

"I'm so sorry, Brian. I had no idea," she said with remorse in her voice.

"I felt bad leaving you…with him," Brian said looking out the window again.

The conversation lulled as neither knew what else to say, so they said goodbye and exchanged phone numbers before giving each other a light hug.

***

On the drive home, Julie thought about her conversation with Brian, allowing her mind to wonder what life would have been like if Brian would have told her about Jim's visit. Would she have left Jim for Brian? They never even kissed, but there was no denying that they had a deep connection. Her mind shifted to Marc, and she wondered what he was doing and if he was still with that woman.

"Why am I never enough?" she said out loud, above the music playing on the radio. As she pulled into the garage, Julie looked over at Jim's precious truck. Anger growing in her belly, she walked into the kitchen, looking around at her artwork. The anger subsided to the feeling of pride in the work she had done in the last couple of weeks. "I. AM. ENOUGH!" she shouted.

Chapter 28

"Memories" by Dean Lewis

The New York City skyline provided the perfect backdrop and just enough shade to shelter Julie and Max, her classmate, while they sat enjoying a much-needed break from their watercolor class. The sounds of honking horns and distant chatter mingled with the smells of freshly brewed coffee, solidifying that she was still in love with this city.

"There's something magical about this city. Don't you think?" Julie asked, before taking a bite of her sandwich.

Max took a long drink of his soda before answering, "I mean, I guess. I grew up in Brooklyn, so it's just home to me."

Julie sighed, "I would have loved to grow up here. There's so much inspiration."
Taking a sip of her drink, she peered out at the busy street beside them. "It's full of non-stop energy."

Max shrugged his shoulders, taking another bite of his sandwich. "What drew you to watercolor?" he asked in between chews.

"I think it's because it's so versatile. When most people think of watercolor, they picture the pastel florals or beach scenes, but there is so much more depth to it. It can be dark, bold and mysterious," she said wistfully.

Max looked down at his phone, "Oh shit. I gotta go. My girlfriend just texted that she's at MoMA. You okay to finish on your own? Sorry, between working and this class, I haven't seen her all week." He stood up, throwing some cash on the table for the tip, he added, "See you back at class."

Julie chuckled, "Alone, once again."

Leaning back in her chair, she felt the warmth of the sun on her skin. Closing her eyes briefly, she relished the short respite. For a moment, time slowed down and she's grateful for the chance to simply be present in the midst of the city's hustle and bustle. Lost in thought, she found herself daydreaming about what life would be like if she moved here. She imagines strolling through Central Park on lazy Sunday afternoons, exploring hidden art galleries in Greenwich Village, and sipping coffee in cozy cafes in Brooklyn. With each step, her imagination paints a vivid picture of a life filled with endless possibilities in the city that never sleeps.

Moving her sunglasses down from her head, she pulled out some cash to add to Max's tip money. As she walks back to MoMA, she took in the sounds around her. A dozen or more different languages, music playing, someone singing in the distance; it all makes her love this city even more. She thought about the possibility of selling her home in St. Louis and taking the plunge to move, making this her forever home. A wide grin graced her face as she walks, and then she sees him, or at least she thinks it is him. Holding her breath, she watched the man reach out to open the cab door. He looks up toward her and she lets out the breath. It wasn't Marc, but her heart raced at the thought of running into him. Holding her hand over her heart and willing her pulse to slow down, she let out a light laugh.

***

At the end of class, the instructor told everyone about an art show at Lumas Gallery in SOHO that evening. Excited by the announcement, Julie decided that she couldn't miss this opportunity.

Stepping into the gallery, she was immediately captivated by the kaleidoscope of colors and shapes that adorned the walls. The air was alive with the hum of conversation and the soft strains of music, creating an atmosphere of creativity and inspiration. Picking up a flute of champagne, she moved from one painting to another, her eyes drinking in the beauty of each piece. She imagined herself working in a gallery like this one, surrounded by art every day, helping to curate exhibitions, and sharing her passion with others. Lost in her reverie, Julie wandered deeper into the gallery, her heart filled with dreams of a future where art is not just a hobby, but a way of life. She imagines herself standing amidst the vibrant works, guiding visitors through the gallery with enthusiasm and expertise.

As she lingered in front of a particularly striking painting, Julie felt a sense of belonging come over her. In that moment, surrounded by creativity and possibility, she knew that her dreams of working in a gallery or teaching are not just fantasies. She knew in her heart that she belonged here in New York City, immersed in the world of art.

A tall, dark-haired, slender woman dressed in a smart black dress approached Julie as she made her way back to the front of the gallery. "Beautiful show, isn't it?" she asked.

Julie replied, "It's exquisite. The artist is so talented." She turned around with a champagne flute still in hand as she motioned around the gallery.

"Would you like to meet her?" the woman asks as Julie downed the last of her champagne.

"Oh, yes, please," Julie responded with excitement.

"Follow me. I'm Lauren by the way, the Gallery Director," she said as Julie followed her. "How did you hear about the opening? If you don't mind me asking."

"I'm taking a watercolor class at the MoMA. John, our instructor told us about it after class this afternoon," Julie explained as she followed.

"I love John, he's a fantastic artist himself. He showed his artwork here last summer. The show was a hit," Lauren said as they approached a younger woman with short, brown hair and glasses. Turning to Julie, Lauren said, "Magdalena, this is Julie. She's a fellow artist and wants to meet you."

Julie felt a flush of heat across her face, "Your work is gorgeous. I love your painting, Magenta." She's unsure how much to say or what not to say.
Magdalena stuck her hand out to shake Julie's, "Thank you. It's very nice to meet you. Thank you for coming."

Lauren interrupted, "Julie is an art student at MoMA." Turning to Julie, she asked, "Where is it you're from?"

"St. Louis, but I'm considering moving to New York in the near future if I can find a job in the art field," Julie says, surprised at her the words that come from her mouth. Moving in the near future? Her mind scrambled to get back into the conversation.

Magdalena nodded, "Maybe I'll get to see your work hanging here someday."

"That would be a dream come true. I actually have my first solo art show in a couple of weeks back home," Julie beamed with pride.

"Wonderful," both Lauren and Magdalena say at the same time, with a giggle afterwards.

Julie laughed along. "Magdalena, I'll let you get to your other patrons. Thank you for having me and it was a pleasure to meet you. Lauren, it was a pleasure meeting you."

Magdalena turned around to another group, while Lauren walked toward the front with Julie. Reaching into her pocket, she handed Julie her business card. "Let me know the next time you're in town and we can meet up to brainstorm positions for you. I know quite a few of the gallery owners around town, so I'm sure we can find you something."

Julie shook her head in disbelief, "Oh my gosh. Uh, thank you Lauren. It's been lovely meeting you and seeing your beautiful gallery. Thank you for making me feel at home."

"My pleasure Julie. Take care and keep in touch," said Lauren as Julie made her way to the exit.

Once outside and a block away, she excitedly jumped up and down, raising her fists in the air with pure joy surging through her body. Hailing a cab, she made her way back to the hotel with the biggest, cheesiest grin across her face. She couldn't wait to call Carla and tell her.

***

"Falling" by Harry Styles

The rest of the week passed quickly, and suddenly it was Julie's last day in New York. She didn't have class, but decided to spend part of her morning browsing the MoMA after picking up her portfolio. She slowly walked from exhibit to exhibit, taking it all in one last time. She loves the St. Louis Art Museum, but MoMA and the art here seem some more transforming. She stood in front of Phantasy II by Norman Lewis, mesmerized by how different it was from Twilight Sounds while still maintaining the same vibe.

Turning around, she was startled to see Marc standing behind her. Her breath catches, a wave of heat flushes her face, and her eyes grow wide. Her heart racing as he steps toward her. She takes in how good he looks in his black slacks, dress shirt, and glasses. She smirked knowing he still wears his scruff and mustache the way she likes it.

As he took another step closer to her, she asked, "What are you doing here?" Her emotions are bubbling to the surface, so she takes a breath, trying to calm her pulse.

"I was going to ask you the same thing," he said, biting his lower lip which turns into a smile. "Work. I'm here for work."

"I'm here for an art class," she said, not looking away from his gaze. All the while on the inside she was willing herself to not cry, when what she really wanted was to be in his arms, kissing his lips, feeling his love…"

"That's great, Jules. I'm happy to hear you're painting again," Marc said. "How's everything at home?"
"Good. Things are good," she said, as she looked at his perfect lips under his mustache. Memories of kissing him and making love to him came to mind and she feared she was blushing, so she looked back down. She heard Max call out to her, and looked up to give him a wave. Turning her attention back to Marc, she said, "I'm surprised to see you here, especially to see Norman Lewis' work."

"Someone once told me that he was her favorite artist, so I wanted to stop by and check his work out," he said with a smile.

Julie just smiled and looked down again. She wondered if Marc could tell how nervous she was just talking to him. "Well, I better get going. I have an early flight home tomorrow."

Marc's eyes glanced down and back up, "Do you want to go grab some dinner?"

Julie made a half frown face, "Thank you for the offer, but I don't think it's a good idea. Everything is too fresh and I'm trying not to live in the past, ya know? Making strides going forward."

"I owe you an apology, Jules," he said reaching out

his hand to touch hers.

"Marc, stop. I can't," Julie whispered, shaking her head no. She breathed in deeply, praying that it would keep the tears from welling up.

He grabbed her hand gently, "Jules…you need to hear me, if for nothing other than closure."

She watched his chest rise and fall with a slight tremble. He stood in front of her, holding her hand in the MoMA. Blinking several times, she stood and said nothing as she tried to steady her breath and nod her head, "Okay."

Marc held her hand as he led her out of the building and onto the busy sidewalk to Urban Plaza. He invited Julie to sit next to him on the marble bench. They sat in silence for a while.

Marc turned his body toward Julie, "Jules, I'm so sorry for what you saw. I feel awful for hurting you. When I left St. Louis, I was confused. When I turned around to take a call on your porch, I turned back to see you walk inside and shut down, completely shutting me out. I didn't know what I did to scare you, but deep down you know that I would never cheat on you." Marc picked her hand up, "I'm not Jim."

Julie looked up at Marc, no longer able to keep the tears at bay. Drawing a deep breath, Julie stared into his dark eyes, "Thank you." Thank you? Get it together. Reaching up to rub her forehead, she said, "Uh, for the apology." Tingles of sadness moved down her arms, making her heart beat faster. She whispered, "I can't do this." Her words seem so final, but she couldn't shake the wave of sadness flowing through her. Standing to her feet, she looked down at Marc. "I hope that you are happy with…her." Julie took another breath, "Have a good life, Marc."

Julie turned around as she tried to keep it together. She exited the park area and was halfway down the block before the flood of tears streamed down her face, causing her torso to shake with sobs.

She walked for a few blocks and looked up beyond the skyscrapers, watching the sky turn into a beautiful twilight blue mixed with orange and purple. Life has so much color, but for most of her life all she saw was gray, neutral and plain. As Julie hailed for a cab she whispered, "I'm done being gray."

Chapter 29

"No Choice" – Acoustic by Fly by Midnight

Walking into the gallery, Julie's heart raced with excitement. The soft glow of gallery lights illuminated the sleek, white walls adorned with vibrant artwork. Taking in the sight of her own pieces displayed with cards, each one commanded attention with the various colors and intricate details. She could hardly believe that she was finally here, her dream of showcasing her art becoming a reality. She stood in awe, overwhelmed by the beauty of the setup and the realization of her hard work paying off. She wandered around, stepping back to take in each of the paintings while the caterer's staff set up the champagne table and hors-d'oeuvres. Stopping in front of the painting of Venice Beach, it reminded her of the trip that started her healing process. She took in the soft shades of blues and greens of the tide hitting the shore, the clouds lingering in the sky. It was her homage to the paintings at the house she and Carla rented. Reaching out, she touched the brush strokes and thought back to how serene and simple life seemed sitting on that beach.

Checking her phone, she looked at the time. They will be opening the doors in less than an hour. "This is really happening," she said softly under her breath. Walking over to the champagne table, she asked for a flute to help calm her nervousness. Her mind sifted through her fears about tonight; What if no one shows up? What if no one buys a painting? What was she going to do with all the paintings after the show? Taking a deep breath, she took a sip of champagne, and heard Ashley's voice behind her.

"Mom! This is amazing," Ashley beamed with pride for her mother.

Julie turned to hug Ashley, "Thank you Ash. It all seems a little surreal right now. I feel like I should pinch myself to make sure this isn't a dream."

Carla hollered as she came through the door with Paul, "Where's the artist? I have to meet her!" She approached Ashley and Julie, giving each of them a big hug. "Jules, you remember Paul, and Ash, this is Paul," turning to Paul, "This is Jule's daughter, Ashley."

Paul stuck his hand out to shake Ashley's, "Nice to meet you." He turned to Julie, "This is amazing. I understand that this has been a dream of yours for a long time."

Julie said, "Yes, for a very long time." Her mind thought about the night she met Paul in New York with Marc. Closing her eyes, she willed the thoughts away. "Carla, thank you for helping me transport everything over here yesterday. I would still be unloading if it weren't for you and Ashley." She smiled as she patted Ashley's shoulder. "Please look around and grab a glass of champagne, I need to check on something before the doors officially open."

She walked into the restroom; her heart was beating so fast at just the thought of Marc. As hard as she tried to tell herself otherwise, her heart still yearned for him. Looking in the mirror, she inhaled deeply, holding the breath for the count of four before releasing it. She repeated the process a few times, until her head cleared and her pulse was almost back to a normal beat. "You can do this. Tonight is about you, Jules," she said out loud. Turning on her heel, she walked out to the sight of a group of people milling around taking in her artwork. Smiling, she walked out into the open space of the gallery.

When Carla saw Julie emerge into the room, she began clapping. Everyone joined in as Julie's face flushed a pink hue. Julie smiled as she made her way toward Carla, her eyes growing wider the closer she got to her friend. "Stop," she whispered as the hugged Carla.

Carla said, "This is all you, Jules. They're all here because of you and your talent. You did it! I'm so proud of you."

Julie gracefully navigated through the crowd, a radiant smile illuminating her face as she engaged with each patron. With a keen eye for detail, she effortless discussed the inspiration behind each piece, drawing them into her world of creativity. As the evening progressed, the room filled with the hum of admiration and excitement, punctuated by occasional bursts of laughter and enthusiastic applause. Julie's artwork, a kaleidoscope of color and emotion, captivated the audience, leaving them eager to own a piece of her talent. Amidst the flurry of activity, she remained composed, yet she exuded an infectious energy that ignited the room. It's a night of celebration, where Julie's passion and dedication to her craft were met with genuine appreciation and acclaim.

***

"Die Alone" by Disco Cowboy

The clinking of glasses and the buzz of conversation filled the air as Julie, Carla, Paul, and Ashley gather in a cozy corner of the bar to celebrate Julie's successful art show.

"How many paintings did you sell?" asked Paul.

"I'm not completely sure, but they said it was almost a sold-out show," Julie said graciously as she beamed with pride. "I still can't believe that people wanted my artwork in their homes," she said, putting her hands over her face in disbelief.

Carla pushed one of Julie's arms down, "Jules, you should be so proud of yourself. You put yourself out there and sold a lot of paintings. Everyone that I talked to raved about your work. You did it! I'm so proud of you!"

Amidst laughter and shared stories, Julie's smile flickered with moments of wistfulness as she tried to push aside her thoughts of Marc. She raised her glass to toast the success of her show, but with each sip, the memories of Marc lingered as a bittersweet reminder of what could have been.

Carla noticed the subtle change in Julie's demeanor and gently squeezed her hand in silent support. Paul and Ashley, sensing the shift in atmosphere, engage in lively banter to attempt to lift Julie's spirits. However, as the night progressed, and the drinks flowed freely, Julie found herself succumbing to the numbing embrace of the alcohol, seeking solace in its temporary oblivion.

As the evening wore on, laughter turned to hazy recollections and Julie's thoughts drifted further into the past. Finding herself longing for Marc's presence, she wished he could have been there to share in her triumph. With each passing moment, the weight of her unspoken feelings grew heaver until it became a burden too heavy to bear alone.

In the midst of the revelry, Julie's mask of composure began to crack, revealing the raw vulnerability hidden beneath. As the tears finally spill over, Carla and Ashley gathered around Julie, offering comfort and understanding in the face of her pain. In that moment of shared solidarity, amidst the clatter of glasses and the hum of the crowd, Julie found a glimmer of solace, knowing that she is not alone in her struggle.

***

Julie stumbled into the bedroom and started undressing. She decided to sleep on the mattress in the spare bedroom one more time before getting rid of it. Grabbing the mattress, she tried to drag it out into the living room. All she really managed to do was to knock over her easel and some art supplies, so she left it laying in the middle of her studio floor. She got a blanket from Ashley's room and laid down on the mattress. As excited as she was to have her first showing behind her, she felt lost without Marc being there. He had always encouraged her to paint again. She thought back to when she told him she had an art degree, and he wanted to rush out and buy her some supplies. She smiled and looked up at the ceiling, which happened to look like it was spinning. She closed her eyes, but the spinning didn't stop. It had been a very long time since she had drunk that much. Reaching for her phone, she immediately opened the texts between her and Marc. He was reaching out and she just shut him down. Reading the text thread, she held the phone up to her heart while she wept. It was 2am in St. Louis, so it was only midnight in LA. She clicked the number and waited for him to answer.

"Jules, everything okay?" he asked sleepily.

"No, everything is not okay. You weren't at my show tonight."

"I wasn't invited," he stated. "How'd it go?"

"I miss you," she said ignoring his question.

"Jules, it's 2am there. Have you been drinking?"

"I. Miss. You," she restated slowly, her words slurring.

"I miss you too, but missing each other doesn't solve our problems, Jules. Maybe we can talk more next week, when it's not in the middle of the night."

"Do you remember our first kiss?" she asked.

"I do," he said softly.

"Do you remember the first time we made love?" she asked, closing her eyes thinking back to that moment at the hotel.

"Of course, I do Jules. Why are you trying to rehash our relationship while you're drunk?" he asked with a tinge of frustration in his voice.

"I'm not drunk!" she slurred.

"Jules, I'm so proud of you for going after your dream of being an artist again, but…."

Julie interrupted him, "But what?"

"I'm not your person anymore. It's painful for both of us and I don't mind if we talk, but it has to be when you are sober and can remember."

"I remember. I remember that you supported me getting back into art. I remember how your lips tasted. I remember the scent of your favorite cologne. I remember how you touched my body and made me feel more alive than I have ever felt in my life. That's what I remember."

Marc was quiet. "Jules, get some sleep. I'll call you in the morning so that we can talk."

"But we're talking now. I may be a tiny bit inebriated, but I know what it's like to love you and be loved by you," she said as she started to cry. "Did you know that the anniversary of my miserable husband's death is coming up? Yup! He died almost a year ago. Did you know that?" Her words slurred together as she closed her eyes. "I didn't love him as much as I love you."

Marc drew in a big breath of air and let it out quickly. "Jules, this is just the alcohol talking. Do you need me to call Carla to come be there with you?"

Julie shook her head no, even though Marc couldn't see her, "Nope. She's with Paul. They are in love, like, real love, not fake love. Jim was fake love, you were fake love too, but not mine, I loved you both, but I wasn't enough. Never enough," she spiraled. "I sold paintings tonight and came home all alone. Just like everyone wants me to be… fucking alone."

"Jules, you need to get some sleep. Let's talk tomorrow. Do you want me to stay on the phone and talk to you until you go to sleep?" he asked.

"You would do that for me?" she asked, sniffling.

"Of course, I would. What do you want me to talk about?" he asked.

"You have such a nice voice. I love your voice," she slurred.

Marc started talking about nothing in particular. It didn't take long for Julie to relax. He could hear her breathing, and he assumed that she was asleep, signaling it was time to hang up. "Good night. I love you, Jules," he said before ending the phone call.

Julie heard him say this and smiled before rolling over to go to sleep.

Chapter 30

"Hang on Every Word" by Matchbox Twenty

The moonlight filtered through the windows, casting a pale glow over the bedroom. Julie laid curled up on her side, clutching the pillow from Jim's side of the bed. The room was silent, save for the distant hum of the world outside, indifferent to her pain. Today marked a year since Jim had passed, a milestone that weighed heavily on her heart. She had spent the night in and out of restless sleep, tormented by memories and the aching void beside her. In the dim light, her tear-streaked face glistened, her eyes red and puffy from crying. She hugged the pillow tighter, as if it could somehow bring him back.

When she finally opened her eyes, they felt gritty and swollen. She blinked against the light, trying to ground herself in the present. As her vision cleared, she noticed a figure sitting in the corner of the room. Startled, she sat up abruptly with her heart pounding. It was Marc. He sat in a chair, his posture relaxed yet alert, watching her with his eyes full of compassion. His presence was a stark contrast to the emptiness she had felt all night. He had been there, keeping vigil while she grieved.

"Marc," she whispered, her voice hoarse.

He stood and walked over to the bed; his footsteps soft against the carpet. "I'm here," he said gently, sitting down beside her. He reached out his hand to hers, his touch warm and reassuring.

"How long have you been here?" she asked, her voice trembling.

"All night," he admitted. "I didn't want you to be alone today."

Her heart ached with a mix of sorrow and gratitude. Marc had always been patient and present with her, but she didn't expect him to show up now, to bear witness to her raw grief.

"I didn't know if I could face today," she confessed, her voice breaking.

Marc's eyes softened with understanding. "You don't have to face it alone," he said. "I'm here with you."

Tears welled up again, but this time they carried a different weight. She leaned into him as he wrapped his arms around her, holding her as she cried. His embrace was solid, a reminder that life, though irrevocably changed, still held moments of connection and support. For a long time, they sat together as the silence was filled with unspoken words and shared sorrow. Marc didn't try to fill the space with platitudes or empty reassurances. He simply held her, proving his love through his presence and offering her strength to face another day.

As the sun rose higher with its light growing warmer, Julie felt a glimmer of something she hadn't expected…hope. Marc's love couldn't replace the loss of Jim, but it could help her carry it, making it a little more bearable. In that moment, she realized that she wasn't as alone as she thought.

Pulling back slightly, she looked up at Marc with gratitude. "Thank you," she whispered. He brushed a tear from her cheek, his smile tender, "Always," he replied, as Julie laid back down in bed.

***

Julie sat on the floor by the window, the soft glow of the setting sun casting a golden hue over the room. In her hand, she held a framed photo of Jim, his smiling face bringing a fresh wave of grief to crash over her. The anniversary of his death felt like an open wound, raw and relentless.

Marc moved quietly around the house, his presence both comforting and tender to Julie. He was making tea, understanding that sometimes it was the simple acts of kindness that meant the most. Julie glanced up as Marc entered the room, carrying a tray with two steaming mugs. He set it down on the floor and took a seat beside her, his hand finding hers. She squeezed it, grateful for his support.

"Thank you," she whispered, her voice barely audible over the lump in her throat.

"You don't have to thank me," Marc replied softly. "I'm here for you, always."

Just then, the bedroom door creaked open, and Ashley walked in. She paused in the doorway, her eyes widening as she took in the scene. Julie hadn't expected her to come today, assuming she would be dealing with the loss of Jim in her own way.

"Ashley," Julie said, her voice a mix of surprise and emotion.

"Mom," Ashley replied, her gaze shifted to Marc, a hint of confusion crossing her face. "I…I didn't know you had company."

Marc stood up, motioning for Ashley to come sit by her mother. "I'll let you two have some time alone." He stood at the door, taking in this precious moment between a mother and a daughter.

As Ashley took a seat next to her mother, her eyes softened with concern, "Are you okay, Mom?"

Julie nodded, tears brimming in her eyes, "It's just…today."

Ashley enveloped her mother in a hug, "I know, Mom. I miss him too."

Julie held onto Ashley tightly, feeling the familiar comfort of her embrace. After a moment, she pulled back and looked at Marc, who was watching them with a kind, understanding expression.

"Marc has been a great help," Julie said softly.

"He's…he's been here for me."

Ashley studied Marc for a moment, then nodded, "Thank you for being here."

Marc smiled warmly, "Of course, I care about her very much."

Julie felt a surge of gratitude as she looked between Ashley and Marc. It was a complicated mix of emotions, mourning Jim while feeling the stirrings of something new and hopeful with Marc. She knew it would take time for Ashley and Ben to fully accept this new chapter in their lives, but today, with Marc and Ashley by her side, she felt a glimmer of peace amidst the sorrow.

Julie hesitated for a moment before walking out to join Marc on the front porch. He was gently swaying on the old wooden swing, his presence a comforting anchor in the sea of her emotions. He looked up as she stepped toward him, giving her a small understanding smile. Julie sat down beside him, the swing creaking softly under their combined weight. For a few moments, they sat in silence, the only sounds being the distant chirping of crickets and the rustling of leaves in the evening breeze.

Marc reached over and took her hand, his thumb brushing soothing circles on her skin.

"How are you feeling?" he asked softly.

Julie took a deep breath, staring out into blue sky. "Today's been…hard," she admitted. "Jim and I had a very complicated relationship."

Marc nodded, encouraging her to continue without pressure. He pulled her hand up to his lips, gently kissing her palm.

"Jim was…he was charming when he wanted to be, but he wasn't ever faithful to me." she said, her voice tinged with a mix of sadness and bitterness. "Throughout our marriage, he cheated on me so many times, I lost count. It broke me in ways I didn't realize until it was too late. I felt stuck for most of my adult life."

Marc squeezed her hand gently, his expression one of empathy and support.

"I stayed because of Ben and Ashley…" Closing her eyes, "He made me feel so small and that I wasn't worthy of his love. I was never enough for him, even though I tried so hard to be the best wife and mother. It was tumultuous, every betrayal and harsh word left a scar." She paused, the memories overwhelming her for a moment. Marc wrapped an arm around her shoulders and pulled her in close. "You don't have to go through this alone," he murmured.

Leaning into him, she drew strength from his presence. "Thank you for being here, but I understand if this is too much. If I'm too broken for you."

Marc lifted her chin up so that he could look into her eyes, "Jules, I love you. Your broken pieces, scars, and everything that makes you who you are today, is who I fell in love with. You are perfect to me." Leaning down, he gently pressed his lips to Julie's mouth.

Julie leaned against his chest, "I love you, Marc. I'm so sorry for pushing you away. We lost valuable time because of me."

They sat together on the swing most of the evening, until it grew dark around them. In Marc's arms, Julie felt safe for the first time in a long time, and she allowed herself to believe in the promise of a better future.

***

"I Choose You" by Forest Blakk

Julie stirred awake, her senses coming alive with the familiar, comforting aroma of freshly brewed coffee. The sun's soft light filtered through the curtains of Ben's old room, casting a glow on the faded posters and childhood memorabilia. She blinked, momentarily disoriented, before the events of the previous night came rushing back. She and Marc had fallen asleep here, in her son's room, surrounded by memories. She sat up slowly, before crawling out of bed and her feet sank into the soft carpet. As she walked down the hallway, the sounds of laughter and clinking dishes grew louder. She paused at the entrance of the kitchen, taking in the scene before her. Marc was standing by the stove, flipping pancakes with an easy grace, while Ashley was setting dishes on the island.

"Good morning, Mom," Ashley called out, noticing her mother in the doorway.

Marc turned around, flashing Julie a warm smile. "Morning, Jules," his voice soft and affectionate.

Julie stepped into the kitchen, feeling a swell of emotion. "You two are a sight for sore eyes," she said, crossing the room to pour herself a cup of coffee. She took a deep breath, savoring the rich, inviting scent.

Marc handed her a plate of pancakes. "Sit down and eat," he said. "We've got everything under control here," leaning down he kissed the top of her head as she smiled.

Julie took a seat at the island, watching her daughter and Marc as they finished preparing breakfast. The room was filled with the sounds of sizzling butter, the clinking of dishes, and the soft hum of morning chatter. It was a simple moment, but one that filled her heart with contentment.

After breakfast, Ashley excused herself, leaving Marc and Julie alone again.

Julie looked at Marc, tears welling up in her sore eyes, "I never stopped loving you."

Marc's expression softened, reaching out to cup her face in his hands, "Neither did I."

In that instant, the time that they were separated melted away. Julie closed her eyes and leaned into him, their lips meeting in a kiss that felt both familiar and electrifyingly new. It was as if they had never been apart, all the hurt and distance had never existed.

Marc smiled as he looked at Julie, his eyes pleading, "Jules, come back to Los Angeles with me," his voice was soft but insistent.

Julie hesitated, glancing down at the coffee cup in her hands. She quietly contemplated his suggestion. "Marc, you know I can't just leave," her voice was filled with uncertainty. "This is my home, and Ashley…" she paused.

Marc reached over, gently taking her hand in his, "I understand, Jules, but we can make it work. Ashley and Ben can come visit us, and you can come back whenever you need to."

Julie's heart ached with the weight of the decision before her. She glanced toward the window that faced the backyard. The yard that held so many memories. "I need to talk to Ashley about this. I hope you understand."

"Of course. You said last night that we've already lost precious time together. I will do whatever I have to do to keep you in my life," his eyes filled with compassion at all that she had been through.

Ashley stood at the doorway, overhearing the conversation. Walking over to them, she wrapped her arms around her mother, "Mom, now that I've finished school, I would like to move back to the house. I can take care of it while you are in LA with Marc." She kissed Julie on the cheek. "You've sacrificed so much of your life for me and Ben, and you deserve to be with someone who loves you and makes you happy."

Julie turned around to face Ashley, looking up to her with tears in her eyes, "Are you sure?"

"Mom. It's your turn to live the life you've always dreamed about. You have your artwork, and now you have Marc back in your life. I'll be fine." She winked before adding, "Besides, it's time for me to grow up and be my own person."

Marc smiled at Ashley, mouthing, 'Thank you.'

Julie stood up, taking Ashley in her arms for a big hug, "We need to call Ben, I would like his blessing too before I make a final decision."

Ashley rolled her eyes and nodded her head, "I'll take care of Ben. He'll be fine. I'll make sure of it."

Julie looked between Ashley and Marc, taking a deep breath before exhaling. "I guess I'm going to LA."

Chapter 31

"High Hope" by Patrick Droney

Julie stood by the large window in Marc's cozy cottage, her fingers tracing the edge of a seashell on the windowsill. Outside, the sun dipped low, casting a golden hue over the canal. Her thoughts drifted to the last time she was here, making her heart feel heavy. She tried to push the memories away, treating them as a distant bad dream that she had finally woken up from. Marc approached her, his eyes sparkling as he stopped to take her in. "You're really here," he whispered.

She leaned into his embrace, "I'm really here."

"Ready for that walk?" he asked.

Julie smiled and nodded, taking his hand. They stepped out into the warm evening air, the salty breeze ruffling their hair. The beach stretched out before them, waves lapping gently against the shore. They strolled along the sand, their conversation light and filled with laughter. As they walked, dark clouds began to gather on the horizon.

Marc glanced up, his brow furrowing slightly, "Looks like a storm might be coming."

Julie followed his gaze. "Maybe we should head back soon."

They lingered a bit longer, drawn by the beauty of the ocean against the dark sky. The first drops of rain were barely noticeable, as soft mist quickly turned into a steady drizzle. Mark pulled Julie closer, their footsteps quickening as they turned back toward the cottage. The rain intensified, soaking them through. Julie's hair clung to her face, and Marc was drenched. They breathlessly laughed, as they finally reached the small porch of Marc's home. He fumbled with the key, their laughter mingling with the sound of the rain pounding against the roof.

"I'm going to take a quick shower to warm up," Julie said, making her way down the hallway. Turning around, she took her soaked top off and noticed Marc watching her. She smiled slyly before asking, "Wanna join me?"

Marc quickly walked down the hall toward her, following her into the bathroom. He started the shower as she stripped out of her soaked clothes. The warm water cascaded over their bodies as he took her in his arms. Looking into her eyes, there was an evident longing in his gaze.

He began to kiss her neck as she tipped her head back against the wall. Arching her back, he held her close to his body as he slipped his hand down between her legs, making her moan with desire. Pushing himself into her, she wrapped her arms around him and pulled him closer while kissing him. Closing her eyes, she panted his name as she climaxed. Her body relaxed as he fell against her, the water flowing over them until he pushed himself up. He pressed his lips against hers, in the longest, most tender kiss she had ever experienced. Turning, she reached for the bar of soap and caressed it across his chest as she began to wash his body.

Taking the bar of soap out of her hands, he began to rub it on her stomach, "I love you." She started to say it back to him, but he put his finger on her lips, as if to say, Shh, "Jules, I have loved you forever. I had given up hope of ever having you in my life, but since I found you, I feel whole. I love how selfless you are in your love for me, and I don't want to live another day without you." He took a deep breath before continuing, "I want you to be my wife. I realize this isn't the perfect way to ask you, but I can't live without you, and I want to spend the rest of my life making you happy and giving you the life you deserve. Will you marry me?"

Tears welled up in Julie's eyes as she pulled him into her, "Yes, a thousand times yes! I love you, and I want to be your wife!"

***

"Settle Down" by Fly by Midnight, Zaeden

Marc and Julie sat in the living room, the remnants of their dinner on the coffee table. The candles flickered softly, casting a warm glow across their faces. Marc put his arm around her and in return, she offered him a tentative smile, her eyes filled with a mix of joy and worry.

"I still can't believe it," Julie said softly. "We're really doing this."

"I know," Marc replied, his expression gentle. "You're worried about Ben and Ashley."

She nodded, her eyes growing misty. "Ashley realizes how good we are for each other. She witnessed the evidence when you came to the house, when…well, you know." She hesitated, a pensive look on her face. "Ben has a harder time wrapping his head around the idea of me with someone other than his father."

Marc leaned back in his chair, his expression thoughtful, "He's protective of you. That's understandable. You all have been through a lot in the last year."

"I know," Julie sighed. "I just don't want him to feel like he's losing me, or that his feelings don't matter."

"We'll handle it together," Marc said reassuringly. "We need to talk to him, honestly. Let him know that he and I only want the best for you. Your relationship with him won't change."

Julie nodded, wiping a tear from her cheek. "I don't want to this to create a rift between us."

"We need to tell him soon, so he doesn't think we're planning our lives without him. We will do this together," suggested Marc.

Julie smiled through her tears, cupping Marc's face in her hands. "Thank you. I don't know what I would do without you."

"You'll never have to find out," Marc whispered, leaning in to kiss her softly.

The room fell silent for a moment, the only sound was the gentle flicker of the candle flames. Julie took a deep breath, feeling a bit of the tension ease from her shoulders. Reaching up, she rubbed the back of her neck.

Marc opened a bottle of champagne to toast his soon to be bride. "Mrs. Julia Diaz," he said while handing her a flute of bubbles.

Julie grinned from ear to ear, trying to mask her concern for Ben. "I love the sound of that," she said as they clinked their glasses.

"Should we call our families?" Marc asked after taking a sip, looking longingly into Julie's eyes.

"Let's wait until tomorrow. I don't want to share this with anyone yet." Julie said matter-of-factly.

Marc pulled his head back, "Okay?" he asked with some concern in his voice.

Julie scooted closer to Marc, "I just don't want to share this moment tonight with anyone else. I am wholeheartedly in love with you and no one, not even my kids, can change that. I cannot wait to be your wife," she assured him.

"But?" he said in a strained voice.

"You've never been married before, and I was for a really long time. I want to make sure that you are proposing because it's what you really want and not just because you're afraid to lose me again."

"Babe, I don't want to lose you ever again, but I don't want to be anywhere other than by your side for the rest of my life. I haven't entertained the idea of marriage before, because it wasn't you." Marc pulled her back to him. "I meant it when I said I want to be your husband. Do you believe me?"

"Of course, I believe you."

"Then there isn't a problem. Stop trying to find one. I love you. You love me," he said pointing back and forth between them. "We're going to spend the rest of our lives together."

***

"Overjoyed" by Matchbox Twenty

The next morning, Julie stood in the kitchen, the soft hum of the coffee maker filling the room as it dripped into the pot. The rich, familiar aroma began to waft through the air, offering a small comfort as she mulled over the conversation she needed to have with Ben and Ashley. She thought about Marc's proposal last night. The memory brought a smile to her face, but it was filled with a pang of anxiety. How would the kids react to the news? Pouring herself a cup of hot coffee, she took a deep breath, the warmth of the cup soothing her hands as she searched for the right words to say to them.

"Good morning, my love," Marc said as he walked into the kitchen, rubbing his eyes. Leaning down he pressed his lips to the tip of her nose. He pulled away slightly, breathing in the scent of the fresh coffee, "You made coffee. I knew there was a reason I wanted to marry you," he joked.

"Very funny," Julie said, slapping him on his arm. "I'm going out to the back porch."

Marc teasingly smacked her on her butt, "Be out in a minute, wifey."

Turning around, she joked back, "I think the new rule is, you'll be bringing me coffee in bed every morning." Reaching for the door handle, she smirked.

"I would agree to that, wifey," he laughed with a wink

Joining her on the back deck, Marc took her cup of coffee and placed it on the small table beside his. He wrapped his arms around her waist, gently swaying back and forth. He whispered in her ear, "I'm going to marry you."

Julie smiled as she stared across the canal, placing her hands on top of his as they continued to sway. She had finally found happiness.

"After we're married, we just need to figure out how to get you into the art scene here in LA. I have no doubt that we'll figure it out," Marc said.

Julie turned around to face him. "I need to be honest with you about something."

Marc looked at the serious look on Julie's face, "Should I be concerned?"

Julie swallowed hard before taking a breath, "You know that my dream has always been to live in New York, to teach and be a part of the art community there."

"Okay. Yes, I knew that, but we can't just pick up and move to New York this week," Marc said with confusion in his voice.

"I realize that, but…" Julie paused. "I have given up my dreams since I was 22 years old, and if you haven't noticed, I'm not getting any younger," she said with a forced laugh. "I need to know that you also want to move to New York, as soon as we can."

"I know that, and yes, I want that too. I've talked to my boss about it, and a move like that takes time," he said. Pulling her into his arms, "I want to be wherever you are, so it's not as if I'm stalling to stay here. I've been with this company since the beginning, and I love my job. If it

doesn't work out, then I'm willing to find something in New York, but I need you to be patient."

Julie felt the pang of disappointment, knowing that her face couldn't conceal the thoughts flashing across her mind. "Can we at least set a date on when we'll make that decision?"

Marc let out a breath, "Of course, but I've already put the wheels in motion, so it's just a matter of time."

Julie smiled, "Thank you."

Marc pressed his lips to hers as she wrapped her arms around his neck. They continued kissing until he pulled away, "Believe me when I say that I will do anything to make sure that we end up in New York and that you are happy. I am overjoyed that you've agreed to be my wife." Julie leaned in for another long kiss, as he pulled her close, rubbing her back with one hand while cradling her head in his other hand. "I love you, Marc Diaz."

"I love you, Jules…Diaz," he smirked as he took her face in his hands, kissing her again. "Ready to tell your kids the big news?" he asked with a twinkle in his eyes.

Julie took a breath as a nervous look flashed across her face, "No time like the present." Her hands trembled with a mix of excitement and nerves. Beside her, Marc squeezed her hand reassuringly. They had decided to share the big news at the same time with Ben and Ashley, via FaceTime. Julie glanced at Marc, who gave her an encouraging smile.

"Ready?" he asked softly.

Julie nodded, taking a deep breath, "Let's do this."

She tapped on the FaceTime icon next to Ben's name and waited for the call to connect. After a few rings, the screen lit up with Ben's face. He was sitting in his apartment, a curious
expression on his face.

"Hey, Mom! What's up?" Ben greeted; his eyes shifted briefly to Marc. "Hi, Marc."

"Hi, Ben," Marc replied warmly.

"Let's get Ashley on the call too," Julie said. She quickly added Ashley, and soon her daughter appeared on the screen, her face lighting up when she saw her mother and Marc.

"Hey, Mom! Hey, Marc!" Ashley said cheerfully.

"We have some news to share so we thought it would be best to do it together," Julie began, her voice slightly shaky. She felt her heart race, and looked to Marc one more time for reassurance. He gave her a nod.

"Well, the thing is…Marc asked me to marry him," Julie announced.

There was a moment of stunned silence on the other end of the call.

Ashley squealed, "Oh my God! Mom, that's amazing. Congratulations!"

Ben sat quietly for a few more minutes, as Julie waited for his reaction. "That's big news," his voice indifferent, before adding, "Congrats, Mom, you too Marc."

"Thank you, guys," Marc said, his voice filled with happiness. "We wanted you to be the first to know."

"We're so happy for you, Mom. Right, Ben?" Ashley said, her eyes misting with tears. "You two deserve all the happiness in the world."

Ben finally cracked a smile, "Absolutely."

Ashley asked, "When is the wedding?"

Julie laughed, "We just got engaged last night, so we don't have a date picked out." She looked at Marc with a grin, "You'll be the first to know when we set the date, I promise."

Ashley said with excitement, "Let me see the ring!"

Marc laughed, "Uh...I wanted your mom to pick out whatever ring she wants, so we're going shopping soon."

Julie added, "I don't need an engagement ring, a simple band will suffice."

Marc gasped, "You're getting a ring, not another word otherwise." He let out a chuckle.

"Tell us how you proposed, Marc. I love a good story," chimed Ashley.

Marc looked at Julie with wide eyes as he realized that people would actually be asking this question. That didn't even enter his mind when he popped the question while rubbing soap on Julie's naked body. His face flushed, with embarrassment.

Julie looked over at Marc's red face and laughed. "We had been walking on the beach, when a storm blew up and soaked us as we ran back to his cottage. We just got caught up in a moment and he told me that he couldn't live without me and asked me to marry him," she explained. "It was simple but perfect."

Marc leaned back on the sofa out of sight of the phone and relief washed over him. Julie just smirked, as she winked at him.

As Julie continued chatting with the kids, she felt a sense of peace settle over her. Sharing this moment with her children, and seeing the joy and support, made the occasion even more special. She squeezed Marc's knee, grateful for the new chapter they were about to begin together.

Chapter 32

"Sky is the Limit" by Mark Ambor

Julie couldn't help but glance at her hand every now and then, admiring the beautiful princess cut diamond ring that sparkled in the sunlight. It was a perfect symbol of their love, chosen together, and reflecting both elegance and strength. It was hard to believe that two weeks had passed since Marc asked Julie to marry him. Coffee cup in hand, she sat on the back porch of the Venice Beach cottage, soaking up the fresh sea air and the warm California sunshine.

Marc joined her on the porch, leaning down to kiss her before he headed off to work. Pulling the mug from her hand, he lifted it to his lips to take a sip, before returning it to her with a smile. "I have an idea," he said.

"What's that?" Julie asked with a smirk, looking up at him.

"My buddy has a beach house out in Malibu. He's gone for the weekend, so he said we could use the place. Let's spend the weekend up there, to celebrate our engagement," he said nonchalantly.

Julie's eyes met his as she pursed her lips and squinted in the sunlight. "Something tells me there's more to your 'idea'," she said with air quotes. She grinned, "I'm kidding. Sounds dreamy."

"We could head up there tonight, hang out on the private beach and just relax and unwind," he offered, before leaning down to kiss her on top of her head. "Wear that silky red dress."

"What silky red dress?" she asked, thinking of what clothes she brought from St. Louis.

"The one I snuck home last night," he winked. "It's in the closet. I'll be home by six," he said turning around. "I love you, babe."

"Love you too," Julie said as she waved him away. "You're incorrigible," she laughed.

***

As they drove along the scenic coastal highway towards Malibu, the anticipation inMarc's eyes were palpable. Julie smiled, wondering what Marc had up his sleeve. He loved to surprise her; bringing her flowers, art supplies, or her favorite bottle of wine. Smoothing the silky red fabric down on her lap, she felt Marc's hand reach over and grab hers, intertwining their fingers together. Lifting her hand up, he smiled at the ring and pressed the back of her hand to his lips to kiss it gently.

"You look gorgeous," he said, licking his lips.

"Thank you. My fiancé picked it out for me," she gushed before letting a giggle bubble up to the surface.

They arrived at a stunning beach house; a hidden gem nestled against the cliffs with sweeping views of the ocean. As they stepped inside, Julie was taken aback by the warm glow of lanterns and the sound of waves gently crashing in the background. The living room opened up to a spacious deck, where a small crowd had gathered. Friends and family, who had flown in from various parts of the country, were there to celebrate this special moment. Julie gasped, her eyes welling up with tears of joy as she saw Ben, Ashley and Carla amongst the crowd.

"Surprise!" Marc said softly, holding her hand and leading her towards the crowd. "I wanted to make sure we celebrated our engagement with all the people we love."

Ashley rushed to hug her mother, with Ben right behind her. When they embraced, Ashley whispered, "It was so hard to not tell you that we were coming."

Julie wiped a tear running down her cheek, pulling Ben into their hug. "I'm so happy to see you both, I've missed you so much."

Carla and Paul walked over when Julie stepped back from embracing her kids. "Hey Jules!" Carla said with a big smile as she grabbed Julie's hand to inspect the ring. "Nice," she said before Julie pulled her into a big hug. "Can't breathe, Jules," Carla joked.

"I'm so glad you're here, Car. I've missed you too," Julie gushed. "You too, Paul," she said as she pulled him into a hug.

"I'm just glad you gave this big lug another chance. I couldn't take him sulking over you any longer," Paul joked, pretending to punch Marc in the stomach.

Marc put his hand on the small of Julie's back, "Babe, there's someone here that you need to see." He turned Julie around towards his sister, Lizzy, who was standing behind them.

Julie's hand shot up to cover her mouth, as her eyes grew wide, "Lizzy!" she exclaimed as she stepped forward to hug her old friend. "Oh my gosh, it's so good to see you. You flew from Spain to be here tonight?"

Lizzy smiled, "I had to be here to make sure my baby brother was really engaged to the girl that he dreamed about for…oh god, forever!" Looking over at her brother, she winked. The two girls chatted, catching up. Julie beamed with pride to introduce Ashley and Ben to Lizzy.

"We were inseparable in middle and high school," Julie said with a big grin. Ben and Ashley said their hellos, before going back to talk with Carla and Paul.

"I'm so sorry to hear about your parents, Jules, and Jim," Lizzy said, taking Julie's hand.

Julie patted her hand, "Marc told me about your parents, that had to be hard on you. I wish you would have reached out to me. I would have been there for you."

Lizzy shook her head, "It was a different time, then. It's much easier to communicate nowadays. You and Marc will have to come to Spain to meet my husband and boys."

"I can't believe we're finally going to be sisters!" Julie said with a little squeal.

"I couldn't believe it when he called to say he ran into you. I swear that day changed his life forever," exclaimed Lizzy.

Julie smiled, "It changed mine too."

They joined the rest of the party, but Julie noticed that Ben and Marc were nowhere to be seen. She chatted with some of Marc's co-workers as she kept watch for her two boys. She finally broke away to go look for them. She had an uneasy feeling in the pit of her stomach. Julie walked down the hallway, but stopped short of entering the bedroom, when she heard Ben and Marc's voices.

Marc said to Ben, "I would like your blessing before we go any further with this wedding."

She held her breath, wondering how Ben would react.

Ben spoke, his voice nervous, "I don't like that you showed up out of nowhere and pursued my mom, only months after my dad had passed. I don't like the idea that you are so much younger than her." Ben paused before continuing, "But…I don't think I've ever seen my mom so happy. Not even with my dad. She's carefree when she's with you. Maybe that's just an age thing, you know, with Ashley and I not being little kids anymore. I don't want to see her cry and be depressed anymore, and she's not that way when you're in her life, so…yeah, I give you, my blessing."

Marc's voice sounded at ease, "I have one more question for you. Will you be my best man? I know we had a rocky start, but I respect how protective you are of your mother."

"Yeah…I can be your best man, but I would also like to walk my mom down the aisle. Can I do both?" asked Ben in a hushed voice.

"I don't think your mother would have it any other way, Ben. You and Ashley are her entire world, and I'm just happy to have a small piece of it," Marc said with pride. "She's an amazing woman and mother. Nothing is going to change that."

Julie peeked in around the corner to see Marc pull Ben into a hug. This made her momma heart so full of joy. Moving into the room, she smiled at the sight and said, "What's a girl gotta do to get in on a hug from her two favorite men?" Ben and Marc looked at each other before rushing over to hug and lift Julie off her feet.

Julie's heart was filled with such peace hearing Ben give his blessing, and being surrounded by their friends and family was more than she could have hoped for. Marc introduced Julie to his boss, Oscar, his co-workers, and friends. They mingled; people made toasts to the happy couple, and just as things were dying down just a little bit, Oscar used his wedding band to clink his champagne flute.

Once he had everyone's attention, he made a toast. "I would like to make an announcement." A hush fell over the crowd as everyone's attention was on Oscar. Marc and Julie made their way over to stand next to him. "Marc has been an instrumental part of my company since day one, standing by my side as we worked together to get this business off the ground. He's been like a brother to me. I was thrilled to find out that he found his dream girl." Turning to Julie and Marc, he said, "Julie, I hope I'm not breaking your California dreams with this announcement, but your fiancé is the new President of our New York office," he said holding up his flute of champagne in the air. "Congratulations to Marc and Julie. Cheers!" Everyone cheered, drinking to celebrate this new milestone in Marc's career.

Julie turned to Marc, excitement filled her eyes, "Did you know about this?"

"Yeah," Marc said sheepishly. "It's been hard keeping it a secret."

Looking up into Marc's big brown eyes, Julie asked "We're moving to New York?"

Marc wrapped his arms around her, "Yes, baby. We're moving to New York. You are going to be an artist in your favorite city." He pulled her chin up to kiss her lips. Julie kissed him back, as everyone clapped.

***

As the evening progressed, they toasted with champagne, shared laughter and stories, and danced under the starts. The beach house, with its serene ambiance and the presence of their loved ones, felt like a perfect setting to mark the beginning of their lifelong journey together. The night was filled with happiness, love, and the promise of a bright future. After saying goodbye to all their guests, Marc led Julie out to the deck, the moonlight beaming down around them and illuminating the magic of the evening. He brushed her hair to one shoulder, as he kissed her neck, wrapping his arms around her. She held his arms, stretching her head to one side.

Spinning her around to face him, he gazed into her eyes as he took in a deep breath. "Let's go to Vegas and get married. I've spent more than enough time without you. I don't want to wait another moment."

Julie chuckled, before realizing that he was serious. "I want my kids and Carla to be there, and I know you want Lizzy, Gabby and your mom to be there too." She moved her head to rest on his chest, feeling it rise and fall with each breath. An idea came to her. Pulling her head back, she turned to him, "What if we get married here tomorrow?"

Marc laughed, "Tomorrow? How could we pull that off?"

"Our families are here, and your friends are here. How difficult could it be?" she asked, a serious tone in her voice. "We just need a marriage license and someone to do the ceremony. I don't need anything fancy, Marc. I just want to be your wife."

Marc pulled her back to his chest as he thought about her idea. He kissed her on the forehead, "If that's what you want, then let's do it!"

Chapter 33

"What is it to Love" by Ruxley

Julie rubbed her eyes, glancing at the clock on her phone; 5:30am. It was still too early to call anyone, but she couldn't sleep another minute. The excitement, mingled with a touch of anxiety, kept her wide awake most of the night. Today was the day she and Marc would finally tie the knot, and they had to do it in a way that was so them, spontaneously, with the sound of waves as their backdrop. She slipped out of bed, careful not to wake Marc, and padded into the kitchen. The house was silent, other than the sound of coffee brewing. With a steaming mug in hand, she settled at the kitchen island and opened Marc's laptop. The soft glow of the screen illuminated her determined expression as she navigated through the various tabs.

First, she looked at dresses, because she had nothing that looked close to wedding attire. She scrolled though several online boutiques, her eyes lingering on simple, elegant designs. She knew she wanted something that felt natural, fitting for a beach wedding. She made a note of two of them, because she knew that Carla and Ashley would want to be involved.

Julie stood, staring into the full-length mirror at herself in the big, puffy, white dress with matching veil. She nervously chewed her perfect manicured cuticle, a habit she had picked up shortly after she began dating Jim. She had sent her bridesmaids out of the room, to have a moment alone to calm her nerves.

Drawing in a deep breath, she whispered, "Am

I really doing this?" Lifting her hand up to her mouth again, she looked down at the mangled cuticle next to her perfectly pink nails. She wiped a tear that had ran down her cheek.

Julie turned when she heard a knock at the door, it was her mother. Julie turned her attention back to the mirror, smoothing the front of her dress down. "How do I look?" she asked through a pained smile.

"You look lovely, like a princess," her mother said, as she reached out to touch Julie's hand. "I can't believe my baby girl is getting married."

Julie's smile fell, "Am I doing the right thing?"

"Oh heavens, yes, Julia. We love Jim. You love him too," she exclaimed. "Why on earth would you be thinking about that, today of all days?"

Julie gazed at the pensive look on her face in the mirror. She spoke softly to her mother, "I wanted to move to New York after graduation, to teach art." The words seemed heavy, as she spoke them out loud.

"Well, honey. Sometimes, you have to do what is best for your husband and his job is in Chicago. Being a wife takes sacrifice. You have to give up a piece of yourself, to become whole with Jim. He's going to be a good provider and he'll make sure you have everything you need."

"Did you sacrifice a piece of yourself to marry Daddy?" Julie asked quietly.

"We didn't discuss things like that back in my day, but I guess I did. I wanted to be a kindergarten teacher, but my parents couldn't afford to send me to college, so that dream died before I met your father. I love him, just like you love Jim. You'll see, this is a good thing. Jim is the perfect man for you, honey," her mom said in a tone, that made Julie think that her mother was trying to convince herself as much as she was trying to convince Julie.

The clock now read 6:45am. Almost time for her to start making calls. She took another sip of her coffee and leaned back, her mind shifting to her kids. Pulling out her phone, she drafted a quick group message, her fingers tapping rapidly on the screen:

Hey, big news! Marc and I decided to get married tonight at the beach house. Call me when you're up.

She hit send and felt a rush of relief. As the sun began to rise, casting a soft glow over the kitchen, Julie felt the weight of the day ahead start to lift. She had a wedding to plan and a lifetime of memories to begin. In just a few hours, she would share this whirlwind of a day with the people she loved the most.

***

"It's Always Been You" by Caleb Hearn

Everyone pitched in to make this day special for Julie and Marc. Julie didn't care if the day was perfect or not, she had lived that life, and she craved the spontaneity of being a creative person who was madly in love with her soulmate. She never believed in that word before, because deep down, she knew that Jim was never her soulmate. It had been Marc, all along. From the pretend dates to the movies while Lizzy was off with her boyfriend, to shooting hoops in their driveway. His love for her was pure.

Julie stood in the bedroom, looking at herself in the mirror, but this time, she couldn't keep the big smile on her face at bay. She was genuinely happy, and there were no doubts. It was through her healing, and Marc's incessant love for her, that made this day so special. She pondered the first time she saw him at the beach café, thinking he was a creep, and she chuckled. They had come so far from that day. She had come so far from that day. Looking down at her engagement ring, she sniffed a tear back.

Ashley and Carla walked into the room, both gasping at the same time. Julie's dress was a simple, flowing ivory dress that was perfect for a beach wedding. She looked radiant.

Carla said, "I've never seen you look so serene before."

Ashley held her hand out to Julie, "I brought grandma's pearls for you to wear. I knew you would want something of hers today."

Julie turned to give Ashley a hug. "Thank you. Will you please hook the clasp?" Ashley slid the pearl necklace around her mother's neck, hooking it from the back. "You look stunning, Mom."

***

"I Will" by Matchbox Twenty

Ben stood in the doorway, adjusting his tie for the third time. The sound of waves crashing softly against the shore filled the air, mingling with the sound of the song "I Will" by Matchbox Twenty drifting from the speakers near the beach. He glanced at his reflection in the hallway mirror before turning to look towards his mother walking to meet him.

A huge smile came across his face. "Mom, you look beautiful. Are you ready?" he asked softly.

Julie turned, a radiant smile lighting up her face. She was a vision in her simple, elegant dress, "I'm ready."

As Julie took Ben's arm, he said, "Marc is a lucky guy."

Julie's eyes glistened, "I'm a lucky woman. I love you, Benny."

Ben tightened his grip on her arm, steadying her as they moved across the sandy path. The beach was set for the intimate ceremony. White chairs adorned with delicate flowers were arranged in a semicircle, facing a small wooden arch draped with flowing white fabric. Ashley stood beneath the arch, her bright eyes shining as she watched them approach. Across from her, Marc waited, his face a picture of calm and joy. He looked every bit the groom, handsome in his tailored suit and his eyes fixed lovingly on Julie.

Julie squeezed Ben's arm as they reached the edge of the aisle, "Thank you for walking me down, Ben. It means the world to me."

"Of course, Mom," he replied, his voice thick with emotion. "I'm so happy for you."

Guests turned to watch, smiles breaking out, and Julie noticed a few people discreetly wiping their eyes. She looked toward Ashley, noticing her eyes brimming with happy tears. Her gaze drifted over to Marc, who dabbed at the corner of his eyes as he watched her walk closer. When they finally reached the arch, Ben kissed his mother on the cheek before handing her off to Marc and then stepping beside him.

The officiant began to speak, and nothing else mattered in that moment. No more thoughts of the past, of fights, or misunderstandings. The only thing that mattered was the love and happiness that radiated between Julie and Marc. In that moment, everything else faded away.

***

"Birds of a Feather" by Billie Eilish

When everyone had left, Julie found herself feeling a bit melancholy, as she stood on the deck looking out at the moonlight hitting the ocean surface. She closed her eyes and inhaled the salty sea air.

Marc walked up behind her, pulling her close to him. "Hey there, Mrs. Julia Diaz."

Julie could tell he had a smile on his face without turning to look at him. "I love the sound of that," but she couldn't hide that her voice fell flat.

Moving to her side, he turned her toward him. "Babe, what's the matter?"

Julie smiled halfheartedly, "Just memories haunting me."

"How can I help?" he asked gazing into her eyes.

Julie nodded her head, "I was just remembering my first wedding day and how I wasn't as happy then as I am today."

Marc furrowed his brow before pulling her into an embrace. "I'm sorry that I wasn't the one that you married and built a life with, but I'm so thankful that we found each other again.

I can guarantee that I will do whatever I have to do to make sure that every day is filled with love. I adore you, Jules."

Julie smiled, because she knew in her heart that Marc meant every word he spoke to her. Closing her eyes, she embraced the happiness that filled her heart and mind. Her dreams of being in love, living and working in New York, were finally coming true. "I love you, Marc Diaz."

Epilogue

Julie sat at the small kitchen island; her phone propped up for a FaceTime call with Ashley. The warm golden light from the pendant lamps overhead gave the apartment a cozy glow. In the background, Marc was busy chopping vegetables as a delicious aroma wafted through the air from a pot on the stove. Glancing up toward the living room, she stared at the three painting from her first visit to Venice Beach, a wedding gift from Marc. Her heart felt full.

Julie smiled as Ashley's face appeared on the screen. "Hey Ash! How are things in St. Louis?"

"Hi Mom. Things are going great. The house is coming along nicely. We finally got the main bedroom renovated and it looks amazing. Liam has been such a huge help."

Julie grinned. "That's awesome. I'm glad you're making the house your own." She smiled up at Marc before looking back down at her phone, "Marc and I were just talking about how much we love Liam. He's a great guy and a good fit for you."

"Yeah, he's pretty wonderful," Ashley said. "I can't believe it's been almost a year since yours and Marc's wedding. Are you two planning something special for your anniversary, since you didn't exactly get a honeymoon?"

"We've discussed going to Spain for a week to see Lizzy and then a week in Italy, but we haven't nailed anything down yet. We've also talked about going back to the cottage in Cali to soak up some time at the beach," replied Julie as she looked up and winked at Marc, who blew her a kiss.

"I want to hear how the teaching is going?" Ashley asked.

Julie beamed; the excitement evident in her voice. "It's been amazing, Ash. The kids are so creative and full of energy. It's really inspiring. We've been working with all kinds of mediums; paint, clay, watercolor, the list goes on. Guess what? I'm prepping for my own art show at a small gallery in SOHO!"

"That's incredible, Mom! I knew you'd do great things in New York," Ashley said with genuine admiration. "I wish I could be there to see it."

"I'll send you photos and you'll be there in spirit," Julie replied. "And who knows, maybe you and Liam can make a trip up here soon."

"Definitely," Ashley agreed. "We'll plan something soon. Have you talked to Carla?"

"Only, every day," Julie laughed. "She's moving to LA to be with Paul."

"Wait, what? Her business is here, in St. Louis," exclaimed Ashley.

"She'll keep the office open there with minimal staff, but she's opening a new one in LA," explained Julie.

"I can't see her putting up with the California heat," laughed Ashley.

Julie looked over at Marc, "Love can make you do crazy things."

"I can see that," Ashley said. "Hey, what did you think of Ben's new girlfriend, Elizabeth, when they came to visit?"

"She's a lovely girl, definitely a little shy. I just want Ben to be happy and he seemed very happy with her when they were here last week. It's still new, so we'll see what happens," Julie said with a lilt in her voice.

"I'm dying to meet her. Ben promised he would

bring her to St. Louis sometime. Maybe you and Marc could come home that weekend too," offered Ashley.

Marc glanced over from the stove, giving Julie a supportive smile. "Dinner's almost ready, hon."

Julie nodded, turning back toward the screen. "Well, I should probably go. Marc's making his famous pasta and you know I can't resist."

Ashley laughed. "I remember. Enjoy and give Marc my love."

"I will. Love you, Ash," said Julie, smiling at how well her daughter was doing. Thankful that Ashley broke the cycle of loving the wrong kind of person, and by putting her own wellbeing ahead of a relationship with a man.

As the call ended, Julie opened her music app, turned it on as she looked up at Marc with a sigh. "Life is good, isn't it, Mr. President," she joked.

Marc walked over, wrapping his arms around her. "Yeah, it really is. May I have this dance?" he asked with a smile.

As they swayed back in forth in each other's arms, Julie felt a sense of fulfillment wash over her. She had her art, her family, Carla and Marc, who she loved fiercely. Everything was coming together in the city that never sleeps. It was just the beginning of a beautiful chapter.

Printed in the USA
CPSIA information can be obtained
at www.ICGtesting.com
CBHW031834101024
15670CB00006B/48